JUL 15 2021

TELL ME WHEN YOU
FEEL SOMETHING

TELL ME WHEN YOU FEEL SOMETHING

VICKI GRANT

3939263

Penguin Teen

an imprint of Penguin Random House Canada Young Readers, a
division of Penguin Random House of Canada Limited

Published in hardcover by Penguin Teen, 2021

1 2 3 4 5 6 7 8 9 10

*Publisher's note: This book is a work of fiction. Names, characters, places
and incidents either are the product of the author's imagination or are used
fictitiously, and any resemblance to actual persons living or dead, events,
or locales is entirely coincidental.*

Manufactured in Canada

Library and Archives Canada Cataloguing in Publication

Title: Tell me when you feel something / Vicki Grant.
Names: Grant, Vicki, author.
Identifiers: Canadiana (print) 20200213032 | Canadiana (ebook)
 20200213075 | ISBN 9780735270091 (hardcover) | ISBN
 9780735270107 (EPUB)
Classification: LCC PS8613.R367 T45 2021 | DDC jC813/.6—dc23
Library of Congress Control Number: 2020936851

www.penguinrandomhouse.ca

Penguin
Random House
PENGUIN CANADA

For my dear friend, Leslie Gotfrit.
Brilliant, funny, creative, open-hearted—Les is truly more.

Your body does weird things. Bloats, bleeds, oozes, shrivels, itches, burns, freezes, plays dead, dies. You can be a perfectly normal specimen and you're still a freak of nature.

And if that's not bad enough, your body also lies. Your eye will lie to your head, your head will lie to your heart—and your heart?

It's the biggest sleaze of all.

Davida Williamson

3 days after the party
11 a.m.

The cop is nice enough, but I can tell he doesn't believe me.

He listens to what I have to say then props himself on the front of his desk and dangles one leg over the edge. It's the standard just-having-a-little-chat pose of an adult trying to show he's on your side. Principals love that one too.

I'm sitting in a plastic chair right in front of him. He's too close. There's this starburst of khaki crotch-wrinkles that's basically staring me right in the face. I'll give him the benefit of the doubt and presume he doesn't realize it's making me uncomfortable.

Viv says everything makes me uncomfortable.

"Look." His eyes go big and sad. "A smart, talented, well-loved girl is in a coma. We all want to find someone to blame—but here's the truth. Opioids don't care who you are. They don't care whether you're an addict or a good kid who just goes out and does something stupid one night. Taking 'party drugs' these days is playing Russian roulette and, unfortunately, your friend was unlucky and took a bullet."

Thanks. Like picturing her with all the tubes sticking out isn't bad enough.

"I want you to know this though. We're going to find out who supplied Vivienne with the drugs and prosecute him or her to the fullest extent of the law." He makes a frowny closed-mouth smile and nods. He's given his speech. He wants me to go now, and I should—this is useless—but I don't. It took me days to get up the guts to come in. I'm not leaving now.

"No one 'supplied' her with the drugs. That's what I'm saying."

He puts both feet on the floor and tilts his chin down at me like I'm a little kid who's said something cute. Cute but stupid. "Someone must have. She had to get them from somewhere."

"No. Viv wouldn't do that." I say the words slowly, hitting the consonants hard. I need him to take me seriously. "Viv would not take drugs on purpose."

"Were you at the party?" He knows I wasn't. The police already interviewed everyone who was there. When they didn't come to me, I realized I had to go to them. It's the least I can do for my "friend." (Viv gets quotation marks now. Little cartoony ones that flash in my brain as if they're just another one of her jokes, which they aren't.)

I shake my head but don't break eye contact. Just because I wasn't there doesn't mean I don't know.

Do I know?

Stop.

All he needs to think is I'm not sure—then he'll never believe me.

"You saw the video though?" He walks back to the other side of his desk. "Or videos, I should say. Plural."

"I saw one, but it didn't prove anything."

"No?" He sits down, grabs the edge of his desk and pulls his chair forward with a squeak. He looks at the computer screen through the bottom of his glasses. "Well, there were quite a few videos. Perhaps the one you saw was different. Multiple people recorded Vivienne taking a pill at the party. I've got it from at least six different angles."

"That wasn't a 'pill.' It was a vitamin."

"Again, not to put too fine a point on it, but in the footage, we see Vivienne holding up a pill between two fingers and saying, 'This is E.' I presume by E she meant Ecstasy—or am I wrong?" He looks at me over his glasses and smiles. The long eyelashes surprise me. He must have hated them as a kid.

"No. She did mean Ecstasy—but that was a joke. She always says that."

"Always?"

He's doing that TV cop thing. Trying to trap me with my own words. "Okay, not always, but a lot. She takes vitamins with iron for anemia. We both do. We were at lunch once and someone asked her what the pill was and she went, 'This is E,' and the girl actually believed her."

He doesn't get how ridiculous that was, Viv and Ecstasy, so I tell him. "It was funny. She started saying it all the time, like it was her catchphrase or something."

I shouldn't have worn this sweater. I'm too hot all of a sudden.

"Her catchphrase," he says.

"Yes." I fold my arms so he can't see and pinch my sleeves away from my armpits. I'd take the sweater off, but I'd have to pull it over my head and that would be weird, like I'm undressing or something. "She was just joking around."

"Okay." He pooches out his lips and shrugs.

I let that go. I mean, what am I going to say? He's a cop. I'm some off-brand seventeen-year-old girl. Then I think, no. No chickening out. Viv wouldn't chicken out.

I go, "Why are you saying it like that?"

"I just said okay."

"Um. Well, not really. You actually said 'okay-ay,' which is kind of the opposite."

He at least has the decency to laugh.

"Ask anyone," I say. "Ask her boyfriend. She called it E all the time."

"You're talking about Jack Downey?" He picks up a paper clip and tumbles it through his fingers.

3

"Yeah."

"I've met his mother. She's the preacher at First African Baptist, isn't she?"

"I don't know the name of the church."

He gives his head a little jiggle, as if details aren't important. "He's taking it pretty hard, I understand." He opens his top drawer, drops in the paper clip and closes it again. "Jack is Vivienne's ex, though, isn't he? Not her boyfriend?"

"They had a fight," I say. "Doesn't necessarily make him her ex."

He raises his eyebrows. A girl ends up in a coma after a fight with her boyfriend? The guy might not be her ex but he's sure as hell a suspect. Even I know that.

I picture Jack and Viv, cross-legged on the green-and-black floor of the high school hallway, back to back, textbooks open on their knees, a big yellow clump of her hair hanging off his shoulder like a feather boa. The two of them totally quiet, totally focused, until the bell rings or one of their alarms sounds. Then they're up, kissing, laughing, then kissing again and running off in opposite directions to some class, rehearsal, practice, game, meeting, whatever.

That was before Viv knew me of course—or, I guess, *remembered* me—but I knew her. Everyone knows Viv. Everyone knows how much Jack loves her.

"So what if they did have a fight? What difference does that make?" I say.

"Maybe none." The cop wiggles a little breathing room between his neck and his clumpy beige tie. "But people do strange things when they're under stress. Things they'd never normally do."

"What are you saying? That Jack gave her the drugs? Just because he's Black, you're thinking—"

"Whoa, whoa, whoa." He sticks his hand out like a traffic cop. "I was thinking no such thing. I wasn't talking about Jack. I was talking about Vivienne doing something out of character."

4

"Oh. Sorry."

"You think that could be it?"

"Viv doesn't even drink," I say.

"No?" Like that's so hard to believe.

"Not at all." It's a well-known fact. "So who would go from, like, kombucha straight to Ecstasy, just because of some little argument?"

"People do it for less," he says. "I've had girls tell me they took street drugs because they didn't want to waste the calories on booze. Kids who've bought meth because they don't have ID to buy beer." He lays his glasses on the desk and rubs his eyes.

"But you saw the video. Everyone had alcohol. Viv could have gotten it if she wanted it."

"True." He puts his glasses back on. He drums his fingers on the desk. "So maybe she was more upset about the argument than people knew. Maybe she took the pill as a call for attention."

The last thing Vivienne Braithwaite needed was attention. "She just won this big internship. Her father's getting married and she's a bridesmaid. She's got a new little stepsister. Every guy who's ever met her wants to, like, go out with her. She wouldn't trash all that over some stupid argument."

"What was the argument about?" He totally ignored everything I just said.

"I don't know."

"But it was something stupid?"

"Yes. I mean, I don't know. Probably. They've been together since they were fourteen. They've no doubt had their, um, *ups and downs*. All couples do."

As if I would know. I was a couple for roughly a nanosecond. Just long enough for one "up," one "down" and an "over and out."

"They do indeed . . ." He chuckles, then makes prayer hands and taps them against his chin. "One thing I don't understand though. Why would Vivienne take a multivitamin at a party? Things have probably changed a bit since I was a teenager"—another chuckle—"but something about that doesn't sit quite right."

"You don't know Viv."

"True. I don't. So help me. Taking vitamins in the middle of a party was normal behavior for her. That's what you're saying? You'd seen her do it before?"

"Not exactly. But stuff like that."

"Such as?"

I try to come up with an example but all I can think of is Viv in the hospital, Viv in the van, Viv lying. Looking me straight in the face and lying.

I hold my breath and remind myself why I'm here. It doesn't matter whether she's good or bad. What matters is that somebody did something to her. I need the cop to believe me.

"I dunno," I say. "Viv's always super-busy. Work, lifeguarding, volunteer stuff, family stuff. Maybe that was just the first chance she had to take it."

He picks up an elastic band and runs it through his fingers, squinting as if there's something encoded on the rubber. "Any chance you know what kind of vitamins she took?"

"Same as me. IronPlus Multivitamins for Women."

"What do they look like?"

"Bright pink, oval, about, I don't know, this big . . . I can show you one if you want."

He raises his hands like *by all means.*

I open my backpack. Dad twisted up some pills in plastic wrap and put them there at the beginning of the summer. He's always been weirdly concerned about my iron count. He's super-sensitive that he'll miss some important girl thing, that I'll somehow be horribly wounded growing up in an all-male family.

I hand him one. "She took these exact same pills."

"Big suckers, aren't they?"

"I'm used to them. I can swallow them dry, but Viv hates them. Always needs to wash them down with something."

He holds the pill up like Exhibit A. "These were the only pills she took?"

"Least that I ever saw. She complained so much about them I doubt she'd take anything else for, like, *fun.*"

He hands me back the vitamin. "Would it upset you to see the video of the party again?"

I shake my head rather than lie outright.

"Here's my problem." He swivels his monitor around to show me. It's not the exact video I saw but it was obviously taken at the same time because all the same people are there doing the same things.

"There was some drinking game going on here." His finger circles a bunch of guys horsing around by the kitchen table. "That's what people were interested in. Nobody seemed to be filming Vivienne on purpose. She just happened to be in the way. Now look here."

He points to the area by the sink. "I'll stop before the, ah . . ." He gives me a non-smile. We both know what he means. Viv losing it. Crumpling at the knees, eyes rolled back, spit bubbling out her mouth. The party going on around her while she convulses on the floor. Just another one of her jokes, until suddenly it isn't.

I stare at the screen so the cop can't read my face.

Ariana Cohen's kitchen. Not that I'd recognize it, but everyone knows where the party was. The cupboards are all open, the granite countertop covered in red cups and beer bottles and bright yellow bags spewing barbecue chips. I can name a few of the kids in the video, but I doubt any of them could name me. Sam Fougere walks through the screen with his shirt off. Charlotte and Erica are in the corner and, judging by their faces, fighting about something. Patty Chu is sitting on the counter by the sink, Felix McSomething standing in front of her, his hands on her knees. In the background, Tommy G has Ollie in a headlock. In the center, the game of beer pong. Everyone is doing

7

their Insta-best to look like they're having an epic time. I was supposed to be there with Viv but, for obvious reasons, was not.

Someone scores and arms fly up. The cheering drowns out the music.

For a second, everything goes black. Then Viv's waist-length volcano of kinky blond hair comes into focus. Whoever's videotaping goes, "Hey. Out of the way!"

Viv goes, "Sorry," and hunchbacks it over to the sink. She picks up a fresh bag of Doritos, squeezes it open, then pours a bunch into her mouth.

In this particular video, I can't make out what she says but I've heard it before, so I know. She's asking if there are any clean glasses.

Felix nudges a plastic cup toward her. "This one hasn't been puked in. Like, recently."

She makes a face and pushes it away. "Don't need it that bad. I'm just popping a pill!"

Felix laughs. "Oh yeah, what? Special K? Kibbles 'n Bits?"

Viv goes, "Pah. None of that fancy brand-name stuff for me. This is E." Then she holds up the pill, puts it in her mouth, twists her hair around her wrist, and drinks right from the tap.

Someone goes, "Chug, chug, chug, chug."

She stands up and shudders. "Let the magic begin," she says and lets her hair go.

The cop stops the video.

"Notice anything?" he says to me.

"The sound of her voice. She was joking about it being E."

"Maybe . . ." As if he doesn't want me to feel bad for getting the answer wrong. "Anything else?"

I look at the screen, Viv frozen in time, her hair mid-swing, one side of her mouth turned up into a smile.

How awesome she is. That's what I notice. Because she *is* awesome; doesn't matter what she did to me.

"No," I say.

"The pill." He scrolls back. "See?"

He zooms in. Viv holds it up again. "It's not pink and oblong. It's blue and round."

How did I miss that?

"So," he says, "it couldn't be her usual Iron Woman, ah . . ."

"IronPlus Multivitamins for Women. No . . . but . . ." I can't let this throw me. "Lots of pills are blue. She could have been on some medication I didn't know about."

"Not according to her mother."

"So maybe someone gave her something and said it was a supervitamin or an energy pill or something legit like that. I could see her taking one of *those*."

The cop wobbles his head.

"Why not?" I say. "Why couldn't someone have tricked her into taking the pill?"

"I didn't say that." He acts as if he's got such a poker face, but I can tell what he's thinking.

I say, "Or someone could have spiked her drink and it had nothing to do with the pill."

"What drink? She drank straight from the tap."

"Before that then."

A little smile here. "Great thing about you kids and your phones. We were able to pinpoint exactly when she arrived at the party and what she did. There's no evidence of her drinking anything in the short period she was there. Nothing."

I sit back and cross my arms. "All I know is that Viv didn't take it on purpose."

He stares at me for a few seconds then nods. "We have CCTV footage of her getting out of a blue or maybe black subcompact about a block from the Cohen house just before the party. Any idea who might own a car like that?"

"You're thinking that's who gave her the pill?"

"We're not thinking anything. Just following up."

"A blue or black subcompact?" My brain races through my contact list. It doesn't take long. I barely know anyone, let alone what kind of car they drive.

"Sorry."

"That's okay. Not much to go on, especially since we can't identify the make. We could only tell it was Vivienne by her hair. . . . Know anyone called Jed?"

"Jed?"

"Yes. J-E-D."

"No. Why?"

"Just another lead." His smile lasts maybe half a second. Then he says, "Does Vivienne have any enemies you know of? Someone who'd have a reason not to like her?"

Me. I'm honestly the only person I can think of.

"No," I say, a little too loud. "Viv's really popular. Everyone loves her."

"You good friends?"

"Yeah." *Were*, I think, but leave it at that.

"How do you know her?"

I give him the short version. "We work as SPs."

"SPs?"

"Simulated Patients."

He shrugs as if he doesn't understand.

"We're like pretend patients for med students to practice on."

"Oh, right. Her parents mentioned she worked part-time at the med school. Tell me a bit more about that. How exactly do they practice on you?" He looks slightly horrified.

"They don't operate on us or anything if that's what you're thinking. They just, like, examine us, take our pulse, splint our arms, stuff like that . . ."

"How long you been doing it?"

"Middle of June?"

"Meaning you've only known Vivienne a little more than a month?"

"We'd, like, crossed paths before, but yeah."

He shakes his head and smiles. "You get to know people pretty fast at your age."

I shrug.

"Fast enough for you to get a gut instinct that something wasn't right."

"I guess."

He leans back in his chair and holds his belly the way pregnant ladies do.

"Okay. Look," he says, as if he's got it all figured out. "There's not a cop alive who doesn't believe in gut instincts but, unfortunately, I need a bit more than that to go on. My daughter starts high school next year and I gotta tell you, this scares the bejaysus out of me. I'm going to do everything possible to find out where the drug came from but—"

There's a knock. The cop lifts his finger at me and goes to see who it is. He leans out the half-open door. I hear him say, "Gimme a sec. Almost done here." By the time he turns around, I'm standing, ready to go.

"Sorry, Davida." He pronounces it Da-Vide-A.

"Da-VEE-da." Not that it matters. Everyone gets it wrong.

"Da-VEE-da. Excuse me. Afraid I'm going to have to cut this short." He shakes my hand. "I know you didn't hear what you wanted to, but that doesn't mean we aren't listening."

He steers me to the door. "If you remember anything else that might be important—a change of mood on Vivienne's part, a suspicious new person on the scene, an unexplained absence, really just anything out of the ordinary—please get in touch."

He hands me his card. "It says Alan Eisenhauer but ask for Pidge. That's what everyone calls me."

I mumble thanks but we both know I'm never going to call him.

By now, we both know I was wrong about Viv.

From: Lt. Pidge Eisenhauer
To: Sgt. Tinatin Karchava
Re: **Vivienne Braithwaite Inquiry**

Sarge—

Starting to think the Vivienne Braithwaite case might not just be another party-drug overdose. Talked to a friend of hers this a.m. Very agitated. Implied VB may have been inveigled into taking the drugs. No evidence but the girl seemed convinced.

She met VB through their work as "simulated patients" (SP) at MacKinnon med school. Did a little calling around. No obvious red flags there. The SP program's been going +/- 20 years. Squeaky clean reputation. SPs mostly retirees, out-of-work actors or A+ high school students like VB. They're given an alias and a script telling them what disease they have/how to act/what to wear/where it hurts, etc., then have "appointments" with med students in mocked-up doctor's offices. Even have "moulage" (special-effects makeup) to fake symptoms/injuries. Sounds pretty innocent, like that cosplay stuff my daughter's into these days, but something's got my spidey senses tingling.

Questions:

A) Could the overdose be the result of a prank gone wrong? In which case we may be looking for both the supplier and the idiot who pranked VB.

B) Could the med school be the source of the drugs? Lab tests are back. Wasn't ecstasy she took. It was actually oxycodone. Lots of people at med school could have access. Any of them got light fingers?

Just my gut talking but I think there could be something here. We didn't explore the med school connection initially so I'd like to bring a few people into the shop for questioning ASAP. You ok with that?

Pidge

From: Sgt. Tinatin Karchava
To: Lt. Pidge Eisenhauer
Re: **Vivienne Braithwaite Inquiry**

Pidge—

Go for it. I'm not getting in the way of that big gut of yours.

—T.K.

PS How's the diet going or should I ask?

What Davida Didn't Know

Viv
37 days before the party
10 p.m.

It was as if someone had shouted at her to wake up. Viv's head jerked and her eyes popped open. She'd had a revelation.

She got them every so often, but never when she was actually trying. They just showed up, and at the weirdest times too, when she didn't seem capable of thought at all, let alone a big one. She could be almost totally out of it then, suddenly, there it was, right in front of her—this life-changing insight, fully formed and gleaming.

Stu's the only person who knows me.

That's what her revelation was this time.

Other people think they do but they don't, not really.

She rubbed her nose with the heel of her hand. She wasn't surprised. Maybe a little hurt or embarrassed to see—like, actually *see*—what a fraud she was, but mostly she was just relieved. She felt herself relax. The weight of having to make the rest of the world happy or proud or even momentarily charmed vanished. She let her eyes close. She had a sense of herself as a little kid again, lying on her back in a pool, floating aimlessly, perfectly content.

But then another revelation shouted at her: *Not even Jack.*

She didn't care that much about the rest of the world—at least not right then—but Jack? He didn't know her either?

Obviously. *You think he'd go out with you if he did?*

She felt like shit again.

Her neck was bent awkwardly against her backpack. She sat up, pounded it flat, then flopped back down on the car seat and took another gulp. Cold liquid dribbled into her ear. She didn't bother wiping it away.

But Stu knows me, she thought. *He doesn't hate me.*

She looked at Stu in the front of the cab. The only light came from the parking lot's one working streetlamp. It lit up his face in some spots and cast long, dark shadows in others. He was a big sloppy guy—baggy T-shirt, neck beard, elastic-waist gym shorts barely covering his crack—but his car was weirdly pristine. His evening snacks were lined up neatly on the dashboard in individual Tupperware containers.

She took another sip and chuckled into the bottle. "Good old Stu."

He was studying. He put down his tablet, lifted an earphone and looked at her in the rearview mirror. "What now," he said, not even bothering to make it a question.

"Nothing. Just, you know—good old Stu!" She kicked off her flip-flops and planted her feet flat on the side window.

"Hey." His tiny eyes tightened into pinpricks. "Down."

"Wha-aat?" She loved bugging him.

"You know damn well. Get your frigging feet off—"

She laughed. "Chill." She put her feet on the seat. "Geez."

He hauled himself around and checked the window. "Jesus Christ."

The streetlamp turned her footprints white and ghostly against the dark glass. Such a dickish thing to do, she realized. Her gecko toes were gross at the best of times. "Sorry, bud. I'll wipe it off." She sat up and started rooting through her backpack for something to use.

"Forget it," he said.

All she had was crap. Empty chip bags, the remains of a banh mi, a notebook with a few lame podcast ideas for the Barking Robot internship.

When's the application due? She couldn't remember. Her heart thumped. *Did I miss it?*

She was such a fuck-up.

"Shit," she said.

"You heard me? Stop. You'll just make it worse."

"I got this." She kept tossing stuff out of her backpack until she found a piece of "origami roadkill." That's what Jack called the piles of dirty, randomly folded papers she seemed to collect.

"You're picking everything up before you go." Stu tapped the dashboard with his finger. "Every goddamn thing."

She checked to make sure the paper wasn't important. There was a crest at the top and a scrolly thing below. Many questions to answer. It took her a second to realize it was the scholarship form her mother had given her to fill out months ago. Her mother had won the same scholarship when she was Viv's age. It would mean a lot to her if Viv did too.

Viv knew that—but had she done anything about it? She still hadn't asked that friend of her parents' for a reference letter. She still hadn't written the essay. She still hadn't updated her résumé.

"Shit." She tossed it too. Her mother was going to be so pissed.

"Oh, for Christ's sake." Stu made a move as if he were going to get up and put a stop to this nonsense, but she was reasonably certain he wouldn't. More bark than bite.

She turned her backpack over and dumped everything on the seat. Crushed tampons. The linty wand from an old lip gloss. An empty bottle of IronPlus Multivitamins. Lulu's community center card.

Viv must have forgotten to leave it when she'd babysat the other day. Now Lulu's mother would be pissed too—but so what? As if Katie could talk. Which was worse? Viv taking off with Katie's kid's membership card or Katie taking off with Viv's dad?

The answer was obvious. Viv snorted righteously. *Least I'm not as bad as her.*

She bounced up on her knees, leaned into the window and started scrubbing at the footprints with the hem of her T-shirt.

"Would you stop?" Stu groaned.

"No." *Katie* was the type who didn't clean up her messes, not Viv. "It's. My. Job."

"It is, but you're shit at it. I'll do it."

"You do too much for me already."

"Yeah, I do—because otherwise I have to deal with horseshit like this."

Viv plunked back onto her heels to see how she'd done.

Stu was right. She'd made it worse. The footprints were mostly gone, but now the window was smeared with something dark and waxy. *What is that?* Viv held out her T-shirt. It looked like something ugly and brown had exploded on her belly.

Blood.

She remembered.

Fake blood from that day's SP session. She'd been a victim in a workplace accident. Ruptured spleen. Multiple lacerations. All over Stu's window.

She banged her forehead on the glass. "Stu. Stooo." She scrabbled around on the seat until she found her bottle and took a gulp. "Why do you let me do this to you?"

"Like I got a choice."

"What's the matter with me?"

"You're a drunk." He slipped his tablet into its sleeve and put it in the glove compartment.

"I fuck everything up for you. You can't study. You can't work. You can't eat your little"—she flapped her hand at the dashboard—"whatever they are because, like, here I am! All sprawled and shit-faced and, I don't know, just fucking blah-blah-blah, boo-hoo-hoo poor me. Why don't you kick me THE HELL OUT OF HERE?"

She shook the bottle, so angry at him for being such a sucker, such a pussy. Then she took another drink, since she had it in her hand anyway. She was going to stop tomorrow for sure.

"Tried it. Didn't work." Stu turned to face her, his belly squeaking against the steering wheel. "You're too stupid."

"You're the stupid one. Buying me booze." She sloshed back another drink.

"Yeah, well, I don't buy it for you, someone else will. Then what? You're passed out on a park bench with some letch waiting to pounce on your skinny ass."

Viv laughed, one big *pah!* "That old guy? He wouldn't hurt me!"

"What I said. Stupid."

"He just bought me a little Grey Goose. He wasn't going to *do* anything."

"Ya think?" Stu pulled at the armpitty whiskers under his chin. "That's why he volunteered to hang around and help you polish off the bottle?"

"Hey. You reminded me . . ." Viv lifted her hips and reached into her back pocket. "Take this." She waved a twenty-dollar bill at him.

"You paid me already."

"No, I didn't."

"Yeah, you did."

"That was for the Goooooose," she said, enjoying the vibrations on her nearly numb lips. "This is *danger* pay."

"For what?"

"Looking after me."

"Oh, you mean *irritation* pay. Only danger here's what you're doing to yourself."

"Wow. Way to sound like a grown-up, Stu."

"'Cause I am."

"That's my point!"

"What point?"

"Danger pay!"

He groaned through clenched teeth. "God, I hate drunks . . . What are you talking about?"

"How old are you?" she said.

"Why?"

"Just tell me."

A long pause and then, because he knew she wouldn't shut up otherwise, he told her. "Twenty-five."

"Correct! Twenty-five—i.e., a grown-up. A man." That cracked her up. "Whoa, Stu—you're a *man*! Ever think of that?"

"Yeah. I have. So what?"

"Buying booze for a minor."

"Whatever."

"That's illegal, buster! Hence—danger pay." She flapped the twenty in his face and whispered, "You know you want it."

He gave a quick jab with his elbow and she fell back down. He looked into the mirror and said, "You planning to tell someone who buys it for you?"

"No."

"Yeah, well, me neither. So keep your goddamn money."

"Oh, c'mon! Take it! I got loads." She threw it at him. "Great thing about parents who hate each other. Always someone willing to buy my love!"

She raised her bottle in a toast then sucked back another long, sloppy drink.

Stu took one of the containers off the dashboard and jiggled it at her. Inside were four plump crescents of pastry, oozing something dark and meaty.

"Eat," he said.

She flipped her face away. She couldn't even look at them.

"Eat, for Christ's sake." He jiggled it again. She could smell the grease. She burrowed her nose into the upholstery.

"Goddamn it." He sighed and took it away. "Nothing's worse than you on an empty stomach."

Nothing's worse than you.

"Gee. Thanks, Stu." She held the bottle against her mouth like a bugle, her lips almost closed, and let the vodka dribble in and down and away.

What was she doing here again? How had this happened?

She'd had no intention of seeing Stu that day. Of seeing Stu ever again. She was starting fresh, turning over a new page, et cetera, et cetera. She was sure she could do it this time.

And she did, for a while. She'd gotten out of bed, showered, gargled, gagged, gargled again, put on clean clothes, even brushed her hair and choked back an iron pill. When she'd gone down for breakfast, there was a note from her mother saying she was out for a walk, which meant her mother was trying too. Viv fed the cat then texted Jack: Ardmore 15 mins?

They were trying to squeeze in as much time together as possible before he left for rugby camp, but it wasn't easy. They were both so busy. She figured breakfast would be their only chance that day because he had work then practice then weight-training then a family thing, but she was okay with that. Jack and banana pancakes in a squeaky red-vinyl booth at the Ardmore Diner? That should do her.

But then at noon swim, she'd been blowing her whistle at this mouthy little dweeb who kept jumping into the shallow end and she looked up and there he was. Jack. Draped across her lifeguard chair, big smile on his face, holding out a drippy cone of her favorite ice cream. She'd laughed out loud.

"No running on the pool deck!" he shouted, because he knew what she was like.

He'd picked up the cone for her at Dee-Dee's Creamery then cycled over on his lunch break, his handlebars mauve and sticky with Moonmist Ripple. They only had two minutes together before he'd had to turn around and head back but that was Jack. Always ready to go that extra mile.

Thinking about him had kept Viv in a dreamy state all afternoon. Luckily, the accident victim she was playing was supposed to be in shock, so even that worked out. The SP sessions were just wrapping up when she got a text with more good news. Her mother was going to a gallery opening with Aunt Christie and had left sage gnocchi in the fridge for her. Would Viv mind eating alone?

Mind? Viv was thrilled. A little downtime. Maybe even a chance to work on that podcast pitch. Minutes later, she was on the bus, heading home, absentmindedly shuffling through potential ideas, when something pinged in her brain.

A meeting.

She'd forgotten she had a meeting that night.

It started at six, she was pretty sure, and it was all the way back at the community center. She had to go. People were counting on her. *She* was counting on *them*. She wouldn't get the scholarship without volunteer work. She wouldn't get the scholarship without writing the essay. Getting the reference letter. Beefing up her résumé. Making herself worthy. The world was suddenly full of angry, disappointed people all needing stuff from her immediately.

She jumped up and pulled the cord for the next stop. She got off the bus, crossed the street and waited for the Number 12 heading the other way. She scrambled through her backpack for her transit pass while passengers piled up behind her and the bus driver leaned his beefy arms on the steering wheel and sighed. There were lots of seats, but she stood in the aisle to make the bus go faster. She got off and ran the last block there.

No cars in the parking lot, the front doors all locked. She went around to the side and banged at a window until the janitor looked up from his floor polisher and noticed her, jumping and waving like some psycho team mascot. He turned off his machine and opened the door.

"Yes?"

"I've got a meeting," she said.

"Which one?"

"Um . . ." For a second, she honestly couldn't remember. "Street fair. The waste-free street fair." She got it. She had to calm down. This wasn't helping.

"Hon." He winced. "That was *last* night." He shrugged apologetically then closed the door on her face. Her gruesomely smiling face.

It was just a meeting. Viv slid down the brick wall. Lots of kids missed meetings.

Lots of kids screwed up. Lots of kids disappointed their parents. Lots of kids did nothing with their lives. Viv was just having trouble accepting that she was one of them.

She texted Stu. Paying by cash. That was their code for "buy me a bottle."

He replied, 10 mints, by which he meant *minutes*. By which he meant an eternity.

Just when she thought she couldn't wait another second, Stu's silver cab pulled up under the streetlamp. There was something almost fairy-tale-ish about it, the way it arrived all bright and shiny to rescue her.

She leapt in, sunk into the back seat and tried to yoga the buzz out of her brain.

"Home?" he asked, as if that was an actual possibility.

"Ha," she said, eyes closed, no time for this, a part of her literally dying for a drink. He never let her drink while he was driving so she just had to hang on, think of something else, dig her nails into her palms, try like hell to remember a single relaxing thing that stupid Bikram teacher said week in, week out, until finally, a lifetime later, Stu glided into the deserted parking lot of the boarded-up InnovaGear warehouse. It wasn't far from the med school but it felt like a world away. He turned off the car then, with agonizing stop-action slowness, reached under the passenger seat, picked up a bag and handed it to her. She pulled out the bottle, unscrewed the cap and sucked back her first drink.

That was hours ago. Who needs yoga? She took another swig now.

"You know what my grandfather calls this?" she said, holding up the bottle. "Firewater. Isn't that perfect?"

Stu had finished his snacks and was snapping the lids back on the Tupperware. He didn't answer.

"Stooby! Think about it! *Fire*water!" She laughed. "The way it burns everything away! All the stuff you worry about, torture yourself about . . ."

"All the brain cells . . ."

"I'm serious." And she was now. This suddenly felt like a deep thought. "The only time I feel like I actually have any control is when I'm drunk. And you know how I love control."

"Oh my God." He'd opened the driver's door and flicked crumbs off his shorts.

"What?"

"You." He shook his head. "Control."

"I do. I love it."

"What? From afar or something? Because this"—he pointed his hand at her and moved it up and down—"this ain't control. Not even close." He closed the door.

She caught a glimpse of herself in the sideview mirror. The matted hair, the dirty T-shirt, the basset-hound droop of her face. She was drunk but not too drunk to see how funny that was.

"Okay. I *might* not look like it, but control is my—" She struggled for the right word then, just like that, it swaggered in like a rock star. "It's my *passion*."

He put on his earphones. "Since when?" He meant it as a jab, but Viv, in fact, knew exactly when.

"October 12."

She'd never even thought about control until then. The only reason she did that day was because she'd suddenly found herself without it.

23

Like, 100 percent without it. She was riding her bike back to school to pick up a book she needed for English before meeting Jack, then going to student council, then going to Pilates with her mother, then dinner with her dad. In other words, a normal day. Totally doable.

"Ever tell you about my bike accident, Stu? Changed my life."

He ignored her.

"Changed. My. Life."

He sighed and dropped his earphones onto his neck. "Okay. Make it quick."

"I got doored. Like, doooored. Riding along. Minding my own business. Then this lady steps out of her car without looking and boom! Flying. I must have been in the air for, I don't know? A couple of seconds? But in my head? It was for-*ever*. I was terrified, but I also kind of wasn't. Part of me was just *la-la-la*, looking down at the road, all chill and everything, like, *hey, whaddya know? I'm going to break my neck*."

"Let me guess. You didn't."

"Nope. Landed on my hands and knees like I was going into cat pose or something." She laughed, remembering the shock. "Totally shredded my palms—you should have seen them—and the car behind almost creamed me, but whatever. Five minutes later I was back on my bike, totally cool. I figured it was over. But it wasn't. Know why?"

"Just tell me."

"Because I saw something terrible." She blinked into the darkness. She'd been so scared.

"You waiting for a drumroll or something?"

"The truth. That's what I saw."

"Wow. The Dalai Lama. In my cab. Drunk. So honored."

"I realized then that I have no control over anything. Freaks me out." She took a swig. "Except when I'm drinking. Then it doesn't bother me at all. See? Control. That's what I'm talking about."

Viv took another drink. It felt as good and necessary as water after a long run, until suddenly it didn't. Her insides seized. She lurched up.

Stu said, "Don't."

Her cheeks puffed out; she shook her head.

"Don't," he said.

She fumbled with the window button, burping and swallowing and gagging.

"Goddamn it." He closed his eyes.

The window lowered just enough for Viv to hurl pure alcohol and random bits of a 3 p.m. Greek salad down the side of Stu's impeccable car.

"You know what *I* just realized?" he said after she'd flopped back down in her seat, panting and ashamed. "I only really like you when you're passed out cold."

He got out the spare T-shirt he kept in his glove compartment so she could wipe/hide her face. Viv laughed when she blew her nose on it, but she was sort of crying too because now she cared again. She hated how disgusting she was, and what a failure she was, and it had really hurt, too, when she'd shot little bits of black olive out her nose.

She balled up the T-shirt like some giant nightmare dumpling and dropped it in the liquor store bag. Stu tied it closed, his giant fingers raised as if he were putting a bow on a Christmas present. He got out, splashed water from his Thermos against the barf on the door and wiped it down with paper towels. He climbed back into the car and said, "So?" Stu-Speak for "ready to go?"

Viv checked the time. Almost eleven. Her mother would be starting what Jack called her "textual assault" soon: Where are you? I thought the library closed at 10. Come home don't leave me you're all I have. Her mother never actually said that, but Viv could read between the lines.

She filled her water bottle with vodka and handed the empty to him. "Home, James!" she said.

She shoved her junk into her backpack then waited while he adjusted his mirrors then his seat then started fiddling with his mirrors again.

"Stu! What the hell?" Viv was suddenly desperate to leave, get this train wreck of a day over with. "Why are you doing this?"

"I'm a stickler."

"Hilarious," she said and closed her eyes.

She'd taught him that word the first time they'd met. She'd been passed out on a park bench. (This was back when she was stealing booze from her mother's liquor cabinet, before her mother fired the cleaning lady for it and Viv realized she needed a new supply.) Stu had pulled over to study for his high school equivalency course and noticed her there. Viv jolted awake to him going, "Hey. You okay? Hey!"

She'd scrambled up, knees to her chest, fists against her mouth, everything shaking. "I'm okay."

"No. You aren't," he said.

"I, um. I was just resting." She picked up her bike. "I'm going home now."

He grabbed the handlebars. "You're too drunk," he said, which was true, but she was sober enough to be afraid of him, some Hagrid-wannabe with an unsmiling face and a too-quiet way of talking.

"In the car." He loomed over her until she got in the back then he put her bike in the trunk. She thought about running but it was dark, and she really *was* too drunk for that. She took out her phone to dial 911. She had to squeeze her eyes shut a few times to keep the numbers from moving around. She hit 9. The trunk slammed shut. It was so loud and sudden it reminded her of her parents and how that had ended. She realized she'd rather the cops found her dismembered remains than her parents found her like this. They'd kill her. They'd blame each other. Nothing would ever get better.

Stu squeezed into the driver's seat and said, "Where d'ya live?"

She should have made something up, but she wasn't thinking straight so she told him. He drove her right there. When he noticed the light on in an upstairs window, he said, "Your parents home?"

Her dad hadn't lived with them for almost a year. "My father's probably at the door, waiting for me. He's a real stickler about curfew." She wanted to scare Stu away but it only seemed to piss him off.

"What the hell's a stickler?"

"It's, um, like someone who . . ." She looked out the window and thought of her father and wished for like the ten millionth time that he really was there, and her life hadn't turned to such shit. "It's someone who expects you to do things right." Even when they don't.

"*Stickler.*" Stu opened his glove compartment, took out a head of garlic, broke off a clove and said, "Then you better eat this. Covers the stink."

She wondered for a second if it was poisoned but she didn't have much choice. She forced it down then said, "I'll get some money and come right back. Promise." Another lie. She was going to run in and lock all the doors.

He flicked his fingers at her. They were as thick and not-quite-human as a gorilla's. "Gimme your phone."

She gave it to him. It was new but she didn't care. "Just don't hurt me."

He snorted, which could have meant a lot of different things. "What's your password?"

"It's Jack—capital *J*—exclamation point, small *a* . . ."

"Christ. Put it in."

She keyed in her password. He took the phone, typed something and handed it back.

"That's my name. That's my number. Don't be an idiot. You know what happens to idiots?"

"Yes."

"You don't, but whatever. You get like this again, you call me. I'll pick you up."

"You don't have to. I don't do this all the time. I . . ."

"And quit lying to me," he said. "Understand?"

She could feel her mother standing at the window, blinds bent open a crack, wondering what was taking Viv so long.

"Yes." She was never, ever, ever going to call him. "I'll get your money."

"No. Just fuck off. I got a fare."

He took her bike out of the trunk and gave it to her. Her mother was down at the front door by then, her housecoat pulled around her new scrawniness, her feet bare. She gave Viv a hug then turned away, her nose puckering. "Whoo. Have you been eating pizza?"

Her mother didn't suspect a thing.

Since that first night, Viv always kept garlic in her backpack. She broke off a clove now and ate it as Stu drove her home, yet again.

It was only a twelve-minute drive from the InnovaGear parking lot to her house. The meter read $14.85. Viv gave him a twenty and said keep the change. He didn't. He never did.

She blew him a kiss and got out of the cab. "See ya, Stooby."

"Hope not."

It was sort of a joke but not really. They both knew if Viv saw him again, it would be because she was still drinking.

She stepped into the house and caught her reflection in the hall mirror. Her skin was a whitish-gray and there were tiny burst blood vessels under her eyes from barfing so hard. She had to be at the med school the next day at nine. She was supposed to be bulimic. *At least I'll look the part*, she thought.

Davida

It takes me almost an hour to walk home from the police station. I turn the corner and there's the white Zanger & Sons Heating and Air Conditioning van parked across from our house again. Not like I'm surprised or anything but, today, after all that stuff with the cop? I can't handle it.

I see Tim's profile reflected in the massive sideview mirror. He's not exactly handsome—most people probably find him kind of dorky, what with the old-man glasses and the bad white-kid Afro—but I like his nose. I wish I didn't.

He's looking down, reading probably, which I guess is an improvement. The last couple of days, he just sat there for hours. No phone, no book—nothing—just waiting.

When he first started showing up, I did my best to ignore him. No way I was going to talk to him, not after what he'd done. I'd go to my room, wait as long as I could, then peek out the window, hoping he'd left or at least started playing on his phone like a normal person, but it never happened. He just sat there in the van all still and, like, stoic for hours. I tried really hard not to find it romantic or tragic or anything like that because I knew that's exactly what he wanted. He can't charm me with his weirdness anymore.

The first time we worked together, he told me he'd joined the Simulated Patient Program because he was obsessed with abnormal psychology. He loved playing schizophrenics or kids with borderline personality disorder because he got to "get into their heads." You'd think that would have been a warning sign for me but no. It didn't stop me.

Standing here now, seeing the stupid van again, I don't know who I'm madder at, him or me. He should have been at the police station with me this morning—but that would have been awkward, wouldn't it? "Was Vivienne a good friend of yours?" I'd love to hear him trying to answer that if the cop asked him.

He's right in front of the house so I don't have a choice. I have to walk by him.

I just go for it. I don't turn when he says, "Hey." I just keep walking, eyes straight ahead, until I reach the driveway. I'm basically home free. I can open the door, step inside and forget he ever existed.

But I don't. It's as if someone slams me in the back of the head with a rock or something. That's how hard it hits me—this, like, *rage*.

I storm over and go, "Hey, what?"

"Huh?" He blinks and pulls back his face.

"You said, 'hey.' Hey, what?" I'm not screaming or anything, but there's a definite *you asshole* tone to it.

"I, ah, have your phone." He gives this lame smile. "You left your phone in the van the other night."

"I know."

"Oh . . ." He blinks some more. "Why didn't you come get it? Or ask me? I would have—"

"I don't need it anymore. Viv's in a coma and you're a liar and I don't talk to liars so why would I?"

"What? I'm a what? You're saying—"

"You're a liar. You know you are. Viv is too, but she gets a pass. I mean, considering." My face is hot and red and thumping.

"Dave . . ."

30

"You don't get to call me Dave."

"Sorry." He tries to open the door, but I slam it closed with both hands.

"Davida. I don't know what you're talking about. I don't know why you're like this. This thing with Viv. It's terrible. It just sucks *so much*. But we should be dealing with it together. We—"

"Seriously? You're seriously saying that to me?" If you can scream and whisper at the same time, that's what I'm doing.

He swallows twice then goes, "Yes."

I turn away because I'm too mad to say anything back and too stupid to leave.

"Are you upset about the, um, overdose? Is that what this is about?"

"Don't insult me. Like you're so innocent."

"I don't understand." He's almost whimpering. "It's about us? . . . I thought everything was going good. It was, like, uh, perfect—you and me—and then suddenly you won't talk to me, you won't come to the door, your stepdad goes all evil automaton and asks me to leave. If you're mad because I had to cancel, I—"

I do this little "ha!" and shake my head.

"Okay. I didn't think it was that, but I didn't know. So I thought maybe it was the other night . . ."

"Don't talk to me about that."

"I have to. If I, you know, pushed things too far, it's important—"

I lunge at him, my teeth bared. "That's not the problem and you know it." I'm furious he'd bring that up. And embarrassed. I don't want to think about us like that ever again.

He says, "Good. I mean, I think," as if that's going to make me laugh, and then, "Sorry . . . I don't know what to do. Or, like, say. You're telling me I'm a liar? And Viv's a liar? How? Just tell me what's wrong. Please. I want to fix this."

"Where were you Saturday at noon?" I had no idea that was going to fly out of my mouth until it did. I cross my arms to keep from shaking.

"Saturday . . . ?" He's trying to sound all nonchalant like *hmmm, let me think*, but his eyes are open too wide and his voice is too high. "Oh, right. Saturday. I was working for my father. I texted you, but I guess you'd left your phone—"

"Liar."

"No. Seriously, look—" He holds out my phone, as if a text can't be a lie too.

"Give that to me." I put the phone in my pocket. Phones cost money. Why should I pay for him being a jerk?

"I'm going to ask you one more time—What were you doing in the van . . . outside the Wedgewood Motel . . . on Saturday around noon . . . for almost an hour?"

There's a long pause. We stare really hard at each other, as if we can see right into each other's brains. We're both breathing too loud.

What he says next is going to make all the difference.

"Working for Pa," he says.

"Liar," I say, and walk away.

Why Tim Couldn't
Tell Davida

3 days after the party
2:10 pm

I was in agony the whole way back from Davida's. Personal relationships aren't my strong point, let alone *multiple* conflicting personal relationships. My social skills were already stretched to the limit. I was on the verge of giving up then this thought came to me: "What would a Knight of the Round Table do?"

That's not quite as random as it sounds. King Arthur made his Knights swear to uphold twelve oaths. Davida and I had once sworn to uphold them ourselves but I looked them up when I got home just now to refresh my memory. There are lots of different versions on the Internet so it took me a while to find the right one especially since I was semi-crying the whole time so my vision was less than ideal. (I kept picturing Davida in that Lady Guinevere dress, reaching out to take my hand. Deadly.)

Nevertheless, I'm glad I persisted. Get past the slightly cringey references to damsels, "the weak" and a weird obsession with bearing arms, and the oaths are quite instructional. Sort of Twelve Steps to Living an Honorable Life.

I reviewed them and it became abundantly clear that
a) I cannot break the promise I made to Viv but

b) I also have to tell the truth, which is obviously

c) Impossible to do. It's either one or the other.

This was a pretty depressing conclusion until I noticed this old bio notebook sticking out of my desk drawer. It dawned on me that writing everything down here would allow me to examine my emotions and plot my strategy while simultaneously honoring my promise to Viv, provided, of course, I keep the notebook's existence a secret and destroy all evidence of it when I'm done. (I'm thinking of burning it in a small twilight bonfire at the breakwater although that may be too corny even for me.)

In the meantime, my plan is to give a more or less chronological account of what led to

Pa just barged in the door claiming I have his precious voltage meter. I told him I didn't—why would I?—but when he sensed I was hiding something, he went full SWAT team and ransacked my room. All he found was some old notebook half-filled with last term's bio homework although that didn't stop him, of course, from cuffing me in the head on his way out the door and calling me a "flapdrol."

Flapdrol. (That's his new name for me since Ma told him he can't say "idioot" anymore because it doesn't sound nice.) It's not easy to translate, but break it apart and you more or less get the gist of it. In Dutch, *flap* means "to dither" and *drol* means "shit."

A dithering shit. Not nice either but no doubt accurate, or at least I bet that's what Davida thinks. She must have found my desperate last-minute attempt at an excuse utterly pathetic. I can't even lie well.

This whole conundrum reminds me of that kids' game, "Which would you rather?" Which would you rather: Have your nose torn off by a grizzly or have a lungworm burrow through your eyeball? Have genital leprosy or elephantiasis of the face? Spend the rest of your life alone in a magnificent mansion or live in an overflowing outhouse with Beyoncé?

Which would I rather: Tell the truth and break a solemn promise to my comatose friend—or lie and lose the only girl who ever looked at me like I wasn't some idioot flapdrol? It's a game I can't win.

Viv

When Viv arrived at the med school for her SP session the next morning, the moulage artist was leaning into the mirror touching up her own makeup. Mandy Chan wore a lot of it, especially eyeliner, but it never looked tacky to Viv. It just looked like pure Mandy. One day Viv hoped she could be that honest with the world too.

"Gimme a sec," Mandy said. "Almost done." She started on her other eye. Viv looked around the room.

Mannequin heads with crushed orbital bones and tumorous growths. Stacks of newborn babies. Eyeballs trailing rubbery pink muscles, like a school of prehistoric jellyfish. Viv always laughed when she thought of how Tim described Mandy: "Dr. Frankenstein with a hoarding issue."

A severed leg was lying on a rectangular metal table at the back of the room. A new addition. The thigh end looked raw and ragged, as if it had been torn off by a chainsaw or, maybe, fangs. The bone shone white against the glistening redness of the innards.

"Niiice . . ." Viv knew it was all wax and silicon and cherry Jell-O, but still. It was almost real. She bent down for a closer look.

It might have been the gore or the smell or maybe even just leaning over too fast. Her stomach flipped. Her brain followed.

The pressure on the back of her eyes.

The barf splashing down the side of Stu's cab.

The humiliation.

She snapped up, her hand flat over her mouth.

Mandy sniffed. "Aw, quit it. You're just doing that to flatter me."

Viv said, "You're on to me," and wiped her lip with her thumb.

"I've been on to you for a long time, girlie . . . Take a load off." She motioned to a high metal chair in front of a mirror. "Let's see what you're dying of today."

Mandy ran her finger along the notes she kept taped to a wide gray counter. "Hmm. Bulimia. Insomnia. Anxiety. So . . . We're talking pallor, petechiae, discoloration . . . da-da-dum. Got it."

She snapped a black cape around Viv's neck, patted her shoulders and sized her up in the mirror. "My Jesus, girl. You look halfway there already."

"Thanks, Mandy. You look fabulous yourself."

"No. Really. You're white as a ghost." She clamped her fingertips on Viv's temples and turned her head from side to side to inspect her.

Viv flicked her away. "I'm *anemic*. For real. Give me a break."

"But the purple circles, the spots under your eyes . . . What in God's name you been up to?" She twisted Viv's hair into a massive bun and clipped it out of the way.

"Oh, you know. Living the life."

"Well, keep it up, sister. You cut my job in half. Just have to shave a few pounds off your face and I am done." She wrapped a stretchy cotton band around Viv's hairline, took a cotton pad from a glass jar and wiped her face with cleanser.

Mandy needed a crazy amount of stuff for moulage. On the counter in front of her were bottles of food coloring, Vaseline, sponges, wax, cocoa powder, chicken bones, something that looked like a kid's paint box, something else that looked like playdough, and tons of regular drugstore makeup. She tapped her nose while she decided what she was going to use then chose a pasty-colored foundation, a palette of grayish contouring powders and a mauve lipstick.

Viv closed her eyes and let her get to work. When she opened them ten minutes later, she looked emaciated and sad and even less able to take on the world than she actually was.

"Whaddya think?" Mandy said, screwing the lid back on the foundation.

"*Very* Día de Muertos." Viv leaned closer to the mirror and checked her reflection. She found it weirdly comforting to see herself like this. "I *love* how you bring out the real me."

Mandy laughed—loud, gravelly—then took off Viv's cape and wiped down the chair. "If that's the real you, darling, thank God there's doctors handy. You need all the help you can get."

"This is true." Viv enjoyed the irony. She blew Mandy a kiss and left.

The hall was buzzy with SPs all off to their next simulation. They were done up to look homeless or mentally ill or tubercular or jaundiced, but everyone was laughing and chatting like they were all perfectly A-OK. It made Viv feel lighter somehow. It was as if someone had said, "You be you," and actually meant it.

She said *hi, hey, wassup* all the way to Room 302. When she got there, another SP was just leaving. Makayla was seventeen too, but something about her always made Viv think of a toddler. She was short and solid with big round glasses and blue hair cut into a cockatoo-like swoop in the back. Today, she had a giant purple bruise on her chin, a black eye and fake blood coming out her nose. She looked like an autopsy photograph of a cartoon character.

When she saw Viv, she jiggled her hands and mouthed, *Oh my God!*

"What?" Viv's cheek was itchy, but she didn't want to scratch it and ruin the moulage.

Makayla laughed. "You seen the med student we got today?" Charlotte Ito and Erica Pelourd ran up behind her. They both had casts on their arms. They were giggly too.

"Which one?" Viv said. There must have been thirty students there.

The girls squawked with laughter. Makayla went, "You *obviously* haven't seen him then. This guy, he's like. I don't know. He's like the most perfect human being you ever saw, and he touched me."

Charlotte said, "She's not even exaggerating."

"All I could do to keep my clothes on."

Viv went, "Oooh, nice," but mentally she shrugged. Makayla was prone to gushing. She toodled her fingers at the girls and stepped into the examination room.

It was the typical doctor's office: a sink, a set of scales, pastel-colored body parts on a faux wooden desk, and an examination table decked out with a crispy paper cover and horror movie stirrups. At Viv's last real-life appointment, her doctor had threatened to get her up on one of those for her pap smear. She'd lied and said she was on her period. The thought of a relative stranger sticking a metal thing up her vag and going on a Magic School Bus sightseeing tour revolted her.

She sat down and answered a couple of texts from Jack then switched off her phone. Putting it away, she noticed a cottage-cheesy splodge of puke caked in the ends of her hair. Her heart sped up—she was going to barf, she was going to get caught, this was it, it was over—but it slowed down just as fast. She remembered where she was. She'd be fine. Simulated patients were *supposed* to leave clues for the med students to pick up on. It was part of their job. They all had their tricks. When they played alcoholics, they'd sprinkle liquor on their clothes. If they were homeless, they'd slick Mazola through their hair, maybe a little onion powder in their armpits, to make it seem like they hadn't showered in a while. When they were bulimic, they'd rub Parmesan cheese on themselves for a subtle whiff of puke. Everyone did it. No one would suspect a thing.

Two points for verisimilitude, Viv thought. Her English teacher used to say that whenever someone said something that sounded true but wasn't. She reviewed her lines.

Three minutes later, a med student walked in. Tallish, messy dark hair, big white teeth. He was obviously the one the girls had been talking about. His gorgeousness registered with Viv but that was about all. She had Jack.

Then the guy sat down on the swivel chair in front of her and smiled.

It was the power of suggestion maybe, but something about him hit her like a drug. She bit her lip, turned away and tittered into her shoulder. (The word *tittered* even flashed in her head. That's how bad it was.) Was she still drunk or something?

She looked at his shoes. She had to pull herself together.

Plain black sneakers, shoelaces missing the little plastic tips, raggedy ends. One black sock, one navy.

"Arlene?" That was her character's name.

She looked up. He was still smiling. Random dark hairs sprouted between his eyebrows. Her face felt like it was on fire. She thought of female baboons in mating season, their red asses flashing *Take me* at the first sign of an available male.

"I'm George Pineo. I'm a first-year medical student here. How can I help you today?"

He was leaning forward like the world's cutest football coach, his elbows on his knees, his eyebrows raised. He was polite. He was listening. He was ridiculously hot. He was killing her.

The SP script Viv had crammed for on the bus ride that morning? The two-hour practice session at the med school last week? Poof. Gone. She felt nervous in a way she never did. Viv had always been weirdly confident in her ability to improvise.

Her brain reared back from her mouth, like a horse balking at a jump. There was no way she could talk to this guy about gorging on double-cheese pizzas and buckets of Nutella and all the things the script told her to say. She couldn't tell him about her compulsive purging or her anus-shredding four-a-day laxative habit, even if they both knew it was all pretend. She couldn't bear the thought of someone like him picturing her

40

hurling into and/or squatting over the toilet. Because that's what he'd do. Picture her like that. She would have, if the roles had been reversed.

"I understand you've been having some eating issues?" he said, checking his clipboard.

She shrugged.

"Like to tell me about them?"

"I'm, it's, well . . ." That was as far as she got. Jack was her best friend. Her rock. The love of her life. She didn't care about this guy. She rubbed her face and opened her mouth to try again.

George started laughing. He was trying not to, but he was definitely laughing.

Viv was making a mess of this. "Sorry."

"No. You, ah, just kind of"—he waved his hand vaguely around his face—"removed one of your cheekbones."

Viv touched her face then looked at her hand. Her fingers were covered in gray powder.

There was a pause then she laughed, then he laughed, then they both looked away and laughed some more.

"Now you're going to think this is all in my head," she said in her best Southern accent.

"Not at all. A lot of people's faces rub off."

"Really?"

"Happens all the time. Disappearing Face Syndrome." He frowned earnestly and nodded.

"Oh, right. DFS. I've heard of that."

His eyes went twinkly, as if he was enjoying the banter, but then he glanced at the camera attached to the wall. He pulled down his mouth and got serious again. His profs were watching.

"I understand your parents are concerned," he said.

Viv cleared her throat and made herself focus. He was getting evaluated. She'd be shitting herself if someone was goofing around and ruining *her* marks.

"I don't know what's with them." She sighed so hard the papers on the desk rustled. "They think I've been 'starving myself' or something."

He nodded, a real doctor again. "Why do you think that is?"

"I dunno." Viv was supposed to be "surly and uncooperative." It said so in the script.

"Have you been losing weight?"

"A little, but it's summer. I don't want to look like some big whale on the beach."

"Do you *think* you look like a whale?" Viv found his concern unnerving, or maybe he was just a better actor than most of the other students.

"Okay, not a whale, maybe, but I'm not, like, my ideal weight either. Nothing the matter with having a goal."

"Depends on how realistic the goal is. Generally speaking, the word *ideal* is not, well, ideal. Giving ourselves unreasonable expectations can get us into trouble, emotionally speaking."

He said other stuff too, lots, but Viv missed it. She was stuck on the look in his eyes, the look the camera wasn't picking up, the one that cut right through the make-believe problems and went straight to her real ones. She couldn't help thinking he'd figured her out, or would if she'd let him. (Had he smelled the alcohol on her?)

He pulled his stool up even closer, his knees on either side of hers. He put his hands on her arm and took her pulse. He checked her glands, her breathing, her wildly pumping heart.

When his prof stepped in at the end of the session to get Viv's feedback on his performance, Viv gave George Pineo top marks for bedside manner.

Excerpt from police interview with George Pineo, 4 days after the party

Lt. Alan (Pidge) Eisenhauer: I understand you're a student at MacKinnon Med School.

George Pineo: Yes.

Eisenhauer: That where you met Vivienne Braithwaite? Through the, uh . . . "Simulated Patient Program"?

Pineo: Yes.

Eisenhauer: Tell me about the program.

Pineo: Um, well, it's basically role-playing. SPs are shown how to present with a certain medical condition then we—the med students—diagnose and/or treat them. Theoretically, that is.

Eisenhauer: Interesting.

Pineo: Yeah. Teaches you a lot of things you can't pick up in books.

Eisenhauer: Such as?

Pineo: Patient interaction, I guess.

Eisenhauer: Hmm . . . how would you describe your relationship with Vivienne?

Pineo: What do you mean my "relationship with Vivienne"?

Eisenhauer: I'll leave that up to you.

Pineo: Why would you think I have a relationship with her? . . . It's not like I . . . um . . .

Eisenhauer: Like you what?

Pineo: Look . . . I didn't do anything wrong.

Eisenhauer: Then you have nothing to worry about.

Pineo: No. I know. It's just that . . . people assume stuff.

Eisenhauer: Such as?

Pineo: I don't know . . . You smile at someone. Help them out. There must be something going on. But it wasn't like that.

Eisenhauer: You seem defensive.

Pineo: Sorry. I . . . I just feel a little guilty. I wasn't as professional as I could have been with Viv.

Eisenhauer: In what way?

Pineo: . . . With a patient, you're supposed to be a doctor and nothing else. You don't recoil, you don't judge—and you don't hit on teenage girls. I didn't quite manage to do that with Viv.

Davida

"Well, you'll be happy to know he's gone."

That's the first thing Dad says when I come down for breakfast.

"Who?" I rummage through the fridge for a yogurt or, actually, for an excuse not to look at him. He'd know right away I hadn't slept.

Dad laughs and slathers almond butter on a slice of seed bread. "Who do you think?"

I give him a little ha-ha smile and sit down with my feet on the chair next to me. The sun's coming in behind him, turning the tips of his ears almost see-through. I squint as if it's too bright and look away.

"Have a banana with that." He pushes the fruit bowl toward me. "You're not getting enough fruit."

I break one off the bunch and start to peel it, even though he's wrong. I'm getting plenty of fruit—bananas are about all I can stomach since everything happened—and I'm not happy Tim's gone either. I wish I was, but I'm not. That's just the truth.

I used to think the truth would be easy to recognize. Undebatable, like your shoe size or your street address or the location of the duodenum, but I don't think that anymore. Now I think the truth is more like one of those shape-shifting villains in a sci-fi movie. It somehow manages

45

to be a whole bunch of different things—*opposite* things—at exactly the same time. Like hating Tim with every furious little molecule in my body and also feeling like I'm going to die if I don't see him again. Both of them equally, undeniably and impossibly true. How can I know what to believe?

"He might just have parked around the corner to surprise you." Dad's trying to make a joke of it. Lure me in to telling him what's going on. He'd been so thrilled I finally had a boyfriend—*any* friend—that it seemed almost cruel when I told him it was over.

"Doubt it. I ran the loop three times this morning and didn't see hide nor hair of him," Steve says. He's lying on his back on the kitchen floor, his T-shirt soaked, one thin, furry leg pulled up to his chest. (What is it about middle-aged guys and their short shorts? I can't look at him either.) "Muriel doesn't like him parking in front of her house. She had a word with him about it the other day. Must have scared him off."

"Poor kid." Dad pops a capsule into the Keurig machine. "I know staking out the place is a bit much—but he's suffering, sweetie. You don't think you're being too hard on him?" He leans his elbow on the top of the machine while coffee sputters out.

"No." I dip the banana into the yogurt and take a bite. I am not.

"You just decided he wasn't your type? Is that it? Or did he say something? Did he do—"

"Leave her, Pete," Steve says and starts on his deep lunges. "She's got this."

I aim my banana at him in thanks. He gives me a little salute. Steve knows I haven't got this either, but he's not the type of parent to meddle.

"Of course she does," Dad says. "She absolutely does. And any decision she makes will be the right one. But can I say one more thing?" He sets the mug down in front of me. Hazelnut mocha. A bribe. "Guys are stupid, Davida. Like, double-*o* stoopid. It takes us way longer to figure things out than you girls. If Tim did or said something wrong, my bet is he didn't mean it."

"You don't know that," I say, kind of singsong, because I can't let that go but I'm not getting into it either. I just want to forget about the whole thing. Go back to my boring old life. Before Tim, before Viv, even before happiness. I was better off when I didn't know what I was missing.

Dad opens his mouth like he's about to say something else but then snaps it closed and nods, a sad little smile in his eyes. "You're right." He starts putting stuff in the dishwasher then says, "Oh, listen. I heard a girl from your school overdosed the other day. You know her?"

I blow on the coffee. "Not really." I take a sip.

Not at all, in fact. It's so embarrassing. I couldn't sleep last night remembering myself telling the cop he was wrong. Insisting, "Vivienne Braithwaite would *never* take drugs!" I was so confident. Like I was her closest friend or something. I'm amazed the cop didn't laugh in my face.

But there it is again. That two-faced truth thing.

I saw Viv take the pill on the video.

I saw for a fact it wasn't an IronPlus multivitamin.

Worse, I saw Viv and Tim in the van with *my very own eyes*.

I absolutely believe everything I saw. But I absolutely don't too.

Viv isn't like that. She's not the type of person who takes drugs. She's not the type of person who, like, *betrays* a friend. She just isn't.

Or maybe she is.

Round and round and round. It's like I'm on some demented Ferris wheel and I can't get off. It's crazy-making.

"Got to run," I say. I push my chair back with a screech. I leave the coffee and the yogurt and the banana with one bite out of it and grab my backpack.

"Right now?" Dad says. "Why?"

I kiss his forehead. "For my health." Which sounds sarcastic but isn't. My SP session doesn't start for over an hour, but I can't keep torturing myself like this. I need to get out of here.

Viv

Viv looked at her hands. They were shaking so hard she was worried the next med student would think she had Parkinson's or Huntington's.

Or Somethington's.

That just popped into her head. She smiled. It was a classic Jack joke. Random. Sort of stupid. The kind he loved.

The kind she couldn't tell him. He'd go, "Hahahaha . . ." Then, "Why were you shaking so bad?"

She rubbed her index finger up and down her forehead. She hated hiding stuff from him.

She needed a drink, and not just because of that. Anyone would, she told herself, after having a guy like George Pineo check their vitals. She pictured Makayla and those other girls and how they'd reacted. At least she wasn't that bad.

And anyway, it's not like she needed a big drink. Just a sip. Just enough to calm her down, get her back on track. Then she'd be fine.

She unclipped her water bottle from her backpack. Half the kids in the SP program were on Zoloft. Alcohol or anxiety medication—what was the difference?

Nothing. Everyone needed something.

She glanced at the camera but only out of habit. She was "staying hydrated." If someone was watching, that's all they'd think. She pulled the nozzle up with her teeth, tipped back her head—then there was a knock on the door and the next med student walked in. She could hardly take a swig now.

The student was pretty nervous, so Viv pulled herself together. They both couldn't be a mess. She slapped her water bottle closed with the palm of her hand and put on her best Arlene-face.

The other girl took a big, juddery breath and said, "My name's Christina Zajic. I'm a first-year medical student here. How can I help you today?" She tacked on a smile at the end, no doubt because that's what the textbook said to do. Viv smiled back then they did the same simulation she'd done with George. She did it with five more medical students (none of whom noticed she was missing a cheekbone) before it was time for lunch. She was hungry. Arlene might have had food issues, but Viv sure didn't.

On the way to the lunchroom, she switched on her phone and scrolled through her messages.

There was a text from Jack with a selfie comparing the size of his head to the giant sandwich he was holding.

That a chicken nugget on the left? she texted back.

couldn't be. chicken nuggets made with white meat

Hahahaha Jack always made her laugh.

She was really happy there for a moment, until she read the next text.

Just a reminder. Appt at Smitten Bridal Wed 27th 7 pm!!! So excited to start this journey with my new stepdaughter!!!! Love ya! K8E xox

K8E?

Kay-Eight-EEE?

Seriously? This was the woman her father was going to marry? Katie may have been twenty-two years younger than him, but she was still too old for that.

Viv wished she'd just quit with the reminders. Katie must have told her about this thirty times, as if Viv was irresponsible or something. She texted great, which looked a bit stark, but there was no way she could write love ya.

Tryin not to hate ya was more like it.

The next text was from her mother.

I checked your schedule and, if I'm correct, you're free Wednesday, June 27th. I thought it would be nice to spend a little mother-daughter time together. What if I get tickets to see the Good Lovelies? They're only in town one night. How does that sound?

It sounded like a small act of heroism. Her mother actually getting out of bed, checking Viv's agenda, making a plan, taking a stab at living again.

Shit.

Shit. Shit. Shit. Shit. Shit.

Oh, no! she answered. Sorry. I just took another shift. Can we do something another day instead? Xoxoxox

Such a liar. A sniveling, two-timing liar.

No response.

Viv pictured her mother hearing the ping, reading the text, dropping the phone and crawling back into bed, fully clothed.

Viv needed to get to a washroom.

There was a ladies' room directly in front of her, but that wasn't the one she needed. The med school was a patchwork of mismatched buildings: MacKinnon Hall with the brick turrets, white columns and stained-glass windows, where the simulations took place; the ugly mid-century concrete cube with the staff offices that everyone called the Bunker. And shiny new I.P. Keppo Tower, where the med students took their classes. The buildings were connected by a wonky maze of walkways, elevators and dark little staircases. It would be really easy to get lost if you didn't know your way, but Viv did. She knew there was a washroom at the end of the hall that led to the Bunker pedway. She knew the pedway was blocked off because of a massive leak in the skylight, so hardly anyone used that washroom.

That was the one Viv needed. She went there.

The washroom door swung closed behind her. A tap dripped, but otherwise it was eerily quiet inside. She heaved herself up onto the counter, leaned back against the mirror and unclipped her water bottle. She already felt more relaxed.

She'd just raised the nozzle to her mouth when she heard something. A squeak, more chew-toy than human. She lowered the bottle and listened. A few seconds—nothing—then the jagged little *he-he-he-he* of someone sucking in their breath.

Viv stopped, gritted her teeth.

Someone was crying.

She slid off the counter and bent down at the waist to look. There were feet in the third stall over.

Damn. All she'd wanted was a few seconds alone.

She'd find somewhere else to go. She started tiptoeing out but didn't get very far. It was as if Stu, her inner Stu, was right in front of her, blocking her way, a life-sized hologram squinting at her, his hands on his hips.

Stu hadn't left Viv on the park bench.

He wouldn't sneak off and ditch a person in need.

Viv kind of hated him. Right at that moment, she kind of hated everything. She sighed and turned around. "Are you okay?"

The whimpering stopped. The feet disappeared.

Did the girl actually think Viv didn't know she was still there? Viv pictured some kid crouched like a gargoyle on the toilet seat. It would be funny if it wasn't so sad.

"You all right?" She waited a couple seconds. When there was no answer, she thought *fine*. She'd tried. The girl didn't want her help. Stu should mind his fucking business. Viv slipped out the door and into the hall.

It was empty, not that it mattered. Viv wasn't waiting any longer. She popped open her water bottle and took a gulp. She closed her eyes, hoping to feel better, to feel human, free, something, but she didn't. Stu was still there, staring at her. She took another swig then headed back toward the washroom to help the girl.

That's when she saw Janice Drysdale beetling around the corner. She sort of ran the SP program. She'd know what to do.

"Janice!" Viv ran toward her.

"Well, hello there." Janice stopped, but not before they were weirdly close together—so close Viv could tell she used Pears soap and had a wiry white hair growing out of her chin.

"Wow." Janice peered right into her face. "Excellent moulage. Are you alcoholic?"

Viv jumped back. "No. I'm . . . I'm bulimic."

"Oh. Of course. I saw that on the schedule. Don't know why I thought that."

"I got a new piercing and my ear's infected. I just put some alcohol on it. Maybe that's what you smelled." Viv's face felt warm. Her three piercings were old and not infected and Janice would know that because she was a nurse and she hadn't even said anything about smelling alcohol in the first place.

"Could be." Janice smiled. Her lips were striped with dry, white cracks but the files she was carrying were crisp and orderly. Viv had the impression Janice was one of those people who's super-anal about everything except herself.

Janice said, "You need me for something?"

"Yeah. Um. There's this . . ."

"Walk with me." She took Viv's arm and picked up the pace. Viv remembered Tim Zanger telling her once that sharks had to keep moving or they died. A weird thing to think right then. Janice was so not a shark. She was way lower on the food chain than that.

"What's up?" Janice said.

"Someone's crying in the women's washroom."

She stopped. "Oh dear. Which one?"

"Near the pedway."

"Any idea who?"

"She was in a stall," Viv said, meaning "no," but then she pictured the feet, the beat-up Vans, the toes pointing out, and it hit her. "Maybe Eva?"

"Eva Federov?"

"Yeah. You know how she does that ballet thing with the duck feet." Viv put her wrists together and bent her hands out into a V. "I'm pretty sure it's her."

Now Janice went, "Oooh," way more serious. "Thanks for letting me know." And then she was gone.

Excerpt from police interview with Janice Drysdale, 4 days after the party

Lt. Alan (Pidge) Eisenhauer: Mrs. Drysdale?

Janice Drysdale: Ms., actually, but call me Janice.

Eisenhauer: Janice, then. Thanks for coming in. Let's get started with you telling me how you know Vivienne.

Drysdale: Through the Simulated Patient Program.

Eisenhauer: And what's your role there?

Drysdale: I'm the co-ordinator and a registered nurse, but I think of myself primarily as Dr. Keppo's "right-hand man" . . . Oh, sheesh. I have *got* to stop saying that—but "right-hand woman" has always sounded odd to me. Right-hand person. How about that?

Eisenhauer: Dr. Keppo?

Drysdale: Yes. Ivan Keppo. He's the med school's Dean of Education and also the director of the SP program. I just take care of the practicalities so that he can be free to work on "big picture" stuff. He likes to call me his "fixer," and I guess that's as good a definition as any.

Eisenhauer: What do you fix?

Drysdale: Oh, wow. Whatever! I write the scripts, train the SPs, oversee the simulations, "put out fires," the whole shebang.

Eisenhauer: You're busy.

Drysdale: Not as busy as Dr. Keppo! Frankly, the hardest part of my job is making sure he doesn't spread himself too thin. He teaches, does clinical work, community outreach, donor relations—not to mention makes himself available 24/7 to discuss any little thing the med students or SPs might be worried about.

Eisenhauer: So he works directly with the SPs?

Drysdale: Not if I can help it! But that man and his open-door policy . . . I have to shoo them away. Honestly. The teenage SPs—they're the worst! (*laughs*)

Eisenhauer: Worst? How?

Drysdale: I shouldn't say worst. I mean "most demanding"—which isn't fair either. We've got to accept some of the responsibility.

Eisenhauer: For what?

Drysdale: We take young, inexperienced people—kids, really—and say, "Imagine yourself in this scenario. You've got cancer or you're mentally ill or watching your mother die of a horrible illness and you don't know how you're going to look after your younger siblings when she goes." It's all simulated, of course, but it can be very triggering for some of them. The irony, of course, is that sensitive kids make the best SPs even though they're often the ones most affected by it. It's my job to weed out—again, wrong word—to *select* appropriate candidates, but I have to admit I've never quite found the magic formula. Some can be quite problematic.

Eisenhauer: Was Vivienne Braithwaite problematic?

Drysdale: Vivienne? . . . Oh, no. No! A great girl. Always well prepared. Full of beans. Upbeat. I was thinking of someone else. A former SP who recently kind of spun out of control.

Eisenhauer: Who was that?

Drysdale: Oh, ah. Her name's Eva.

Eisenhauer: What's her story?

Drysdale: Hmm . . . well . . . She's one of the sensitive kids I was talking about. She has an *amazing* ability to produce tears on demand . . . I shouldn't laugh, but really. In our line of work, that's a very handy skill to have.

Eisenhauer: "Spun out of control"? What happened to her?

Drysdale: Family problems. Her dad died, must be a year ago. She was having trouble coping and the SP program was no longer a good fit for her. All those mock traumas. Very triggering, as I said. We tried to help but not much we could do. She's eighteen. An adult—at least in the eyes of the law.

Eisenhauer: Were drugs involved?

Drysdale: I'm the wrong person to ask about that.

Eisenhauer: Were she and Vivienne friends?

Drysdale: They'd know each other, but friends? Probably not. Although,

Vivienne being Vivienne, so warm and fun-loving, she . . .

Eisenhauer: Do you need a tissue?

Drysdale: No. I'm fine. Sorry. It's just hard, thinking about Vivienne the way she was then and the way she is now . . . Heartbreaking.

Eisenhauer: How well did you know her?

Drysdale: Vivienne's been an SP for almost three years. Just summers and the odd shift during the school year, but nevertheless, I'd say I know her quite well. But I know all the SPs quite well. I make it my business to. Since Mother died, I live alone. This program is my life. Most of the SPs are older, but I really gravitate toward the young ones. They're kind of the children I never had. I like to think I'm there for them when they need me. I hope that doesn't sound pathetic.

Eisenhauer: That doesn't sound pathetic at all.

Davida

Normally, I'd take the bus to the med school but normal is officially over, so I walk. I have to think.

Just out of habit (or maybe hope), I glance at the place where Tim's van used to be. The parking spot is empty. A gaping hole. The type of hole meteors leave when they destroy civilizations.

Muriel, the old lady across the street, sees me looking. She's in her Montreal Canadiens nightie watering her garden, a hose in one hand, a cigarette half-hidden in the other. She tips back the giant *Breakfast at Tiffany's* straw hat she's wearing and calls out, "Sorry if I shooed your friend away, honey, but I—" She's about to launch into one of her strangers-in-the-neighborhood, can't-be-too-safe rants. I wave and cut her off.

"That's okay! He shouldn't have been there anyway. He's lucky you didn't call the cops."

That's what she likes to hear. I smile and keep going.

The cops.

Pidge.

What a stupid name.

The way he talked to me. I growl and give my head a shake. Who does he think he is? The smirk when he said, "So you've only known Vivienne a little more than a month then?"

I stop at the corner. Was it really only that long? All that stuff happened—*my entire life changed*—in, like, five weeks?

It's hard to believe. I do the math. There were those two weeks we were at the same camp, but forget about that. That was ages ago. But this time? June 15th—that's when I met her at the med school—to the party on July 21st. I count it out on my fingers.

Yup. Thirty-six days.

So, "Yeah, Pidge. Not long."

No wonder he was smirking. There's no way I could possibly know what was going on in Viv's life—in Viv's *head*—after only knowing her five weeks. The truth is she fooled me again. That's all that happened. I've just got to accept it and move on.

I turn and look back at the house. The cup of coffee I barely touched. The rest of that banana. My empty room. Oblivion. It's so tempting. I could call in sick and forget about the whole thing.

Muriel sees me looking and her face lights up, as if maybe I do want to talk about stranger-danger after all. The spray from her hose catches the sun and turns into a rainbow.

Muriel made a rainbow. Cranky old Muriel. It feels like a sign.

I do the count again. I still get thirty-six days but this time it's broken down a little differently. Now I get five awesome weeks and one day that totally sucked.

One day.

The worst day of my life, but still. No matter how sorry I feel for myself, no matter how much I blame her, that day was still way worse for Viv.

I wait until a car passes then cross onto Robie Street.

Stupid, but I feel like I owe Viv. And if I don't owe her, I at least owe myself. We both deserve an explanation.

Did I just miss something? Did everybody else know what was going on except me? Exactly how stupid was I?

I might not have known Viv very well, but someone at the med school must have. She was there for three years.

I'll just ask around. Pidge clearly isn't going to.

Viv

36 days before the party
2 hours later

Alcohol on an empty stomach was a bad idea. Viv needed food.

She also needed camouflage. She was standing in the doorway to the lunchroom, rifling through her backpack for garlic, when Makayla ambushed her.

"Soooo?" Makayla made jazz hands. "Seriously. Right?"

Viv glued her lips together and went, "Hmm?"

"George Pineo! Dr. Hotness! Come on!"

Viv chuckled, but carefully. She didn't want to give off any fumes.

"Did you freak? I mean, he can*not* be real. Real guys don't look like that. What is he? A next-generation sex doll or something?"

Viv raised her eyebrows like *hilarious!* then covered her mouth and pretended to cough.

"You okay?"

She nodded and did that red-in-the-face, can't-quit-coughing thing.

"Come sit with us." Makayla jerked her head toward the far side of the lunchroom where Charlotte and Erica were leaning into each other, whispering and laughing.

Viv shrugged and pointed at a random table as if she'd made plans. Luckily, Tim Zanger just happened to be there. He pointed back at her, hand flipped sideways, gangster-style. She hadn't spent much time with him outside the SP program, but he always cracked her up. He was what her mother would call an odd duck and she'd call a weirdo. (She loved weirdos. She found them so brave. She'd have been one if she could.)

Makayla looked surprised that Viv would choose Tim over her, but went, "Next time." Viv gave her a thumbs-up and headed to the food table. She snuck the clove of garlic into her mouth then grabbed the last cupcake. Enormous grocery-store chocolate with a poo-emoji mound of icing gone crunchy along the ridges. Sort of her dream lunch. It was amazing how fast life could turn around.

A girl she didn't recognize was sitting across from Tim, so Viv grabbed an empty chair from another table. The girl moved over to make room for her.

"Yo," Tim said, perhaps ironically.

"Hey," she said, sitting down. "What's with the hair?"

Tim was a skinny white kid with an Afro the color of a cardboard box. That day, he was wearing it picked high and parted. It looked like a giant beige tennis ball with a wedge carved out of it.

"You like?" He swiveled to give her the full one-eighty. The light caught the lenses of his oversized aviator glasses, briefly blanking out his eyes.

"*Love*," she said. "What is it about putting a part in big hair that just seems to scream 'crazy'?"

"My theory? It's not just because the hairstyle itself is unattractive, it's because the person rocking it took the time, effort and fashion risk to make it so. It's like announcing to the world that here's an individual who either wittingly chose to be an outsider or is so disconnected that he-slash-she-slash-they just naturally became one."

"Didn't actually expect an answer—but, hey, good one." Viv took a bite of the cupcake. Icing smooshed up almost into her nostrils. "What scenario you doing today?"

"Domineering boy—seventeen, mild dyslexia, socially isolated— bullies girlfriend into going through with unplanned pregnancy."

"Whoa. Typecasting 101." She wiped the icing off her upper lip and into her mouth. "Who gets to play the lucky gal?"

"Davida."

Viv flinched as if he'd snapped her with an elastic band. "Davida?" she said.

He pointed at the girl beside her.

Viv pulled back her face to look. "Davida?" She had to say it again.

"Yeah," Tim said. "It's just David with an *a*," as if she hadn't quite understood.

The girl Viv was gawking at didn't look familiar, but she asked again anyway. "Davida Williamson?"

How many Davidas could there possibly be?

Davida

By the time I get to the med school, I'm all fired up. All Special Victims Unit. All Harriet the Spy. I'm going to do some snooping, ask some questions, get to the bottom of this. For Viv, but for me too. I finally understand what people mean when they say "closure."

I'm not nervous or anything, but then I walk into the lobby and I think I hear Tim's voice—I hear *someone's* voice at least—and I panic. I bolt down the basement stairs.

I go straight to the nook under the steps and hide, my head in my hands, praying, praying, praying that he didn't see me, didn't see me run.

Dad and Steve are always talking about how much more confident I am since joining the SP program, but look at me. Worse than ever.

How sad is that? The whole reason Dad talked me into signing up for the program in the first place to "get me out of my shell." I needed to open up, I knew that, so I went—mentally kicking and screaming, the way us pathologically shy people do—but I still went. I memorized the script, attended the practice session, chose an appropriate outfit. I was ready.

Then I walked in the door that first day and just knew there was no way I could handle a bunch of strangers poking me and prodding me and asking me mortifying personal questions. Didn't matter the questions weren't actually about me. I couldn't do it.

I froze. Classes started to change. Perfect laughing people with stethoscopes and active social lives crisscrossed in front of me.

I saw a red exit sign above a gray metal door and took it. That's when I found this place. I hid here until I could make myself move again then snuck out the back door and went home.

It was kind of a stupid thing to do. I should have gone to the session and sucked at it, rather than not showing up at all, because that only set off alarm bells. When Janice, the lady from the SP program, called wondering where I was, Dad got really worried. After supper that night, he and Steve asked if we could have a little "chat." I knew exactly where that was headed, so I made up some story about cramps and gushing blood—periods still kind of horrify them into silence—then I signed up for an SP session on another day. I figured if that kept them from dragging me to yet another "confidence coach," it was worth it.

I didn't go back to the med school until the middle of June. That's when I met Tim. We were paired up on this boyfriend/girlfriend scenario. I was supposedly pregnant but didn't want the baby. He supposedly did. The med student's job was to help us work through our differences.

I thought Tim was kind of weird at first, like creepy-weird, although it was hard to tell how much was an act and how much was him. The script said the boy was "confrontational," but I still think Tim went too far. He called this one student a "baby-killing doctorette" when she gave me a brochure on Planned Parenthood. He pushed another guy so hard I was worried they were going to call security. Every session, he did something that made me uncomfortable.

I tried to brush Tim off at lunch, but I guess I was too subtle. We ended up eating together.

That's when I met Viv. Or, actually, re-met Viv. She remembered my name but clearly didn't have a clue who I was.

I wasn't surprised. Three years at the same school and she hadn't recognized me once. Still, it kind of hurt. Making friends with Viv when I was little had been such a big deal for me.

You'd think after all the agony I went through back then, I'd have known better than to let her do it to me again, but here I am, worse than ever.

No.

No, I'm not.

I make myself get up off the stairs. I'm going to do this thing. Get it over with.

I have moulage soon. I'll ask Mandy Chan about Viv. See if she knows anything.

Tim

4 days after the party
9:10 a.m.

The big problem is Davida doesn't understand my relationship with Viv. No one does. Most people can't even believe I *have* one.

Perfect example: that time at the lingerie store with Avram and Wendell.

We needed tights for our Medieval Living History group so there we were, in this shiny pink basically porn shop, trying like hell not to get a boner, and who do I see? Viv. Two aisles over, studying a miniscule black lace bra like it was some kind of masterpiece (which, IMHO, it kind of was).

I went, "Hey. There's my friend." Avram and Wendell both turned, saw Viv, went *ha-ha*, then went straight back to arguing about whether it was worth paying extra for pantyhose with the reinforced toe, even if it's not historically accurate. (Unlike ye old spandex.)

I went, "Seriously, she's my friend," and they were like, "Right." So I went, "No. Seriously. I know her from the SP program." And they went, "Fuck off," and then it was just basically back and forth:

"Quit shitting us."

"I'm not."

"Asshole."

"It's the truth."

"Like you got a nine-inch dick is the truth," etc., etc., until I finally went, "Oh, yeah? Well, watch this."

I zigzagged through this kinky obstacle course of plastic butts and insanely perky breasts right up to Viv, who by then had like five or six ridiculously sassy bras hooked over her wrist. She saw me and, I swear, it was like God Him/Herself smiled down upon me. She screamed, "Timmy!" (which was somewhat infantilizing but whatever) then gave me this giant hug then spun me around and tangoed me up and down the aisles with her hair and her bras and her actual body draped over me as if I'd written the whole fantasy dream sequence myself. The sales associate asked us to leave before Viv got her bras or I got my tights, but who cares? It shut those morons up.

And, sure, I played up the sexual nature of the encounter just to put them in their place, but did I believe it?

Please.

No sane person, including myself, would ever believe I had a chance with Vivienne Braithwaite. It's the whole reason we can be friends. Other guys get all anxious around her because they foolishly believe they have a hope in hell. I, on the other hand, have no such illusions, therefore no reason to be nervous, therefore no reason not to act normal around her. (By normal, I mean *my* normal, which admittedly is not setting the bar particularly high, although it's higher than Wendell's and several stratospheres above Avram's.) Viv was just like any other person to me, albeit poured into a smoking-hot body. Whenever I saw her at the med school, we goofed around, shot shit, bugged the hell out of each other. We were comfortable together.

That's why, in the end, I was the one she came to when she was in trouble. She told me so herself. (Strange how the most popular girl of all time had only one friend to confide in. And, yeah, downright bizarre it was me.)

On the other hand, the person I *did* feel nervous around was Davida.

I know that sounds like I was only interested in her because she was lowly enough to be in my league. And, admittedly, Davida probably isn't A-list material for most people. She's too shy, too blotchy when you say anything to her, too sort of invisible.

But that doesn't matter. To me she's beautiful. The eyes. ("Luteous" is the word I think, although more green than yellow.) Skin, the color of milk. (Whole, not skim.) Hair—I don't know what color you'd call it. Not blond. Kind of the color of a really, really light pencil mark. I saw her that first SP session and it was like, *zing*. Big pink arrow, straight to the heart. When I realized she was actually going to have lunch with me that day, I got twitchy and sweaty and, even on the open-ended Tim Zanger Dorkiness Scale, incredibly awkward.

It started out okay. When Davida told me her real name, I asked if it was Sanskrit. (Trying too hard perhaps, but seriously. Dah-*vee*-dah. Does that not sound like some ancient Indian goddess?) She blushed and said, no, it was just David with an *a*. Like Roberta or Alana or something.

I could have left it at that, but why carry on a perfectly normal conversation when you can totally torpedo it?

"Funny how many female names are like that," I said. "You ever hear of Leonarda Cianciulli?"

She shook her head, which was all the encouragement I needed.

"Leonarda, as in the feminine version of Leonardo," I said to clarify. "She was a serial killer who baked her victims' bodies into cakes and fed them to unsuspecting guests as a human sacrifice to the gods. True story. This was during World War II and her son was a soldier, so she was just trying to keep him safe."

Just. Like that was perfectly reasonable. I mean, "Leonarda, darling, I really *must* get this recipe."

Wendell and Avram—even Viv—would have been all over that, but I could tell by the look on Davida's face she was a tad disconcerted.

So I cleverly changed the subject to Juana—that would be Juan with an *a*—Barraza, a professional female wrestler from Mexico who killed between forty-two and forty-eight elderly ladies. (Not in the ring, although that would have been epic, come to think of it.) I proceeded to give a short dissertation on Juana's reign of terror, based entirely on her Wiki entry, which I'd just happened to read while on the toilet that very morning.

Am I nuts?

Was I trying to impress Davida with my encyclopedic knowledge of the deranged?

Or was I just trying to spare myself further mortification? Up until the moment I first laid eyes on her, I'd never honestly thought a girl-friend was a possibility for me. Maybe, in my tiny lizard brain, I realized I wasn't ready.

Frankly, I don't know what was motivating me. All I know is I couldn't stop. When I ran out of female "names-with-an-*a*" serial killers, I segued into my totally fabricated "passion" for abnormal psychology. I just could not turn that ship around at all.

So I was like, "Thank you, Jaysus!" when Viv sauntered into the lunchroom. I figured having the Braithwaite stamp of approval was the only thing potentially powerful enough to change Davida's impression of me. I waved her over to our table. She worked her magic.

Viv is my friend. She was the one who brought Davida and me together. That's why she means so much to me. I explained that to Davida but she didn't believe it. She thought it had to be something more.

And that was *before* she saw Viv and me in the van. No wonder she won't talk to me now.

Viv

36 days before the party
A second later

"Davida *Williamson?*" Viv bent her head practically onto her shoulder to get a closer look at the girl beside her.

The girl gave the tiniest nod but kept staring into her single-serving tub of fruit salad. Her skin was pale and her shoulder-length hair was fine and shiny, almost like it was made of threads of glass.

It took Tim a couple of seconds to understand what was happening. "You *know* each other?"

"Knew," Viv answered, because by now she was sure. It was the dimple in the girl's chin. Just a little notch, not a full-on face-vulva or anything, but Viv remembered how Davida used to hate it. "We were at camp together," she said, then to the girl, "I didn't recognize you! Wow. Contacts?"

Davida blushed so hard it made them all embarrassed. "No. I only needed glasses for a while. To fix my lazy eye." Her voice was husky, as if she'd just woken up or didn't use it much. Viv recognized that too.

"But your hair and . . ." She raised her hand as if Davida was so tall, even though she clearly wasn't. She just wasn't tiny anymore.

"Um," she said, almost making eye contact. "My hair got darker and, I don't know, I guess I grew."

Viv laughed, not at what Davida said but at the mere craziness of seeing her again. They'd been friends for maybe two weeks, seven years earlier. Viv had almost totally forgotten about her. "What have you been up to? You live around here?"

"Sorta . . . We, ah, go to the same school."

"We?" Viv wagged her finger between the two of them. "You and me?"

"Yeah. Cyril B. Eaton."

"No! How come we never saw each other there?"

Davida shrugged and Viv immediately knew how come. She wasn't proud of it, but she could see herself maybe not noticing someone like Davida.

Which made her an asshole.

"I loved camp," Viv said, doing her best to make up for it. "Didn't you?"

Another shrug.

Some vague memory floated up of Davida, sitting alone.

Of the two of them sitting alone.

They were together somewhere.

Then it came to Viv.

"Remember that day we got stuck in the clubhouse all afternoon?" She hadn't known Davida until then, and had really just wanted to be outside with her friends, but it had turned out okay.

"Yeah." Davida's smile only lasted an instant before she caught it and hid it away again.

Viv turned to Tim. "We got really burnt at free swim and the junior counselor freaked and dragged us inside because she was supposed to make sure we all had sunscreen on. She acted like she was personally responsible for giving us Stage 4 skin cancer."

He laughed really hard, which was so not-Tim. He usually made Viv work for it.

There was a pause then Davida said, "We played Guess Who."

"Guess Who." Viv shook her head and grinned. "Wow." It was as if someone had switched on the TV and there it was, that whole day, playing out in color.

"Arabella got a bunch of games for us." Davida talked into her fruit salad. "But that was the only one we played."

"Ara-bella. Oh my God!" Viv felt weirdly happy. "The counselor. That was her name. She had really curly hair that she was always getting leaves and pinecones and stuff stuck in. Bit of a ditz."

Davida gave a little laugh, as if she'd forgotten that too. Viv noticed how pretty she was, like someone from an old painting. Those glasses she used to wear were brutal.

Viv scraped some crumbs off the cupcake paper and into her mouth. She hadn't thought about that summer in ages. The two of them had ended up spending quite a bit of time together. Davida was really funny when they were alone but got shy when Viv tried to drag her out with the other girls. She'd say hi then sneak away to read a comic or knit squares for the baby quilts they were all supposed to make for the women's shelter.

"Too bad we didn't keep in touch," Viv said.

She wondered why that was; then another memory took shape.

Last day of camp. Her parents had driven in from the city. They'd waved and jumped and whooped when they'd spotted her in the crowd of waiting girls, but Viv could tell they'd been fighting. She hurried through her goodbyes and got in the car, already planning the stories she'd tell to make them laugh, make them forget. Her parents responded with tight smiles and the occasional competitive chuckle. Viv was so worried about leaving them alone in the car when they'd stopped at a gas station for a pee break that she'd run back from the washroom without checking for her phone. They were almost home by the time she realized she'd left it there. Major blowup. Her father got mad at Viv, then her mother got mad at her father for getting mad at Viv. They didn't speak again for weeks. Viv had been afraid to ask for another phone until school started. By then, she'd forgotten about Davida and all the other friends she'd made at camp.

"I guess it happens." Viv really didn't want to think about it anymore. "Camp is, like, your whole world when you're there, but three days later you've moved on to something else."

Davida went white then pink then got busy getting something out of her backpack. A little plastic-wrapped bundle she untwisted and laid flat on the table. Inside was a bunch of pink pills.

Viv went, "Hey! IronPlus multivitamins!" It didn't deserve that much enthusiasm, but she was still making up for being a jerk and not noticing Davida at school. "You take them too? I keep forgetting mine."

Davida pushed them toward her. "Want one? I've got lots. My dad." She gave a little roll of her eyes. "He's obsessed with my iron count."

"Want?" Viv laughed. "No. But I better. I'm so anemic it's pathetic. My boyfriend says my skin's the color of a Vietnamese spring roll. He can see my inner mung beans." She picked a vitamin up and shuddered. "Pills totally gag me. Don't know why. I can stuff half a burger in my face, no problem, but one little pill and I'm, like, retching."

She held it between her fingers and practice-swallowed a few times, trying to get the courage to put it in her mouth.

A voice behind her went, "What's that you got there?"

Viv jumped in surprise.

Makayla had managed to sneak up behind her. "An illicit substance of some sort?" She waggled her eyebrows, which were dyed blue to match her hair. Her desperate need to be cool was almost heartbreaking, so Viv played along.

"Shhhh! Makayla, geez . . ." She looked around as if someone might hear. "This is E. Trying to get me busted or something?"

Makayla's eyes went wide. She bent down and whispered in Viv's ear. "E? You mean, like, Ecstasy?"

"Obviously."

It was a lame joke, pure filler. Viv figured they both knew it, but Makayla went, "Oh. Um. Sorry. Didn't mean to interrupt. Talk later maybe? Or not. Whatever. See you." She scurried off before Viv could reply.

Viv looked at Tim and he looked at her then they cartoon-grimaced and covered their mouths with their hands and tried not to laugh. Viv folded her arms on the table and leaned across, her head low. She whispered, "She didn't actually think I was serious?"

"Yup," Tim said.

"Noooo. Moi? Popping Ecstasy in the med school lunchroom? What does she think I am?"

"Ahhhh . . . someone else entirely?" Tim flipped his palms out. "I mean, you don't even *drink*."

Viv sat up. "How would you know?" She sounded normal enough but inside, she was freaking. Was he being sarcastic? Could he smell it on her? "You stalking me or something?"

"Stalking's such an ugly word. I prefer to think of it as . . . research. I've been collecting little bits of your DNA for years."

"No. Seriously. How do you know I don't drink?"

"Call it a hunch. I'm extremely intuitive." Joking but not really. Viv was pretty sure he was saying that for Davida's benefit. "It also helps that you said so."

Viv squinted at him like *what are you talking about?*

"Please. Ariana's party last summer? You and I were the only two not face-down in the rubbing-alcohol punch."

"Oh, right." She laughed, relieved.

"You shared your kombucha with me. We drank it in chilled aperitif glasses with tiny paper umbrellas handcrafted in postwar Japan. Together we got high on living."

Viv turned to Davida. "We did share kombucha, but the rest, I assure you, is pure fantasy."

Davida bit her lip and smiled. "I don't drink either." Her raspy voice made it sound less like a confession and more like another tough fact of life.

Tim tipped back in his chair. "Well, aren't *we* a bunch of puritans."

"We certainly are," Viv said.

Or at least *were*, she thought.

It was true. She didn't drink back then. She wasn't a prude or religious or even that much of a goody-goody. She just had stuff to do. Stay in shape, ace her exams, impress the world at large. Back then—before the lady doored her and Viv saw her life flash before her eyes—she still thought she could.

Viv put the IronPlus pill in her mouth and washed it down with vodka from her water bottle. She wiped her lips with the back of her hand, took a scoop of icing for coverage and said, "You should come to the party this year, Davida. Ariana Cohen always has one when her parents go away."

Davida looked at the tabletop and shook her head. "I don't know her."

"Doesn't matter. Everyone's invited. There are kids from all over. So come."

"That's okay." Davida shook her head harder.

"Seriously," Tim said. "It'll be fun! Plus, Team Sober needs players. Viv and I get, like, *creamed* every year in the tug-of-war."

"You're coming." Viv was going to make up for ignoring Davida at school. "You have to."

"Attendance is mandatory." Tim smiled in a way Viv had never seen him smile before. No edge whatsoever. *Tim*, she thought. *You hound dog.*

"You're in?" Viv said to Davida.

"I guess."

"Not 'guess.' Promise."

Davida was staring at her little plastic-wrap package, her face pink and almost moist, but she was smiling too. "I promise."

"All right!" Viv was thrilled. "On another note, have you two youngsters decided what you're going to name the baby?"

"What baby?" Davida asked.

"Our love child," Tim said to her. "The SP session?"

Davida laughed. A good sign. Then Tim turned to Viv. "In honor of my Armenian heritage, I'm leaning toward Bagrat."

"I thought you were Dutch."

"I am, but seriously. I'd convert to Armenian if I could name my kid Bagrat. Bagrat Zanger: Master of the Universe. Is that not an awesome name?"

"Why are you asking me?" Viv said. "Ask your lovely girlfriend."

Tim's lips cinched into a happy little knot. Viv looked at him looking at Davida and thought how it was like watching some lab experiment. Bubbles of mercury running into each other's arms. Iron filings performing their mating dance for the magnet. Cesium exploding at the lightest touch of H_2O. Exactly what the laws of chemistry demanded. It was as science-y as that. He'd found his person.

She gave him a big side-eye toward Davida, as in *she's cute, go for it.* Tim's eyes went *don't you dare,* but they were twinkling.

Viv had just found her new volunteer project.

She stuffed the last of the cupcake into her mouth and got up. "You two lovebirds can hash that one out, but I gotta go. Got a podcast to finish." (By which she meant "start.")

"No. Stay," Tim said, but he didn't mean it.

Davida

On the way up from the basement, a song pops into my head. Just a snippet, but it's on repeat. *Something something something* "forever and a day-o." That's all I've got.

It's driving me crazy. I stand at the top of the stairs. The song goes around again and again then it hits me.

It's that camp song. The one we sang every night at the end of campfire. We'd stand in a circle with our arms crossed, holding hands with the girl on either side, swaying back and forth, belting it out. To me, it was just a song, but some girls cried every time we sang it. When it was over, counselors would walk them back to the cabins with their arms around their shoulders, whispering, "It's okay, it's okay, we'll all be together again next year."

Because friends we make at Wappamayo
Are friends forever and a day-o.

That's how it goes.

Is that why the song came to me? Because of the "special bond" Viv and I forged at camp?

Ha. Some bond. She went back to the city and never thought of me again.

I shove open the door into the lobby and notice the clock over the reception desk. I was supposed to be at the moulage station five minutes ago.

I run up the stairs and arrive panting. Mandy is just finishing up with another SP. She's an older lady who's laughing away about something despite the fact that there's a broken bone sticking out of her wrist. It's just a chicken bone but it looks totally real.

Mandy sees me and goes, "Relax, girl. You got plenty of time."

She dabs a little blood on the lady's shirt, musses up her hair, then sends her off.

"I'm going to sit you here today," she says to me. She taps a folding white table then starts collecting stuff on a tray. Sponges, Vaseline, a couple makeup palettes, a blow-dryer, a tube of RadiantU Peel-Off Facial Masque, don't know what else.

I'm all ready to ask her about Viv, but before I can say anything Mandy goes, "I'm so excited!" and it doesn't feel like the right time anymore. She gets me to roll up my sleeve and lay my arm on the table, palm up. "Ever had a bad burn before?"

"No," I say, but immediately realize I'm wrong.

"Well, you're in for a treat then." She starts dabbing red powder onto my arm. "Third-degree burns are the bomb. Barbecued pork with blisters—that's the look I'm going for. Call me sick but I love a good blister."

I smile and nod but I'm thinking of another Camp Wappamayo memory.

Our meet-cute story. The day Viv and I got fried.

Mandy smears a thin coat of face masque onto my arm and starts blowing it dry. She's chatting away the whole time but all I can think of is Vivi.

Vivi.

That's what people called her back then. I don't know if it was because she was only ten and that's what her family called her or if it was her camp name. All the girls wanted to go home with a cute new nickname.

The junior counselor made the two of us stay in the dining hall all afternoon. I was petrified. The only thing worse than being stuck outside with everyone was being stuck inside with Vivi. I was this awkward kid with an ugly name, a lazy eye and brown plastic glasses. Vivi was basically Viv, even then. She walked in with a Hawaiian print towel wrapped low around her hips and her hair all lit up from behind as if it were on fire.

Arabella said, "You know Davy?" She was just trying to help me fit in, but I said, "Davida."

Viv put one leg on either side of the bench and sat down beside me. "I do now." We could hear kids laughing and splashing in the lake but she acted like this was exactly where she wanted to be. After that day, she went out of her way to include me in everything. She always chose me for her partner unless someone got her first, always made sure to grab a hammock so we could spend Quiet Time together every afternoon. Viv's the only reason the other girls paid any attention to me.

On the last day of camp, we exchanged phone numbers and promised to get together in the city. We never did. I was too shy to call first, and Viv never tried. It took me ages to get over it. My family was weird and I didn't have many friends, but that was the first time I'd ever felt lonely.

"And now the pièce de résistance," Mandy's saying. She turns off the blow-dryer and checks to see if the masque is dry. "Excellent."

She takes a little pointed spatula and randomly peels up the edges. "Does that not look exactly like dead skin to you?" she says, tilting her head back and forth to make sure it's perfect. "In my own little way, I'm kind of a genius."

Viv said the same thing to me about Mandy once. I knew they talked a lot. Viv always said how much she liked her—so I just go for it. "Were you surprised when you heard about Viv?"

I've shocked her. Mandy falls back in her chair, like a passenger in a car that's taken off too fast. She closes her eyes and shakes her head. "Oh, God. I've been trying not to think about it."

She picks up an icing bag full of Vaseline and starts squirting pustules of grease under the fake skin to make blisters. "I'm just . . . dumbfounded. And that doesn't happen very often."

"Did you have any idea she was into drugs?"

Mandy shakes her head and smooths down a too-gloopy blister with her fingertip.

We're quiet for a while then I say, "Do you think it could have been a mistake? Viv didn't mean to take it?"

"Did you see the video? She picks up the pill and puts it in her mouth. Didn't look like a mistake to me."

"I know but . . . but do you think maybe she didn't *realize* what she was taking?"

"I'd sure like to." Mandy sort of laughs, but sadly. "I still can't believe she was into that stuff."

She leans in close and studies my arm. "Not burnt enough," she decides then starts sponging powdered charcoal around the edges. "It just doesn't seem like something she'd do, know what I mean? Viv was a party girl, a drinker, not a—"

"What?" Now I'm the one who's shocked.

"Well, 'drinker.' Maybe that's too strong a word, but she sure liked her booze. Pills, on the other hand, that's—"

"Viv doesn't drink."

Mandy laughs.

"I'm serious."

"Oh, come on." She puts down the sponge and looks up to see if I'm joking.

"She doesn't drink." Viv told me so herself that first day in the lunchroom.

"Yes, she does."

For a few seconds, we stare at each other in confusion. "Are you sure?" I say.

"Let me ask you this." Mandy picks up another sponge and adds some more red to the flesh around the burn. "Did you have a banana this morning?"

"I had a *bite* of banana."

"Yeah, well, I can smell it on you. I did Viv's moulage lots of times. Trust me. I know what booze smells like. You kids all think mouthwash or mint or barbecue corn chips are going to cover your tracks, but sorry. They don't. I was a kid once too, you know."

"I'm . . . I'm shocked."

"Yeah, well, me too. You really never saw her drink?" she says. "I thought you were friends."

Viv

36 days before the party
After lunch

"So, Arlene . . . Mind if I ask you some personal questions?"

Viv shrugged like *whatever.*

"Great!" Irving Patel wasn't going to let his patient's attitude get him down. He was a slim, third-year med student with serious glasses he kept poking into place with a stick-straight index finger. "Do you consume alcohol?"

Viv didn't stutter or blush. She said, "Never," totally unfazed, despite the vodka from her lunch with Tim and Davida still sloshing around in her belly. She wasn't lying. In the Simulated Patient Program, it's called acting.

"How about recreational drugs?"

Viv shook her head. Irving nodded, looked down to check the next question—then a girl in the hallway screamed. It was so loud and sudden he grabbed Viv's hand.

They turned and stared at the closed door as if they could miraculously see through it.

The girl's voice was angry, frantic. The only words Viv could make out were "leave me alone" and "he told me he would," or maybe "he told me he did." Whatever. This "he" told her something.

"I'm not sure what the protocol is here." Irving moved toward the door, almost ready to step outside and intervene, but then there was the sound of more footsteps. Someone new started making it's-going-to-be-all-right noises. The girl didn't want to be comforted. She kept screaming and banging into the walls even as they led her away. A few minutes later, everything was quiet again. Viv figured they must have coaxed her into the elevator.

"Whoa. Glad she's not *my* patient." Irving gave an awkward bare-toothed smile then pushed up his glasses and got to business. "So—Arlene—tell me a bit about how you're sleeping. Any problems there?"

Viv pretty much forgot about the commotion after that. Her mind was on her lines or podcast ideas or her mother or Jack or even, occasionally, Dr. Hotness.

She daydreamed her way through the last couple of sessions then she was done for the day. She was heading down the deserted hall, vaguely thinking about the scholarship application she should be working on when she saw Tim, squatting on the floor outside an examination room, reading. He was so deep into his book he didn't notice her until she nudged him with her foot.

"*The Psychopath Within*." She read the title out loud. "Hmm. Story of your life?"

He slid up the wall until he was standing. The pressure made his Afro spread up and out like some weird avian mating display. "How'd you guess?" he said.

"Anyone who'd name a defenseless child Bagrat has to be a psychopath."

"Or an Armenian."

"True. What are you doing here?"

"Waiting for Davida." He bit the inside of his mouth to keep from smiling then cleared his throat. "Just got this from the med school library. We were talking about psychopaths earlier. Thought she might be interested."

"Oooh, look at you. Don Juan. Mover and shaker."

"Man-about-town."

"Indeed. Where is she?"

"In there with Dr. Keppo. She's not feeling well. She had some sort of, I don't know, woozy thing in our last session."

"Ha. You do so know. *'Me? Actually know the correct medical term? You think I'm a nerd or something?'*"

"Okay. She had what I presume was—"

"What you know was . . ."

"What I know was a vasovagal attack."

"In other words?"

"What I said. She got woozy."

"I just love it when you use big words, Dr. Zanger. Were you able to ascertain the cause of this asshole-bagel attack?"

"Vasovagal attack."

"What I said. Asshole-bagel attack."

He flashed a pointer finger at her. "I shall be using that."

"Be my guest . . . So what happened? Why'd she get woozy? All those manly pheromones you're giving off?"

"I thought it was Eva scaring her—but come to think of it, you're probably right. Note to self . . . must dial back the virility a titch."

"Eva Federov?" Viv flinched in surprise. She hadn't heard of her in months and now twice in one day. *"Eva* scared her. How?"

"Didn't you hear the screaming? Fifth session?"

"That was her?"

"Yeah. I don't know what simulation she was doing. Probably a manic episode or something. She was wild. The noise must have shocked Davida because all the color ran out of her face then—" He flipped over his hand like he'd just lost at arm-wrestling. "Not quite on the floor but pretty close."

"She okay?"

"A little shaky, but otherwise, yeah."

"You just reminded me of something."

"What?"

Viv shook her head. It was all a bit hazy. "At camp." She closed one eye and thought about it for a second. "Some kid fell out of her bunk or had a nightmare and Davida lost it. Like, *lost it*. Fainted maybe? She might even have thrown up . . . She really didn't like loud noises."

"She's shy, I guess."

Viv nodded, but something was telling her it was more than that. She couldn't quite put her finger on it.

Tim was talking. ". . . Anyway, the med student and I looked after her until Dr. Keppo came in and took over."

"*You* looked after her?"

"No. I mean. Held her hand. Whatever."

Viv picked something out of his hair and smiled. He was so cute. Holding Davida's hand . . .

"I saw Eva today too." She didn't mention it was only her feet. "I thought she wasn't coming here anymore after what happened."

"First time I've seen her in a while too, but she's right back at it. She must be channeling all that anger and grief about her dad into the acting."

Viv laughed. "Interesting observation, Sigmund."

"No. Seriously. I opened the door a crack. You should have seen her face." He looked genuinely concerned.

"Oh, c'mon. Be honest. Eva's always been kind of hysterical, even before. Remember when Liam broke up with her, or that time she said those girls were picking on her even though they totally weren't? You feel sorry for her at first and then you're just, like, get me away from this person. Not to be mean—but I stopped believing anything she said ages ago. There was always some crisis."

"I know, but maybe she can't help it. Maybe her dad was like that too—always blowing stuff out of proportion. It would be hard if that's what the world looked like all the time."

"Argh." Viv stuck her hand into his hair and mussed out the part. He leaned into it, purring like a cat. "How is it you manage to think the same thing I do and yet sound like a good guy?"

"I am a good guy."

"You are. Had I not already pledged myself to another man-child, I'd be all over you."

"Sarcasm is the lowest form of humor."

"I'm not being sarcastic. I'm taken. That's all it is."

"Right."

"May I make a suggestion?" She nodded toward the examination room. "Ask Davida out."

"Mind your own business."

"Your happiness is my business."

"You sound like some sleazy dating service."

"I am some sleazy dating service. How's next weekend?"

"For what?"

"Your big date with Davida!"

"No."

"Why?"

"Just no."

"All answers must be in complete sentences or points will be deducted." She poked him in the ribs with a finger. "C'mon. Try again. Why?"

"I'm busy."

"Doing what?"

"Working for my dad."

"Okay. The weekend after that then."

"Can't."

"Why?"

"I've got tickets to the taxidermy show."

"You're kidding."

"No. I've been looking forward to it for—"

Viv squawked and slapped the sides of her face. "Oh my God! Taxidermy? That's perfect. Perfect! The quirky charm? So you! Seriously." She poked him again. "Ask her! You have to ask her."

"No," he said. Several times, in fact, but Viv could tell he was thinking about it.

She mouthed, "Do it . . . ," then left just as the door to the examination room opened.

Tim

I just had a great idea.

I bought Davida a gift after our first "date." I'd been saving it for something special but hey, what could be more special than having the girl you're in love with tell you she never wants to see you again? #romanticmoments.

I'll just write her a little note then get a courier to drop it off at her place.

I think she'll understand the significance. I think this might work.

Davida

4 days after the party
10:30 a.m.

I step out of the moulage room, still stunned at what Mandy just said.

Viv drinks? That whole big story about Team Sober, getting high on kombucha—that was a lie? What was the point? Why hide it? Nobody cares. Everyone drinks. I mean, other than Tim and me, and I'm not even sure about Tim now. (Had he been lying about *everything*?)

Someone down the hall is going, "Hey! Ah . . . Hey!" I turn to see who it is.

Makayla is running toward me. "Oh, um, hi!" She doesn't remember my name. I can tell.

"You okay?" she says, touching my elbow as if I'm sick or sore or something. She's changed her hair from blue to a kind of algae green. I wonder if it's a mistake.

"Why?" I say.

"Viv!" She puts her hand on her lips and shakes her head, which I presume is supposed to mean she's holding back tears. "It's really messing me up. I can't imagine what it must be like for you. You guys spent so much time together lately. How *is* she?"

I wobble my neck to avoid saying anything.

"Oh no." She actually moans. "So sad."

Her head is tilted down and her eyes are tilted up, as if she's trying to look deep into my soul.

It's such an act. She doesn't care about Viv. She just wants gossip. It grosses me out.

I go, "Sorry . . . but I have to . . ." I point down the hall.

"I understand. I don't want to keep you but, ah . . ." She still can't remember my name. I nod anyway. "Stay strong." She pounds her chest with her fist and frowns sadly.

It's so lame I kind of laugh. I immediately think about telling Viv, telling her how fake it was, how fake *everything* Makayla said was, and how we'd crack up, but then I realize I can't tell her.

That's the worst part. The forgetting. Feeling happy until you remember you aren't.

My laugh obviously confused Makayla. She looks at me weirdly.

"I gotta go," I say, and I do. My SP session is starting soon.

I get to the third floor then can't figure out which room I'm in. I check the schedule on my phone and realize where I'm wrong: it's 406, not 306.

I turn toward the staircase and see Tim heading into his session. He's wearing a tight gray ski turtleneck with sleeves that go right to his palms. It shows how skinny he is, and triangular too. (Those shoulders.) We'd picked the outfit out together after the practice session last week. His character is a cutter. Tim thought a guy like that would bunch his cuffs into his fists to hide his scars. You always wonder about someone who holds their hands in fists.

He sees me and stops, half in, half out of the doorway. Then someone must call him because he shrugs apologetically and walks in. The door closes behind him.

Did Tim know too? Were he and Viv playing a joke on me? A trick? If I'd gone to the party, would they have made fun of me for not drinking? For thinking they were "puritans" like me?

Maybe he's the one who gave Viv the pill. I'd seen them together.

What else had they been doing in the van? What else were they hiding from me?

How can people seem so nice and be so awful? At least with my mother you kind of knew.

I head upstairs. I don't want to be late for my session.

"Well, I'll be. Davida!" Dr. Keppo is bounding down the steps toward me, grinning. "I was wondering where you'd got to lately. Not trying to avoid me, are you?"

He's this really important guy at the med school but he knows everyone by name, even me. That's just the type of person he is.

I do my best to chuckle because I know it's supposed to be a joke. "No, I . . . uh . . ."

His smile fades, as if he just remembered about Viv. "No. Of course not . . . You okay?"

It's the exact same thing Makayla said to me, but totally different. He actually means it. My neck goes tight. I can feel tears behind my eyes.

"I was disappointed not to see you at the grief counseling session the other day. Tim said he didn't think you could make it."

I nod. I bet Tim didn't say why.

"I hadn't realized you and Viv were such close friends until he told me. Got a second?" He sits down on the gray cement steps and dusts off a space beside him. His knuckles are hairy but his head's practically completely bald. It's weird how that happens.

I hesitate. Dr. Keppo's busy. He's got better things to do.

"How much farther up are you going?" he asks.

"Fourth floor."

"*A whole floor?* Then you need a rest." He pats the step. "Sit."

I do. He raises his eyebrows and says, "So. Viv."

I nod.

"We're all reeling. You never get used to this sort of thing. Even us doctors and nurses—and we've seen it all. For you kids? It's like the end of the world."

That's exactly what it feels like. The end of the world. I know it's not the way he means it, and I know he might not like me when he hears what I'm really feeling, but I get this urge to tell him anyway.

"Yeah. It's . . . hard." I stumble for words. "I feel bad." I *have* to say that. "But I . . . I feel mad too. Viv was this person . . . who was . . . really, you know, special . . . but she . . ."

My throat aches, I'm holding it so tight to keep from crying. I want to tell him what she did to me but it won't come out.

There's a long pause then he puts his arm around my shoulder, just for a second. I pull down my sleeve and rub it across my eyes. I'm not going to fall apart. Not here.

"Anger is normal in situations like this," he says. "Strange but true. You *expect* to feel sad, heartbroken, upset, whatever—but tragedies often want more from us than that. They bring up our deepest, most conflicted feelings. Anger, hurt, loss . . . My guess is you're feeling deserted."

It's more than that, but yes. I nod.

"Why wouldn't you feel angry then? Here's this person you enjoyed so much, up and deserting you! You don't deserve that."

I swallow a noisy gulp of air and hold my breath.

"And it's doubly hard for you because this isn't the first time, is it?"

I look at him in shock then I realize he doesn't know she did this to me before. He's not talking about camp. He's talking about my mother. I'd told him about my weird family when he'd helped me after I'd fainted that first day. I told him why I didn't like loud noises.

"First losing someone to an illness, and now to a drug habit."

"Habit?" That stops me. "Viv had an actual habit?"

He spreads his hands like *I can't say* or maybe *I won't say*. "The person I'm concerned about at the moment is you. This is no doubt unearthing old feelings of hurt and betrayal. Do you have anyone you can talk to about it?"

I shake my head.

"Your dad?"

I shake my head harder. Dr. Keppo kind of laughs. "Oh, come on. You've told me about him. He's not that bad. Pretty damn good, in fact, if I remember right."

"I know. It's just that he's—"

A door above us opens and a bunch of med students come barreling down the stairs. Dr. Keppo and I scooch over to the side. He has a joke or a comment for each of them as they pass, and they all have one for him. Their voices ricochet off the walls the whole way down. We don't say anything until the lobby door opens and closes and they're gone.

He laughs. "This might not be the best time or place to chat."

I nod.

He pushes a hand down on one knee and stands up. "Milady?" He takes my hand and helps me up too. "I have to run, I'm afraid. Janice sent me out of town the last couple of days and she's got me hopping again today, but listen. If you ever do want to talk, best time to reach me is after six, when no one else is around to bug us." He winks at his little joke. "Just pop up to my office. Room 622. Top floor of the Bunker. Or hey, did I give you my cell number last time?"

"You did." It's pinned to my bulletin board.

"No harm getting it again." He pulls a prescription pad out of his pocket, scribbles something and hands it to me. "I'm around if you need me."

I look at it and laugh. Below his number, he's drawn a goofy little character with its paws on the side of its head, screaming, "Help!!!"

"Is that me?" I say.

He raises his eyebrows like *what do* you *think?* then bounces down the stairs two at a time.

Viv

"Hey," Jack whispered, "You okay?"

Viv opened her eyes. She didn't like the sound of that.

He was propped on one elbow, looking at her in that intent, unblinking way of his.

Scary.

She closed her eyes and focused on a hair glued to her lip. She tried flicking it away with her tongue but couldn't get it. Jack put a finger under her chin and scratched at it with his thumb.

"I mean it. You all right?"

"Yes." She whacked his hand away. "What are you talking about?"

It was Sunday morning. His family was at church and would be for hours. (He'd gotten a pass that day because he was leaving for rugby camp on Saturday and he had a lot to do. His parents thought that meant "packing.") Jack and Viv were in his single bed, covered in a sheet and a bright white checkerboard of sunlight.

"You look sad."

What did he have, X-ray vision or something?

"Yeah, well, you may have heard. My boyfriend's leaving for a month."

"Twenty-five days."

"That's like a month."

"No, it's not." He buried his face into her neck and whined in a way she was supposed to recognize, "It's like a *year*! No. A *decade*!"

"Exactly. It's really, really long."

"Oh, c'monnnn, Vivification. Not that long." He took her earlobe between his teeth and gave it a tug.

"Longer than we've ever been apart."

He looked at her, all serious again. His eyes were the same shiny brown as her grandmother's piano. "You going to be okay when I'm gone?"

"Yes! Geez. Like I'm going to fall apart without you or something?" She swung a pillow at him. He grabbed it and tossed it off the bed in one smooth move. She doubted Dr. Hotness could do that.

"I'm worried about you," he said.

"Why? You're the one who's going to be totally alone in some strange place surrounded by a bunch of competitive assholes, all of whom are praying to God you sprain your ankle or pull your hamstring or screw up so massively you don't make the team. *I* should be worried about *you*."

He didn't laugh. He put his hand behind his head and stared at the ceiling.

She'd gone too far. "And I would be," she said, "if I didn't know you are so damn good, you'd make the team even if you had *two* broken legs."

"Yeah, okay," he said. "Can you quit with the stand-up routine for a minute and just talk to me? It's only us. No one's going to take off points if you admit there's actually something upsetting you."

Viv looked at him, serious now too. This would be a reasonable time to spill her guts. To tell him how overwhelmed she was. How freaked out she was about her parents, her future, failing, letting everyone down. How drinking was the only way she managed to hold things together and even then, just barely.

She wanted to tell him. He loved her. He was a good person. He'd help.

But he was also human. She could hardly expect Jack to love a total fuck-up. Jack, who could literally have anyone he wanted.

"I'm just upset you're leaving," she said. "That's all. I'm going to miss you."

"I'm going to miss you too, but you know what the difference is?"

"You'll have all those competitive assholes keeping you company?"

"I've got my family. If I need them, they're here for me, no matter what."

"I've got my family too."

He curled a piece of her hair around his finger. The split ends sparkled against his skin. "I like your parents. They've always been really nice to me. But I don't know where their heads are at these days. It's like they're so deep into their own shit, you don't matter or something."

"I don't matter?"

"Sorry. You don't—I don't know—*register*. They obviously love you. A lot. But right now, all they seem to think about is themselves. They're so busy fighting they don't have a clue what you're doing anymore."

"Lucky us." Viv flashed a boob at him.

He sighed and flopped back on his pillow. She was immediately ashamed of herself. She snuggled into his side and said, "I'm a grown-up." It was almost an apology.

"Not really."

"Thanks."

"Yeah, well, neither am I. We still need, like, guidance or security or something. We at least need to feel like someone's got our back. Everyone does."

"You've got mine."

"But I'm leaving, and I keep thinking you're way more . . ."

"What?"

"I don't know . . . *fragile* than you're letting on."

Viv put her arm across his chest. She could feel his heart chugging away like an engine. The Little Train That Could. That was Jack in a nutshell, doing what had to be done, no matter how hard.

He had enough to worry about.

"You're sweet," she said.

"I don't have to go. I'll stay if you want."

Yes, she thought. *Stay. Please. Don't leave me.*

"Jack." She put her hands on either side of him and pushed herself up. Her hair fell around them like a tent. "Don't be dumb."

"It's just rugby."

"*Just* rugby?!" She pretended to choke. "Just your life, you mean."

"Wow. How to make me look one-dimensional. I'm also interested in football and hockey." He pulled her back down. "And you."

"*Parts* of me."

"No. All of you."

"Joking."

"Which I've asked you to quit doing. I don't want to go. I don't care that much about rugby."

"Such a lie."

"No, it's not."

"Okay. Fine. But you *do* care about a scholarship and your parents do too and that's where the scouts are, so you have to go, period. Plus, it's only twenty-five days."

"That's like a *year!*" He put on the girly whine again. She hit him.

"No, it's not. It's like a *century!*" And then he pushed her and she pushed him back and then they were sort of wrestling and then they were kissing and then were back at it and then Jack went, "Oh, shit." They both heard the car door slam at the same time. He rolled over and peeked out the window. "Dad!"

Jack had gone gray and big-eyed with panic, but Viv was practically peeing herself. They'd just managed to get their jeans half on when Larry called up the stairs to say he was home.

Jack went, "Hey, Dad! You're early," his voice muffled by the T-shirt he was pulling over his head. Viv kicked her bra under the bed and pulled on a T-shirt too. They were both dressed and the bed sort of made when Larry popped his head in the door.

"I'm just here for a sec. Mom asked me to pick up the coffee urn for Fellowship." He looked at the almost-empty suitcase open on the floor. "So? Get much done?"

Jack smiled and said, "Yeah. Lots."

Viv pretended she was tying her shoe, so Larry wouldn't see her crack up.

Excerpt from police interview with Jack Downey, 4 days after the party

Lt. Alan (Pidge) Eisenhauer: Jack Downey?

Jack Downey: Hi.

Eisenhauer: Have a seat . . . I know your mother. Lovely lady.

Downey: Thanks.

Eisenhauer: I know this has been hard on you, but I'm sure you appreciate we have to do this.

Downey: Yeah.

Eisenhauer: How about you tell me about you and Vivienne? How long have you been going out?

Downey: Since we were fourteen.

Eisenhauer: So, what's that? Three years?

Downey: A bit more than that.

Eisenhauer: A long time. Any problems?

Downey: Not usually.

Eisenhauer: But recently? You two were seen arguing.

Downey: Oh. Um. Yeah.

Eisenhauer: What about?

Downey: Nothing . . . It was my fault.

Eisenhauer: What do you mean?

Downey: All of it. The argument. What . . . what happened to her.

Eisenhauer: The overdose?

Downey: Yeah.

Eisenhauer: Did you supply the drugs?

Downey: No! . . . I didn't even know she was into that stuff!

Eisenhauer: So why's it your fault then?

Downey: I shouldn't have left her. I *knew* she was in a bad place, but I went anyway.

Eisenhauer: "A bad place"—how?

Downey: Her life was just, I don't know, a mess. That's why I went to rugby camp. I was trying to help.

Eisenhauer: How would that help?

Downey: We've wanted to go away to university together since, like, forever. Viv's parents have tons of money, so she doesn't have to worry, but the only way I'll be going is if I get a scholarship. My marks are pretty good but, you know, not full-ride good. The guidance counselor, my coach, the scouts—they all told me rugby was my best chance. So when I got picked for camp, I was like *yes*. I'd be training with the best coaches anywhere. The only thing holding me back was Viv. She could fake out most people, but not me. I'd never seen her that messed up. I seriously considered bailing on camp and staying with her, but I thought it's only twenty-five days. You know, "short-term pain for long-term gain." I decided I needed to go to camp, work hard, get a scholarship, then we could go away and I could take care of her.

Eisenhauer: Isn't that her parents' job?

Downey: You'd think. But Viv spent more time worrying about them than vice versa. I'm not saying I'm some big manly man or anything, but Viv needed help. If my life were like that, I'd need someone to look after me too.

Eisenhauer: How long have things been bad at home for her?

Downey: Like, ages. I remember going to their solstice party a few years ago. Her parents had one every summer for their clients. Allie—that's her mom—was in . . . I was going to say in her happy place, but Allie doesn't really do happy. I guess you could say "in her element." Everything was, like, *perfect*. Big long tables set up in the backyard with candles, flowers, those little lights. People playing, like, *harps*. Some fancy restaurant doing the catering. All the guests had to come dressed in white. It was like something you'd see in a movie. Anyway, Katie was there—

Eisenhauer: Katie?

Downey: Her dad's fiancée. Back then, she was just an employee, but first time I saw her, I knew. It was so obvious. Ross—Viv's dad—was all over her.

Eisenhauer: As in?

Downey: Sleazy old-guy stuff. You know, standing too close when he refilled her wine. Whispering in her ear so he could look down her blouse. It would have been embarrassing to see him act that way with *any*one *any*where, but he was doing it with some thirty-year-old in front of his own daughter. I just tried to keep Viv occupied with the gochujang shrimp skewers or whatever they were. She didn't need to see that.

Eisenhauer: I can understand how that would upset her.

Downey: I shouldn't make it sound like it's just Ross. I mean, he was being a jerk, but he's not really the problem. Allie isn't either.

Eisenhauer: What is then?

Downey: They just don't *like* each other. Before the Katie thing, Ross was always giving Allie diamond bracelets for Valentine's Day and she was always flying him to fancy golf courses for Father's Day, but actually talking to each other? Never happened. The only thing they had in common was Viv. It's like when they looked at her, they were happy. When they looked at each other, they weren't. That's why Viv felt responsible for them. She was all they had.

Eisenhauer: Did you two talk about it?

Downey: At first, but later? Not much. I think their behavior embarrassed her.

Eisenhauer: Did anything change recently for Vivienne? Anything that, looking back, makes you think something was up?

Downey: Maybe? I don't know. Viv was always overbooked, borderline stressed-out. I was worried about her being alone when I left but she was all excited about this new project she was cooking up. I thought it might help.

Eisenhauer: What was that?

Downey: (*laughs*) She was matchmaking. Two kids she knew from the SP program. She decided they'd be perfect together. She was spending a lot of time with them. She seemed to be having fun.

Eisenhauer: You think they might know something about the drugs?

Downey: I don't know them very well but doubt it. They're kind of like . . . um . . . I dunno . . . nerds. Goody-goodies.

Eisenhauer: You know their names?

Downey: Tim Someone and Davida . . . Sorry, I should know her name. She goes to my school.

Eisenhauer: Williamson. That's okay. I've already spoken with her . . . Anything else you noticed? Anything at all?

Downey: No. We were both so busy before I left, we hardly got to see each other. Then I was at camp and we were barely able to talk . . .

Eisenhauer: And then you got home and you argued. What was that about?

Downey: Nothing. I mean it—nothing! Me being stupid. Jealous. Asshole-guy stuff. We'd never been away from each other so it was kind of weird being back together. I misread things and I got mad and I apologized and that was it. I thought it would just blow over.

Eisenhauer: But it didn't.

Downey: There wasn't time.

Tim

Why did I send Davida that package? Seriously. Why?? What an idioot.

This is exactly why Pa's always telling me to think first. Use my head.

But that's the thing. I DID think first. I thought it was the perfect idea. I thought it would remind her of how much we had in common and all the fun we used to have and then she'd read my note and she'd call me and we could talk and she'd understand that even though I can't tell her exactly what predicament I'm in, I am indeed in a predicament but it has nothing to do with her/us so let's just forget about it and pick up where we left off.

Now, though, I realize a dead animal might not be everybody's idea of a romantic gesture.

I just called the courier, but I was too late. They've already delivered it.

Viv

33 days before the party
5:15 p.m.

Viv had her feet on the kitchen table and her laptop on her knees. She was supposedly working on the Barking Robot podcast pitch but she'd only managed to come up with a few sort-of okay ideas before she gave up and FaceTimed Jack. He was too busy to talk but agreed to let her watch him work out as long as she didn't distract him.

"Me? Distract *you*? I, at least, have my shirt on."

Jack flexed his pecs. "Excuuuse me, Braithwaite. My eyes are up here."

They were goofing around like that when the back door swung open and Viv's aunt Christie barged in, loaded down with deli bags.

"Vivi, feet off the table—and Christ, Jack. Put on some clothes." She gave Viv's legs a quick flick with her finger and slammed her laptop closed.

"Christie, geez! What's with you?"

"Wha-at?" Christie kissed the top of her head. "My guess is you've been on that thing for hours and he has stuff he should be doing. As do you."

Christie was an emergency room doctor. She was used to taking charge in ugly situations. She put the bags on the table and pulled out a bouquet of tulips, three plastic tubs of vegetables and some fish wrapped in butcher paper.

"Put those in a vase. Set the dining room table. Then warm up the vegetables. The fish should be gently pan-fried but not yet. I'll tell you when. I'll deal with your mother. I've had enough of this crap." She pointedly looked around—at the unwashed dishes, the abandoned clothes, the bowls of week-old cereal curdling on the table—then headed upstairs.

"I can't believe this!" Viv acted pissed, but she was actually happy to have a mature adult in the house. An hour later, Allie was showered and dressed, and the three of them were sitting down to eat at the dining room table. Christie had insisted on the good china and candles. It was the first meal Viv and Allie hadn't microwaved or toasted in months, which made it kind of a celebration. Everything was going fine until Christie started bugging Allie to take up the flute again.

"Oh, for God's sake." Allie sighed and smoothed the napkin on her lap. "I haven't played since undergrad."

"Doesn't matter." With her thick shiny hair and high cheekbones, Christie looked a lot like Allie, only heavier and healthier and not so worried about everything. Viv often wondered how they could be so similar and yet so different. "It's an amateur orchestra. They don't care how well you play. It's about learning. Having fun. Expanding those tight little horizons of yours." She helped herself to more tilapia.

Allie glared at her and started slicing her green beans into stupidly small pieces.

Christie ran her tongue under her lips to keep from laughing. She cleared her throat. "C'mon, Allie. You'll enjoy it. You'll be out of the house. You'll be around people with similar interests . . ."

They all knew she meant "unlike Ross." Christie was not a fan. Never had been.

"I'm not ready to be around anyone, thank you very much."

"You are so, but fine." Christie pointed her fork at her. "You can't tell me you're not ready to be around *music* again."

"Hey, Google. Play Bach's *Goldberg Variations*." Piano music came on through the tiny speakers on the ceiling. Allie gave a smug smile. "Done."

Yes, Viv thought. *Done. Leave her.*

"Hey, Google, stop. Staying home with a robot is not what you need. You need to go out, spend time with the real thing." Christie started whistling some tune Allie apparently used to play. "You'd love it." She whistled some more. "You know you would . . ."

Allie sighed, threw back a gulp of wine, then went, "All right. Fine."

Christie wasn't sure what she'd just heard. "You mean yes? You'll go?"

"I said all right."

"I'm so proud of you!" She leaned over and gave Allie a hug. "That's great! Just great."

Christie refilled their wine glasses then tipped the bottle at Viv with her eyebrows raised to see if she'd like any.

Allie went, "Chris-*tina*! Leave Vivi alone. She doesn't drink—and she's hardly going to start with a couple of old bags like us."

Christie laughed. Viv wasn't sure if that was about her not drinking or them being old bags, but she played innocent. If anyone was on to her, it would be Christie. Viv was actually surprised she hadn't said anything about her drinking yet. Christie was the one who'd given her a box of condoms—and a lecture—for her sixteenth birthday.

"A toast," Christie said. The two women raised their wine glasses. Viv raised her milk. "To new beginnings!"

"That's redundant," Allie said and took a sip. "Beginnings are always new."

Christie and Viv groaned, but lovingly. Allie and her grammar. Not less, fewer. Not who, whom. Not now, seriously.

"It's a joke," Allie said. "Ross said that at our wedding. Don't you remember, Christie? That's how he started his speech."

She smiled when she said it, but her lips quivered. It was like that scene in thrillers when everyone suddenly realizes a bomb's about to go off. Viv froze.

"Al." Christie reached out to hold her hand. "Allie. Don't. This isn't worth it. The marriage was over years ago. You know that. Long before Katie came on the scene. She's evil and she's awful and I promise to say horrible, vicious things about her as long as you need me to, but frankly she did you a favor. She set you free while you're still young and beautiful enough to do something about it."

"Katie's way younger than me." Allie was trying to be brave and make a joke, but her hand flew up to her mouth and her face went red and ugly.

"But not as beautiful." Christie and Viv said it at exactly the same time, and so wildly enthusiastically that even Allie started to laugh.

She dabbed her eyes with her napkin. "Yeah. She's a real *dog* compared to me."

"She is," Viv said then turned up her face and let out a long, loud howl.

Her mother went, "Oh, stop it," but Viv didn't, so Christie started barking too.

"Stop it. I mean it." Allie held out her arm at its full length and waved her napkin uselessly at them. It was such an Allie thing to do—both so regal and so ridiculous—that they all cracked up.

Allie jumped up and grabbed them by the shoulders. Viv was ready for her to cover their mouths or knock their heads together, but Allie started barking too.

This was Viv's mother. The person she loved. Viv was howling and laughing and making weird honking noises because she was sobbing too hard to catch her breath, but she was happy. Really happy for the first time in ages.

After they'd barked themselves hoarse, Christie refilled the wine glasses and cranked up some eighties pop then they danced around the living room until Allie noticed someone on the sidewalk looking in and made them stop. Allie was happy too, and probably a little drunk by then as well. They bullied her into trying on all her clothes so they could tell her which ones to throw out. She resisted—"It's Eileen

Fisher!"; "I paid $400 for it!"; "No one's going to see my underwear!"—
but by the end they'd convinced her she had too much unstructured
linen and needed better bras.

Viv left the sisters in the sunroom setting up a Tinder account for
Allie. She didn't want to know the details. She drank the wine left in
their glasses before she put them in the dishwasher but otherwise no
booze. She felt like the world was fixing itself.

Last thing she heard before falling asleep was the two of them
squealing about some excruciating date Allie'd had in high school with
a Spanish exchange student named Fernando. Viv crawled into bed and
texted it all to Jack.

Excerpt from police interview with Dr. Christina LeBlanc, 4 days after the party

Lt. Alan (Pidge) Eisenhauer: First off, let me say how sorry I am about your niece.

Dr. Christina LeBlanc: Yeah.

Eisenhauer: You're close?

LeBlanc: Like my own kid.

Eisenhauer: You're an ER doctor. You've seen the opioid crisis firsthand. Were you surprised Vivienne got caught up in it?

LeBlanc: *Shocked.* Getting that phone call was the worst moment of my life. I raced to the hospital like a crazy person. I wasn't even dressed. I had cotton between my toes. My nails were still wet. And then seeing Viv like that? White and limp and intubated. And Ross and Allie, crying. Crying in each other's arms? Nothing made sense.

Eisenhauer: Does it now?

LeBlanc: No. I've been racking my brain for something I might have missed but, honestly, there's nothing suggesting Vivi was into that stuff at all . . . I mean, I knew she drank. Don't know how her parents missed it. Garlic can only hide so much. But a little drinking? So what? She's seventeen and it's summer. Jesus. I was partying a lot harder than that by the time I was fourteen. Vivi was still lifeguarding, volunteering, being an SP, doing all the things she was supposed to do, not to mention dealing with the cesspool of her parents' relationship. God knows, I need a few hits of something after a day with Allie myself. She's my big sister and I love her, but Allie's always been "complicated." God. Who am I to talk? I've never been married or divorced so I can hardly comment on how she's handling it, let alone handling Vivi in a coma. *My* heart is broken. It must be killing her.

Eisenhauer: One of the issues we're looking at is where the oxy came from. You ever hear of the med school being a source?

LeBlanc: The med school? . . . No. Frankly, I'd be surprised. I went to MacKinnon myself. Still do a bit of teaching there. It's a great school. Ivan Keppo runs a tight ship. I certainly wouldn't have encouraged Vivi to become an SP if he didn't. Why? What have you heard?

Eisenhauer: Nothing. Just thought you might have an inside scoop.

LeBlanc: I wish I did.

Viv

The bark-a-thon with her mother and Christie was exactly what Viv needed. Like a sauna after a junk food binge. She felt purified. She could practically smell the toxins oozing out of her.

She woke up the next day without a hangover. Hours later, she was still amazed how bearable life could be. The shine off the pool that morning hadn't fried her eyeballs. She'd biked to the med school without having to pull over and puke. And, despite the stale air and nasty lighting in the conference room, she'd actually found herself interested in the two-hour prep session just wrapping up.

"Good work, everybody!" Janice raised her voice over the sound of chairs scraping back. "See you next week. In the meantime, please review your scripts. Everything you need to know should be there, but any questions—any questions at all—I'm happy to help. Okay? Lovely. Off you go!"

Viv checked her phone. Four o'clock and she hadn't had a single drink all day or, she realized, much to eat. The lunchroom would be closed by now but there were machines downstairs, just off the lobby. She waved to everyone—Makayla pretended not to notice her, now that she was a drug addict—then took the elevator down to the main floor.

Davida was peering into the vending machine, rubbing her chin as if she had a monumental decision to make.

Viv came up behind her and whispered, "Got any E?"

Davida jumped back with her hands up, as if Viv had caught her going through someone's locker. She patted her chest when she realized who it was. "Sorry," she gasped. "Sorry."

Viv laughed. "Why are *you* sorry? I'm the one who scared you. Speaking of which—oops."

Davida shook her head and blushed and Viv remembered how little it took to embarrass her. A stupid thing to do, creeping up on her like that. Rule number one: Know your audience.

"What are you getting?" she asked.

"Oh, ah, well, I wanted a Wunderbar but then I saw they've got carrots and raisins and, like, peeled apple slices in here." Davida shrank into her hoodie. "Now I feel, I don't know, guilty."

Viv whispered, "I won't tell anyone."

Davida smiled then turned back to study the vending machine.

"Let me help." Viv put in two bucks and hit D7. A Wunderbar fell into the bin.

Davida gave a little close-mouthed laugh and picked it up. "Thanks. I'm terrible at making decisions."

"I, on the other hand, am a pro. I mean, as long as it's about someone else's snack." This was true, although it sounded like a joke. "Push over. My turn to agonize."

Viv was going back and forth between ripple chips and a Caramilk bar when her phone buzzed.

Chips, she decided.

She put in the money, hit C4 and checked her phone.

A text from **Christie**: Don't look at Facebook. I'm dealing with this.

Viv heard the swoosh of the bag landing but didn't retrieve it. She was too busy scrolling through Facebook.

"Are you all right?" Davida was bent forward, looking up into Viv's face. She grabbed the chips and tried again. "Something the matter? Viv?"

Down the hall, doors started opening. People flooded into the lobby. Viv needed to get out before she saw someone she knew, before someone she knew saw her, before someone asked about the Facebook post, but she couldn't. She couldn't take her eyes off the screen.

"C'mon," Davida said.

Viv let Davida maneuver her through the crowd, across the lobby and down the stairs to the basement. They went through a dim corridor, past the furnace room and the storage rooms and the room marked "Keep Out" to a little triangular alcove under the stairs. Cracked navy-blue gym mats were piled on the cement floor as if someone had meant to trash them but forgot. The only light came from a half-lit fluorescent tube and the red exit sign above a nearby door. It smelled a bit like a rink.

"You'll be okay here," Davida said. When Viv didn't respond, she added, "Anyone comes, I'll just say you're having a migraine."

Viv crumpled onto the mats, her knees bent up to her chin, her hands over her face, her hair flowing over her, weirdly luxurious, like the robe of a high priestess. Davida sat next to her, but not too close, which was good. Compassion would have been more than Viv could handle right then, especially from someone she barely knew, someone who was clearly only there because she'd been in the wrong place at the wrong time.

Viv wanted her mother.

That was almost funny. Her *mother*. As if she hadn't caused this whole mess.

She wanted Jack.

He'd come. He'd come right away if she called.

She couldn't call Jack. He wouldn't go to camp. He'd insist on staying. His parents would hate her.

Christie?

Christie would lie and say it was under control, which it wasn't.

Her father? No way. He'd caused it too.

Stu, she thought.

I'll call Stu.

She slid her hands off her face. Davida was smiling at her, one of those sad smiles, the kind med students aim for when asking SPs to describe their symptoms.

"Can I do something?" Davida said.

"My mother." Viv wrinkled her nose and shook her head. She was trying to make it light, but also not to cry.

"She okay?"

"No. And she's making damn sure no one else is either." Viv coughed out a little laugh. She didn't mean to sound so angry. "She just called my father's fiancée a cheap whore and a gold-digger and a *c*-asterisk-*n*-*t* on Facebook."

Davida gritted her teeth like *ew*.

Viv's eyes stung but she kept talking. "She's totally losing it. I don't know what to do. One minute I think she's going to be fine then the next, she's screaming or crying or apologizing to *me*, which is almost worse because, if anything, I should be apologizing to her. I'm the one who can't stand being around her, even though I know how shitty she must feel being dumped at fifty so my father can get it on with some thirtysomething babe who my mother thought of as a friend, some 'girl' she hired because she figured Katie—that's her name—is a single mother and could use a break. Now Mum can't even work at her own accounting firm, the one she and Dad started. And to top it all off, Mum and Dad are still fighting over 'division of assets' and, as my Aunt Christie says, probably will be until there are no assets left to divide. I mean, I get it. It's a nightmare and Mum has nowhere to turn, which isn't fair because if anyone is the bad guy around here it's Dad, but at least Dad isn't losing it, not publicly anyway. He's doing that 'Now let's all be reasonable here and do what's best for Vivienne' thing, which is making Mum even madder because he's the one who ruined things 'for Vivienne,' not Mum. Saddest part is that if Mum just kept her mouth shut and didn't do anything outrageous for a while, everyone would be on her side. But she keeps doing shit like this, so how can I support her? She's proving Dad's point! She *is* impossible to live with."

Viv threw her phone on the mat. She would have loved to stop but couldn't.

"Last week—*for instance*—Mum parked across Dad's driveway and locked her car there with a big sign taped to the inside of the wind-shield that said, ROSS BRAITHWAITE IS A PATHOLOGICAL LIAR. Which may or may not be true, but still. Uncool. Before that, she wrote the Association of Chartered Accountants saying Katie should lose her CA designation. Mum claims giving your boss blow-jobs is unprofessional conduct. Oh, and what else? . . . Right. She sent Dad's family explicit photos some private investigator took of him and Katie in a hot tub, date-stamped so everyone would know his little 'nothing happened until we'd officially separated' line was a big fat lie. You know. The usual." Viv groaned. "I'll shut up now."

"I don't mind listening. Seriously. It's kind of nice knowing I'm not the only one with a messed-up family."

Viv turned and looked at her.

Davida blushed and looked down at the mat. She picked at a tear in the leather where the stuffing was coming through. "My mother ran away when I was three. I haven't seen her in almost fifteen years."

Viv suddenly remembered something.

The arts and crafts cabin. Campers making vases for their mothers out of tin cans and papier-mâché. Davida was at the end of the table. Was this before or after the two of them got sunburned? Viv didn't know.

She just recalled the counselor crouching down beside Davida and saying, "What about an aunt? Or a neighbor then?" and Davida staring at a string wrapped around her finger, shaking her head, her face painfully red. Even at ten, Viv had sensed something wasn't right at home for her.

"Oh. God." She grimaced. "Sorry. That sucks."

Davida shrugged. "Not like I miss her. I only have one memory of her. Being woken in the middle of the night by this big crash. I got out of bed and peeked out my door and there she was, screaming and waving her arms up and down. The television was smashed to pieces and her mouth was all kind of stretched out and horrible. I thought she was a monster. Like a real monster, the way three-year-olds think of monsters. Dad was trying to calm her down and just the way the light was, I could see the spit spraying out of her mouth, all kind of sparkling. I still don't like loud noises."

"Don't blame you." Viv had been woken by grown-ups making loud noises too.

They were quiet for a while.

"That's how I ended up with Dr. Keppo," Davida said. "I had a little, like, *incident*. When that girl was screaming last week?"

"Eva?" Viv tried to sound innocent. She didn't want to embarrass Davida by letting on she knew about it.

"I think that's her name. Tim said she's this great SP, but I didn't know that then. We were in a session and she was in the hall. She slammed into the wall and I guess the noise must have reminded me of my mother. It was like my body was melting or something. I thought I was going to throw up. Dr. Keppo had to come."

Eva was a bit weird, but she tried really hard at the SP sessions. Viv thought she'd be happy knowing she sounded that realistic. She'd tell her next time she saw her. "You okay now?"

"What's okay?" Davida squiggled her mouth. "Dr. Keppo helped. He made everyone leave then checked to make sure I wasn't having a heart attack or anything, but mostly we just talked. Normally I wouldn't say much, but he asked what I'd thought caused it and he was really nice, so I ended up talking about Mom and Dad and the rest of my weird family."

"Weird how?"

"Other than Mom? Well, I live with my dad and Steve, who I call my stepfather, but he isn't. He's my mother's first husband and my half-brothers' father."

"Oh." It was like doing math in her head. Viv had to close her eyes to figure it out. "So where's your mother now?"

"Don't know exactly. She moves around. When she first left, she went to Nicaragua. Dad and Steve tracked her down and tried to get her to a doctor, but she wouldn't go."

"What's the matter with her?"

"Bipolar. Or at least that's what my dads think. They'd really like to get her on medication, but they can't force her. She may be crazy but she's still a grown-up. She makes her own decisions—I mean, if you can call them that."

"So you have no contact with her at all?"

Davida wobbled her head. "A couple of times a year she gets in touch but it's usually just a letter or an email, which is good because the phone calls are really awkward. She only calls when she's, like, flying—'We're going to do this together and that together, go to Antarctica, start a restaurant, make a movie,' some wild plan like that. When I was little, I'd get all excited. I really thought it was going to happen. But then I wouldn't hear from her again for months and by that time she'd be on to something else, and I'd be crushed. After a while, I stopped taking her calls. I know that sounds mean, but they're really disruptive. Dad or Steve usually tell her I'm out then make me write her an email later."

"That's tough."

"She can't help it. Dad and Steve both tell me how wonderful she was before she got sick. I just try to remember that and not get too down about it." Davida took the Wunderbar out of her pocket and broke it in two. She handed half to Viv. "Chocolate helps."

Viv almost said, "Or booze," but didn't. She remembered Makayla avoiding eye contact with her ever since the Ecstasy joke. Davida seemed even straighter than Makayla. Viv didn't want to scare her away.

She said, "How long have they been living together, your dad and Steve?"

"Long as I can remember. They're not gay—this isn't some switcho-chango romance thing—it was just easier. They were spending a lot of time together anyway, trying to find Mom, figure out what to do with her, all that stuff, and it was costing a lot of money. So they got a place together. Saved a ton on babysitting. Plus, they're the perfect combo. They're both really organized, really boring, really normal. Mom basically married the same guy twice."

Davida took a bite of the bar. Caramel drooped out in two shiny strings. She patted them back in with her finger. "I've always found it embarrassing. Their arrangement, I mean."

"Must be awkward." Viv imagined her mother and Katie moving in together. Two bodies being brought out the next day.

"No. It's not that. It's fine. Mostly. My half-brothers are older. They moved out a while ago so now it's just Dad and Steve and me. They keep saying they're going to sell the house and get their own places but we've got plenty of room and, I don't know, we're a family, I guess. Pizza Friday night, fighting about laundry, opening presents around the Christmas tree, stuff like that. We have our problems, but probably no worse than anyone else's." Davida's neck was covered in pink and white blotches, like a baby's toy giraffe. "Try telling people that though. If I had two gay dads, who cares? But a mother who ditches her kids? That's bad. *She's* bad. So I'm probably bad too because, like, how could a child survive such a terrible thing without being, you know, *damaged*? People either feel sorry for me or start 'wondering' about me. That's why I never tell anyone about it."

"Except me." Viv nudged her. There was a pause then they both sort of laughed.

"Yeah. You're the first person I've told in ages. I mean, you and Dr. Keppo." Davida picked a flake of chocolate off her shirt. "You should talk to him."

Viv made some noncommittal noise but Davida kept going. "It felt good just blurting it all out. You meet someone like him—a doctor and everything—and you think he's going to have this perfect life and there's no way he'd be able to understand what you're going through, but it wasn't like that. He told me stuff you wouldn't believe. He was really poor when he was little and his father was abusive, and when he was ten Dr. Keppo found out his dad had a whole other family back in Hungary. The guy even had another son named Ivan who he'd abandoned. Dr. Keppo said he was always afraid if he did anything wrong his father was going to abandon him too . . . Oops." Davida's hand flew up to her mouth.

"What?"

"I don't think I'm allowed to tell you that. It's supposed to be confidential when you talk to a doctor."

"What *you* say to the doctor is confidential, not the other way around."

"Oh, right." For some reason, they found that hysterical. Davida had to wipe her eyes on her sleeve, she was laughing so hard.

"Anyway," she said a little while later, "he was really helpful. You'd like him. I'm not kidding. You should see him."

"Yeah. Maybe." Dr. Keppo was a big guy at the medical school, a friend of her aunt Christie. No way Viv was going to let him find out she was losing it.

"You know who *you* should see?" she said to Davida.

"Who?"

"Tim Zanger."

Davida went, "Oh!" and turned her face away so fast you'd think Viv had flashed her.

"He likes you. I can tell. I know he seems a bit weird—because he totally is—but he's great. Funny and sweet and he couldn't care less what other people think. Personally, I love the guy. If I didn't have Jack . . ." Viv lifted an eyebrow her eyebrows and laughed. "Anyway, he likes you. I don't know how skilled he is at getting that across so if you like him, I'd just go for it."

Davida didn't say anything so Viv elbowed her until she answered.

"I heard you."

"Chip?" Viv said and tore open the bag.

Davida nodded and took a handful. Viv could see she was trying not to smile.

Davida

I promise Dr. Keppo that I'll call if I need to talk then I head upstairs for my SP session. Because I've got a burn, I'm going to the med school's so-called emergency department. I find the room, pull back the curtain and climb up on the examination table. The white paper covering crackles so loudly I blurt out, "Sorry!" I blush and look around to see if anyone heard me.

Then I laugh. I realize that's the type of thing Viv would have found hilarious.

Which makes me stop laughing. A picture appears in my head: Viv in a real hospital. Real oxygen, real doctors, real emergency.

I shake it away and make myself focus on the scenario. My name's Felicity. I was at home, cooking french fries, when I tripped on the edge of a throw rug. A cast iron frying pan full of boiling fat fell on my arm. I'm in shock. I'm in pain. (That much is true.)

The med student opens the curtain. "Felicity?"

I say yes and look up.

"I'm George Pineo." He gives his little introduction.

I can't take my eyes off him but not because he's so hot. Almost the opposite. I've never had a session with him before. Viv kept going on and on about him—all the girls did. But looking at him now? I don't get it. He just seems kind of awkward. Not cute at all. A customer service rep going through his lines.

"Mind if I leave the drapes open?" He pulls back the curtain surrounding the examination table without waiting for an answer. "Kind of stuffy in here today."

He fakes a smile then sits down on the stool across from me. He looks at the burn for a second then pushes back his stool as if he's afraid he's going to catch something from me. "How did that happen?"

I tell him.

He asks a few more questions then he explains how he's going to treat it, what's going to hurt and what's just going to sting a little. I nod like I'm listening but I'm thinking of Tim.

Tim didn't do anything for me at first either. He made me laugh and he was really nice when I fainted but that was about all.

Then he texted me, totally out of the blue.

I was in my room after supper, watching the snow goose episode of *Planet Earth* for like the eighty-third time when my phone buzzed. He asked if I'd like to go to the taxidermy show that night. I said yes, but only because Viv had told me he liked me so, I don't know, I guess I thought I should. I'd always been terrified of boys.

Ten minutes later, Steve came to my door and went, "Did you call Zanger Heating and Air Conditioning?" He was smiling way too hard. "There's a technician here to see you."

I hissed, "Steeeeve," and pushed past him. I patted down my hair, wiped my mouth on my sleeve and just went for it.

Tim was standing at the front door in his uniform: dark green pants and a light green shirt. The word *Junior* embroidered on his chest just below the Zanger logo. His hair was big but the part was gone.

That's when it happened to me. All of a sudden, Tim wasn't just another terrifying boy. He was cute. I couldn't look at him; I couldn't look away. I remember Viv telling me the same thing about Dr. Hotness.

Laughing about it. How ridiculous it was. The way her heart pounded. Not that it meant anything. She had Jack. It was totally innocent. That's what she said.

But now I remember something. That day, a little while ago, when I saw her talking to Dr. Hotness in the hall. The weird way they were standing. The awkward smiles on their faces. The way she sort of shooed me away. I didn't think anything of it.

Now, though, I'm wondering. Was something going on between them?

Viv

29 days before the party
7 p.m.

"Home?" Stu said.

"No. Metro Exhibition Place. I'm meeting some friends at the taxidermy show."

"You have friends?" he said and pulled out.

Yes, she did, sorta—but she was seeing Stu again too. She had to. The chat with Davida in the med school basement a few days earlier had only helped for a while. Viv had gone home that afternoon to find her mother holed up in her room, door locked, blinds down, but the agony still seeping out through the cracks. Apparently, Allie had thought she'd just sent her little C*NT update to her best friend from high school. She didn't realize she'd posted it for all her Facebook friends to see. Fortunately, she only had twenty-two friends. Unfortunately, ten of them were from the CA firm and seven were major clients.

Christie got the post taken down pretty quickly. Other than a receptionist at Braithwaite & Braithwaite, she was pretty sure no one outside the family had seen it—but the damage had been done. Viv knew the fight was just getting started.

Jack couldn't find out how upset she was. She just had to hold herself together for a little while longer until he was safely off to training camp. A hit of Goose now and then helped her keep up the act.

She took a sip when Stu wasn't looking and checked her phone. She'd be a few minutes late, but that was okay. It would give Tim and Davida a chance to get to know each other. She leaned back into the warm car seat and smiled. Matchmaking. Nudging two lonely people toward love and happiness. It was the one bright spot in the dark shittiness of her life.

Stu turned into the parking lot of Exhibition Place and crawled along behind a line of cars. Viv could see Tim and Davida standing at the entrance, weirdly far apart, staring off in opposite directions. A bad feeling hit her like a wet towel.

As the cab got closer, Viv noticed Tim had something on his head. She couldn't tell what, but it wasn't a good look. A band around his ears had squeezed his Afro into a peanut shape.

Tim, she thought. *Tim, Tim, Tim.* Normally she loved his weirdness, but was now really the time to be showcasing it? Davida dragged one foot back and forth across the sidewalk in what Viv could only assume was misery.

She should have just left well enough alone. Why was she meddling in other people's lives when she couldn't even handle her own?

"Let me out here," she said to Stu.

"I got cars behind me. I can't stop."

"Yes, you can."

"No."

"Stop."

He didn't.

There weren't that many cars. He wasn't going that fast.

Viv jumped out. Stu screamed at her, but she'd slammed the door so missed the worst of it. She ran up to the entrance. "Hey, guys!" She pulled a smile out of her ass. "You made it!"

Tim said, "We did indeed." Davida cupped her elbow with her hand and nodded.

"Goggles." Viv realized what was on Tim's head. "That's what they are. I was wondering."

"*Magnifying* goggles, in fact, with attached head lamp." Tim had them propped on his forehead. He gave his neck a little snap and they dropped over his eyes. They looked like something from *Ghostbusters*. "Sorry, but I only have one other pair. I gave them to Davida."

Davida lifted her hand a couple inches to let Viv see. Poor kid. He'd expect her to wear them too.

"Don't need 'em," Viv said. "Eyes like a hawk."

"There's a taxidermy joke in there somewhere. Gimme a sec. I'll get it." Tim was really trying. Davida smiled weakly.

"Something to look forward to!" Viv took each of them by the arm and gave them a reassuring squeeze. It would be okay. She'd play buffer for a while. Once around the arena to check out the stuffed toys then the nightmare would be over. Someday they'd laugh about it.

They were just heading in through the revolving door when a car screeched up to the curb and someone called Viv's name. They turned in time to see a backpack fly out the window and onto the pavement.

"Quit leaving your goddamn stuff all over my car."

"Sorry, Stooby!" Viv ran over to pick it up. "Hey, wanna meet my friends? This is Da—" But Stu pulled off before she could finish.

Tim went, "Whoa. Who's that?"

Viv laughed. "My personal driver." Stu was going to give her shit for this later.

"Yeah, well, time for a new one. That guy psycho or what?"

"Nah. Just misunderstood." Viv checked to make sure the lid of her water bottle was on tight then pulled on her backpack. "Stu's a gem. He takes excellent care of me. Don't know what I'd do without him."

"May I suggest 'walk'?" Tim said. "Might be safer."

You have no idea how wrong you are, Viv thought.

They headed into the large, echoey auditorium. Animals frozen in various states of play, fear or aggression were displayed on skirted tables. Groups of people huddled around exhibits, leaning over the red velvet ropes like fans crowding movie stars. A giant bear loomed over the entrance, head back, mouth open, elbows bent. *A middle-aged gym teacher getting down at the high school dance*, Viv thought and almost said so.

It was the kind of observation Tim would normally appreciate, but maybe not now. He clearly really loved taxidermy.

And so did Davida. Viv looked up to see the two of them the next aisle over, heads almost touching, peering through their goggles at what looked like a prehistoric pig. Big, black and hairy with long nasty tusks. Viv hadn't known animals like that still existed.

"Viv! You gotta see this." Tim waved her over. He handed her a tiny flashlight. "Up there?" He meant the nostril. "See the ant?"

"Is that alive?"

He laughed. Davida did too.

"No! Duh. Taxidermy show, remember? Warthogs root in the earth. Thus the dirt on the snout. Thus the ant in the nosehole. Authenticity or a little joke? Who's to say—but I love it."

"So good." Viv meant it.

"Told ya." Tim turned to Davida. "Viv only came because she wanted to scoff at the tackiness—but look at this stuff. This is art."

He pointed at the next exhibit: a weasel, up on its hind legs, its neck elongated, its arm out.

"No, it's not," Viv said. "It's Janice Drysdale."

There was a pause; then they burst out laughing. It kind of was Janice. Something about the energy, the eagerness, "the stereotypical weaseliness," as Tim pointed out.

The ice had broken. Now they were having fun. They took tons of videos of themselves hamming it up in front of their favorite displays. Taxidermy, Viv had to admit, was pretty amazing. The way things could be so dead and so alive at the same time. Too bad Mandy Chan wasn't here. She would have loved it.

After the main exhibit, they wandered into the backroom to see the beginner's work.

"At last, Viv, the tackiness for which you seek." Tim swung his arm around the room like he was welcoming her into a strange new world. The displays here were lumpy and awkward and screamingly funny. That raccoon? The moose? Viv couldn't remember the last time she'd laughed so hard.

Or felt so good. They took some more videos together then Viv wandered off on her own. At one point, she turned and saw the two of them, giggling over a baby marmot. She realized they'd forgotten all about her. She realized she loved it. She loved not being the center of attention. She loved knowing that the only time Tim and Davida looked at her was when they'd got caught looking at each other again.

Her work here was done. She walked over to them.

"Gotta go," she said. "You two bushy-tailed opossums have fun. My man needs me."

Tim

Or maybe the package wasn't such a bad idea. I've got to stay positive. After all, I thought the taxidermy show was going to be a disaster too.

Viv was the one who talked me into it. She'd been bugging me to ask Davida out and said the taxidermy show would be perfect. "So you!"— which I thought was an insult but apparently wasn't. Something to do with my "quirky charm." Long story short, after days of Viv hassling me I agreed to ask Davida out as long as Viv promised to go too. I am a wuss par excellence. What can I say?

It turned out to be a stroke of genius. I had no idea Davida was a fellow *Planet Earth* superfan. We pretty much went one-for-one identifying little-known species. She has a near encyclopedic knowledge of marmots. She told me they're also called groundhogs, weenusks and/or whistlepigs, and that their babies—so good—are known as chucklings. (We decided to refer to Bagrat as our chuckling from now on.)

We were at the show for about three hours before Viv had to go. Jack had finished whatever he was doing, so she wanted to see him because he was going away soon. I said I'd drive her, but she was like, "No!" and called her psycho "personal driver" instead.

Davida and I only stayed a little while longer after she left. It wasn't awkward or anything, it's just that we'd seen everything at least twice.

"Taxidermy is grossly underappreciated," I said when we got in the van to go home. This is something I truly believe, but I added, "Don't you think?" because Viv had said the number one mistake guys make is acting like they know everything. (When I asked what the second biggest mistake was, she went, "Hold your horses, cowboy. You're not ready for that yet." This intrigued me.)

Davida and I talked about taxidermy for a while and how even the bad stuff takes skill. Somehow that got us talking about what we want to do when we "grow up," on the off-chance that should ever transpire.

I said, "Pa's still hopeful, but I'm afraid I'm never going to develop a sudden passion for *verwarmingsbuizen*." Davida looked interested until I explained that *verwarmingsbuizen* is merely Dutch for "heating ducts."

She asked me what I wanted to do instead. I told her I didn't know. I said, truthfully, that I feel like I'm at an all-you-can-eat buffet and everyone's saying "try the salmon, try the baron of beef, try the squid-ink linguine," and all I really want at the moment is a dinner roll. I realized immediately that exposing my total lack of ambition was not the best way to impress a date, but it was too late by then. I looked at her and shrugged like the idioot I am.

"White or whole wheat?" she said, which was kind of funny.

I asked if she knew what she wanted to do.

She picked at the bottom of her T-shirt. (Pale green, same color as her eyes, not really tight but tight enough to suggest what was underneath, although I hardly looked at all because that's another thing Viv told me not to do.)

Davida didn't know what she wanted to do either, so we started talking about animals again. Random facts, ridiculous names (you really can't beat the blue-footed booby), top ten episodes of *Planet Earth*. We talked all the way back to her place.

I pulled over across from her house and switched off the engine.

I didn't want Davida to go yet and/or ever. I undid my seat belt, leaned against the door, and desperately started rehashing some of my favorite displays. I did Janice the Weasel and Irritated Moose and this frankly adorable family of ducks—which was actually kind of tragic if you think about how a mother and six babies ended up in a taxidermy show but whatever—then I got to the bears.

I was hovering over Davida with my paws up and my fangs out in what I believed was a reasonably accurate imitation of ursine attack mode when I obviously suffered some sort of mental collapse because next thing I knew I'd swooped down and kissed her. *Très suave*.

I don't know how she didn't scream. It must have been terrifying, but Davida just went, "Oh," and rubbed her lip where I'd bumped it with my teeth.

I went, "Sorry," and hung my head in shame. Even I knew that had to be the worst kiss ever, if you can even call it a kiss. It was more like "assault with a wet mouth." I gross myself out just thinking about it.

Davida touched my shoulder and went, "That's all right," which in itself was more than I could have hoped for, but then she added, "Try again." So we did. I believe it's fair to say that I improved rapidly.

That's why I sent Davida the package. I was hoping she'd remember the magic that happened between us that night, which I know sounds like some corny exaggeration but isn't.

Davida

4 days after the party
Noon

Dr. Hotness dresses my wound. He's polite and everything, but he's not even pretending my burn is real. He's just going through the motions. I must have been here fifteen minutes and he hasn't made eye contact with me once. He clips the bandage closed and stands up. He's about to leave.

My jaw bounces uselessly a few times before I manage to say, "Can I, um, ask you something?"

He digs his hands into the pockets of his white coat and puts on a smile. "Sure."

He's expecting a medical question, maybe even running over some possible answers in his head, but I say, "How well did you know Viv?"

The smile disappears. His eyebrows go flat. "Why are you asking me? I barely know her." He sounds like a pleasant robot.

"Just I saw you guys talking a few times so I thought—"

"I'm talking to you, aren't I? How well do I know you?" He manages another smile.

"No, I know. It's just something doesn't seem right about what happened. I think Viv was hiding some stuff. Someone just told me she—"

"Yeah, well. Lot of gossip out there, especially when something bad happens. You can't believe everything you hear—"

He might have been about to say something else, but I don't know. An instructor steps into the room to give him feedback. She says his technique was perfect.

Maybe it was. But I still can't help thinking there's something weird about the guy.

Viv

It was Jack's last full day in town before rugby camp, but Viv barely got to see him. He was busy with his dad in the morning then she'd promised to stay home with her mother until Christie got off work. As soon as she showed up, Viv raced over to the sportsplex. She hooked her fingers through the wire fence and watched Jack run around the outdoor track. She felt as if everything inside her was going to bubble up and spill over. A love fountain. Dr. So-Called Hotness, she thought, was just so not.

Jack caught sight of her and smiled, a spotlight shining on her. He held up both index fingers when he passed. *Just two more laps, don't go.* Viv pretended to sigh then picked up her backpack and headed to the gate. She was so happy to see him but there was this sadness too—one long violin note of sadness, playing in her head. She plunked herself onto the bleachers, chewed on a clove of garlic and tried to ignore the sound until he came staggering over.

He kissed her. He was hot and salty. "I'm dying." He wiped the bottom of his T-shirt over his face then grabbed her water bottle.

There was a split second before Viv remembered what was in it. She grabbed it back.

"Hey," he said.

"I've got a cold sore." It was the only thing she could think of.

"So? You just kissed me, now I've got it too. So gimme."

"No." She swung the bottle behind her and flicked her shoulders back and forth to keep him away.

"Since when do you get cold sores?" Jack took Viv's chin and inspected her. "I don't see anything. You're just greedy."

She pushed his hand away. "Okay. I was lying about the cold sore. I just don't want your sweat all over everything."

"So that's it!" He pinned Viv to the bench and rubbed his shirt on her face.

"Ick! Ick! Gross!" She was laughing. "You pig. Go shower. Go! I'll get you a Gatorade."

"I'm not sharing with you."

"Bet you will," she sang.

"Bet you're right," he sang back. "I am so pathetic." He peeled off his wet T-shirt and threw it at her then he disappeared into the men's locker room.

Viv ate some more garlic on her way to the vending machine. She bought him a Gatorade. She'd finished almost half by the time he came back, all clean and neat and tucked in. Every parent's dream boyfriend.

He stopped when he saw what was left. "Oh, and *I'm* the pig here? You practically drank it all!"

Viv stuck her blue tongue out at him. He stuck his out at her. They inched closer and closer to each other until they touched.

"Yuck." He pulled back and made spitting sounds. "Next time, do us both a favor and get Listerine instead." He had a number of variations on this joke.

"You don't like garlic?" Viv batted her eyelashes. "I had no idea."

He pinched his nose and kissed her. She had a thought: *If he can stand the garlic, he can stand the truth.*

"Why are you looking at me like that?" he said.

He wanted a joke or a compliment or a declaration of her undying love. She knew that. He didn't want the truth. The truth would disappoint him. *She* would disappoint him.

"You've got a booger in your nose," she said.

"You're so romantic." He took a tissue out of his pocket and wiped. (He was the type to have a tissue in his pocket. That didn't even bother her.) "Better?"

He tilted his head so she could check his nostrils. "Beautiful," she said.

"You too." He put his arm around her shoulder and they left.

It took Viv a while to notice he was leading them the long way home, through the park. They'd always liked the park: the big trees, the big shadows, the little side paths that wandered off to nowhere. They didn't say much on the way there, just the goofy babbling baby talk they reverted to when they were alone. She felt happy and safe.

"Wanna stop for a while?" he said when they got to their favorite bench.

"Sure."

He produced a bag of breadcrumbs from his pocket and Viv laughed. He'd obviously planned this little detour. He poured some crumbs in her hand then some in his, and they sat like statues waiting for the birds to show up. First person to get one feeding out of his/her hand won. That was their game. Jack was really good at it. Even birds knew they could trust him.

A pigeon had just flown onto his side of the bench when her phone buzzed and scared it away.

"Hey!" Jack went. "That's supposed to be off." They had a rule. No cellphones when they were together.

"Sorry. Meant to but, ah, Mum's not feeling well . . . I should just see what this is about."

At the beginning of the Ross-and-Allie elimination match, Viv had dragged Jack through everything: her mother finding the emails, her

136

father lying, her mother kicking him out, them getting back together, the late night screaming, the kissy-kissy mornings, then Christie catching her father and Katie in the London airport, shit totally hitting fan, the whole disgusting mess. But unless someone else had told him, Jack didn't know anything about the Facebook incident. Viv was pretty sure the last time Jack had been on social media was when he posted the picture of them at their junior high prom in matching braces.

Viv got out her phone and checked. A text from Christie. Got an appointment for Allie with a shrink today. Called your dad. Not happy but we're talking. This will be fine. Xoxox

Viv sent back a relieved emoji.

"Sorry. Sorry. There. Done. It's off." She flipped over her phone and put out her hand. A pigeon landed on it immediately. She mouthed, "Booya!"

"No fair!" Jack put her into a headlock. The bird flew away and the headlock turned into a hug, a quiet swaying hug.

"I'm going to miss you," he said.

"No, you aren't. You're going to be so busy you'll totally forget me."

"You're right." He kissed her neck.

She put her ear to her shoulder, squeezing him out. "Yeah, well, I'm not going to miss you either."

"I love it when you put on a brave face, even though inside you're dying." He stroked her hair and stuck out his bottom lip in fake pity. "Know what I *don't* like?"

"What?"

"Your mother being home all the time." When Allie used to work, they'd always had a place to go. "Which is why I'm taking you somewhere else."

"Oh, yeah? Where?"

"It's a surpri-ise!" He put on his scary clown face, which always freaked her out.

"Jack, quit it." He smiled scarier.

She batted her hands at him. "Quit it!"

This was usually where he'd lean in and go full Freddy Krueger on her, but he just said, "Fine," perfectly normal. "I texted your mother. I'm taking you out to dinner."

She bounced in her seat and clapped her hands. "Somewhere fancy?"

"That's what I *told* her, but it's not true."

"So somewhere cheap?"

"Close. Somewhere free." He pulled a set of keys out of his pocket and jingled them in the air. "Geoff's brother's away. The apartment's empty, although he *did* say there's pizza in the freezer . . ."

"That sounds *very* fancy."

"Wanna go?"

"I'll call a cab."

Jack was amazed that the cabbie seemed to know Viv.

Excerpt from police interview with Stu Fenske, 4 days after the party

Lt. Alan (Pidge) Eisenhauer: I understand you bought Vivienne alcohol?

Stu Fenske: Do I need a lawyer?

Eisenhauer: All we're interested in is information. We're just trying to find out where the drugs came from.

Fenske: You think I had something to do with that? The whole reason I—

Eisenhauer: Calm down. I'm not saying that.

Fenske: You think I *wanted* to get stuck with some spoiled rich kid? I'm trying to get my own shit together. Driving my cab. Doing my GED. Keeping sober.

Eisenhauer: You have addiction issues?

Fenske: That's why I picked her up. I know what it's like. No one's going to make her stop 'til she's ready. So I bought for her. If I didn't, someone else would. Then what? A girl like her, with that face and all that money in her pocket? How long before something bad happens? I'm a big guy and I got the shit kicked out of me more than once. I figured this was my chance to do something good for a change. So I picked her up, bought her booze, let her hang out in my car while I studied. She had to be home for curfew and I usually don't take fares until eleven so it was no skin off my nose. She's not a bad kid. Too stupid for her own good but not bad.

Eisenhauer: But you never bought her drugs?

Fenske: No! Jesus. I told you. Booze, that's all. I got a juvie record. I'm not going to mess with any of that stuff.

Eisenhauer: Ever see her take any?

Fenske: I would've stopped her.

Eisenhauer: Ever hear her talk about drugs?

Fenske: No. She couldn't even handle booze. She kept saying she was going to give it up.

Eisenhauer: You think she meant it?

Fenske: Yeah. Most drunks do, doesn't mean they can. I kind of hoped the boyfriend would help.

Davida

4 days after the party
3:45 p.m.

My SP sessions are finally over for the day. So much for my big investigation. What did I learn? Viv drinks, Makayla's pathetic, there's something weird about Dr. Hotness and pain is exhausting. Pretending to have it and pretending not to. I never take cabs, but I see one parked outside the old Innovagear warehouse, a couple of blocks from the med school. I run over and knock on the window. The driver's reading something on his tablet. He turns around.

It's that big guy. I recognize him. Viv's "personal driver," as she called him. The one who threw her backpack at her before the big taxidermy show. The one she said "takes excellent care" of her.

"You available?" I say.

He hesitates for a second then jerks his head toward the back like *okay, get in.*

I open the door and climb in behind him.

"Where to?" he says.

I give him my address. He pulls out.

I can't see his face. It takes me a while to figure out how to bring this up or even if I should.

"I've met you before," I say.

"Oh yeah?" He's not really interested.

"I'm a friend of Viv's."

I see him check me out in the rearview mirror.

"Did you hear what happened?"

He nods, just barely.

"It's so awful," I say.

He doesn't answer, but he's making a left-hand turn so perhaps he's preoccupied.

"She told us you were her personal driver. It was kind of a joke but I know she really thinks a lot of you."

He looks at me again in the mirror. He might have smiled a little. It takes me a few more blocks to get my courage up to say anything else.

"I'm just wondering . . . um . . . She said you really looked after her so I thought you might know. Where'd she get the drugs? Did she do them a lot? Do you think she—"

He swerves over to the curb, doesn't even put his blinker on.

"This is as far as I'm going."

"I'm not going to tell the cops or anything. I just need to know . . . For myself. If you know something—"

"End of the line." He reaches around and pushes my door open. "Adios."

"Please. Something about what happened doesn't make sense to me and—"

"So long," he says. "You're leaving."

He's very large. His eyes are tiny and black. Like they're pointed and he's only showing the sharp tips.

I get out. He slams the door and takes off, not speeding, but not turning around to look either.

I walk the rest of the way home, confused and exhausted and wondering why I even care what happened to Viv.

The house is empty but there's a parcel on the kitchen table for me.

I don't remember ordering anything.

Viv

Ernestina's was Viv's favorite restaurant. Exposed brick, industrial lighting, music she didn't know but should, and a waitstaff with the best tattoos ever. (One woman had her three-year-old son draw all over her arm in magic marker then got the tattoo guy to trace it in ink. Viv aspired to be that kind of mother someday.) The food was excellent too.

This was the restaurant Jack had told Allie he was taking Viv to, so she felt weird actually being there the next night with her father. Not just weird. Guilty. She looked across the table and thought of all the lies Ross had told when he'd been sneaking out with Katie. No wonder her mother was crazed. Everyone lied to her.

It was Lulu's birthday. The little girl was stretched out on the bench side of the table, her head on Viv's lap, tying the ends of Viv's hair into messy knots and talking to herself in a tiny high-pitched voice, the way preschoolers do when grown-up conversation gets boring.

The kid should be at McDonald's, Viv thought, patting Lulu's tummy. *That's no way to treat*

. . . my stepsister.

The words appeared out of nowhere.

Lulu was going to be her stepsister.

Two years ago, she'd just been this kid Viv looked after occasionally for some lady who worked for her parents. Viv liked her. Back then, she'd even liked Katie. She always paid Viv well, made sure there was Ben & Jerry's in the freezer and didn't mind / didn't mention when Jack came over. Katie was young and beautiful and cool. If anything, Viv had thought of *Katie* as her sister. Now Katie was marrying her dad. It did something to Viv's head.

Ross loosened his gray silk tie. Viv had never seen it before. (Katie had at least improved his wardrobe. Allie had given up on that years ago.) He blew a blast of air out his mouth, shook his head and went, "What a week, eh, Vivi?"

He said it as if the two of them were on the same side. The one against her mother.

Viv said, "How was *your* week, Lulu?"

Lulu bounced up. She was wearing her birthday outfit, which should have been neon yellow and sparkly but instead was a stylish shade of charcoal. Katie had given in and let her wear red lipstick, which, Viv was happy to see, had smudged age-appropriately across her cheeks. The Joker as a five-year-old girl.

"Awesome!" She waved her little fists in the air. "It's my birthday and I got cake at daycare and I'm having a party and all my friends are coming except Edgar because . . ." She babbled on like that while Katie beamed at her. Ross couldn't leap in now about Viv's mother even if he'd wanted to.

"So when's the big party?" Viv knew she'd be expected to go.

"When I come back from Daddy's. He's going to have a party for me too. He loves parties. He goes to them all the time. That's what Mommy said, right?"

"I did," Katie said then looked at Ross. Viv knew their eyes were passing coded messages about what a piece of shit Dylan was. Katie's ex was a lazy and not-very-talented musician who'd apparently married her because she had a good job and could support them. The irony was not lost on Viv.

Viv let it pass. Everything was perfectly pleasant as long as she just focused on Ernestina's buzzy, top-ten-places-to-eat kind of surface. She sipped sparkling water out of the champagne flute her father had ordered for each of "the kids." He and Katie drank prosecco. They asked about the SP program and how she felt now that Jack had left and what her plans were for next year. She said all the right things and then, when she couldn't stand it anymore, made her father tell Lulu the story about her own fifth birthday. It was always a showstopper. Viv's parents had given her a pink fairy costume that year, complete with wings. She'd somehow got it into her head that she could fly. She hurled herself off the deck in the middle of the party and broke her ankle. Two hours later, she was in the emergency room, still waiting for her cast when she'd heard a commotion. The curtains opened and there was her dad dressed in a matching pink fairy costume, pushing a giant birthday cake in on a medical gurney. Behind him were the kids from the party—a jabbering swarm of little pink fairies—all out of their minds with excitement at the thought of being in costume, in a hospital, and with a mountain of cake to get through.

Her father stood up to demonstrate his twinkle-toe technique for Lulu. He had his belly out, one foot in the air and his hand up as if he were waving a wand. Everybody laughed until they cried, even Viv, because her father was a good storyteller and the thought of all 225 pounds of him in pink spandex was funny, even if he was ruining her life.

She wiped her eyes with her napkin. She loved her father. She still did.

For a while, she could almost imagine things working out then the server arrived with their meals. Moroccan lamb shank for Ross. Seafood stew for Katie (which she'd barely touch). Squash risotto for Viv. Plain noodles for Lulu.

Everyone made happy groaning noises and dug in. Then Lulu started to wail.

There was butter on her noodles.

Katie went, "Shh, sweetie."

Ross went, "There's hardly any! Look." He leaned over, holding his new tie in place with one hand, and pushed her noodles around with his fork. His fork had gravy on it.

Lulu went nuts.

Viv snuggled her up into her side and said, "It's okay. It's okay," but it wasn't. This was Lulu's birthday. She was five. She was getting fed at eight o'clock at some hipster place that put radicchio on everything. This was about Katie and Ross, not Lulu. Everything was about them. *They screw up our lives and we're supposed to smile and be perfect because they're paying.*

Lulu didn't get the "be perfect" message. She sobbed at the top of her lungs. Her tears left navy blotches on Viv's pale blue dress. At the next table, a white-haired guy with his own thirtysomething Katie-clone side-eyed her, pissed.

"Lulu's tired," Katie said, picking her up by the armpits and lifting her over the table. Ross had to grab her flailing legs to save the glasses. "I'll take her home."

Viv tried to say, "I'll take her," but she knew that wasn't going to happen. All evening she'd had the sense her father had some ulterior motive for getting her there. Katie made Lulu kiss Viv goodbye—mid-scream, snot everywhere—then they left, the noise disappearing with them like an ambulance speeding away.

The white-haired guy raised his hand for another bottle and it was all Viv could do not to wave for one too. Ross, of all people, could hardly complain about her drinking.

"Well," he smiled. "Got myself another handful, didn't I?"

"You did."

"Good thing she's cute. Almost as cute as you were at that age."

Viv took a bite of the risotto. It was cold and the cheese had turned into elastic bands, but it was better than talking. She wasn't going to play this game.

She heard the clink of her father's cutlery against his plate. She knew without looking that his elbows were on the table and his hands clasped in front of him. The lecture was about to begin.

"So . . . there was some upset this week, as you're no doubt aware."

"We're not talking about Lulu anymore, I presume."

"Another childish tantrum, but no. Not Lulu."

She let that go.

"Your mother had some very unkind things to say about Katie."

"It was a mistake. She didn't mean to post it."

"But she did mean to say it."

"To one person. She took the post down as soon as she realized what happened, plus she sent Katie an apology."

"Yes. She took the post down—thank Christie for me—but she only apologized for the asterisk."

It took Viv a second to understand.

C*NT

"It's not funny," Ross said, although if he could have stepped back, he would have seen it was. "Look, I know this is hard for your mother, but she's got to start being reasonable. Life is short. Our marriage was making everyone miserable."

Well, not EVERYONE. Viv had actually been fine with it.

"Have you told Mum you're getting married yet?" she said pleasantly, as if it wasn't designed to sting. "It's happening in September. That's only a couple of months away. She should probably know."

He sat back in his chair, hands flat on his thighs.

"Your mother and I are divorced, Vivienne. We have our own lives now. We don't have to work to each other's schedules."

"So you mean *no.*"

"I mean not yet. Frankly, we're worried about her reaction. Katie wants to get some things taken care of then we'll tell her." He picked up his wine glass as if he was going to drain it but changed his mind and put it back, untouched. "We all need to get on with our lives. Your mother is hurt and angry, but I think even she knows that. She needs to change her behavior or we're going to be forced to act."

"Act?" Viv said.

"Legally."

"You . . ." She wasn't sure what he meant. "You'd what? Sue her?"

"I wouldn't want to."

"But you would?"

"If pushed."

"For what?"

"Slander, libel. She can't be saying incendiary things about me—or Katie. Katie is a chartered accountant. She's going to be my wife. Allie's outbursts have to stop. And not just because it's the right thing to do. She could lose her own CA designation for unprofessional conduct."

Viv's insides started to tick. "What do you want *me* to do about it?"

He laughed like *oh-no-no* then reached out and took her hand. "Nothing. I just want you to hear our side of things in case . . ."

"What?" She pulled her hand away.

"In case things get ugly. I hope they won't. I really do. Last thing I want is to hurt your mother."

Little late for that, she thought.

There was so much Viv could have argued with, but she was stuck on the "lose her CA designation." Her heart hurled itself against her chest. *Lose the last thing she has*, Viv thought. *Other than me.*

The server removed their plates.

"Dessert?" her father said, as if that would make it all better.

She shook her head.

"Oh, come on. How about we share the crème brulée?"

Viv just wanted to go.

"It's your favorite!"

If she said yes, he'd stop. "Sure."

"I shouldn't have a whole one anyway. Have you seen the tuxedo Katie got me? Let me tell you, the 'slim-cut styling' does me no favors.

But oh well. More to love." He winked at the server. "One crème brulée, two spoons and an espresso. Thanks!"

Ross leaned across the table, remembering at the last minute to protect his tie from a splodge of lamb gravy. "This'll be okay, Vivi. Better than okay. Katie loves you. Lulu loves you. You'll finally have the sibling you bugged us for all these years!"

Once again, too little, too late.

"Now, if you'll excuse me, I need to use the facilities."

Ross got up. As soon as his back was turned, Viv downed the prosecco left in Katie's glass. The white-haired guy at the next table wagged his finger at her, laughing. She pulled a pretend zipper across her lips. He winked. All fun and games.

Viv texted Stu. Ernestina's. Now. Paying by cash

6 mints. He must have been nearby.

Ross and dessert arrived at the same time.

"Sorry, Dad." Viv slid along the banquette. "Gotta go."

"What? Now? But the crème brulée . . ."

"You eat it. They can let the tuxedo out. I got a podcast to write."

He pushed his chair back and started to get up. "Gimme a sec. I'll drive—"

"No. That's okay. I can write on the bus. Be here any minute. Got an early shift at the pool. Just remembered . . ."

Viv dragged her backpack off the floor. It caught the tablecloth, rocked the glasses, sloshed her father's espresso, flustered him.

The look on his face. He knew he no longer had the authority to make her stay, and all the commotion of trying to keep dishes from toppling and coffee from landing on his expensive new tie didn't give him time to recalibrate. Viv stood up with a jerk. The prosecco bottle wobbled. He lunged for it. She kissed him on the head and darted out.

She waited in the dark alley next door until Stu arrived. They didn't talk until he'd parked behind the warehouse and she'd had a good hard hit of the Goose.

"Know why I drink, Stu?"

He was scrolling through something on his device. He didn't look up. "You're a drunk."

"Yes." She took another drink. "But not the answer our judges are looking for!"

"You're a hopeless drunk."

"I'm serious."

"Me too. Now would you shut up?" He pointed to his tablet like he had work to do. His nails were bitten to the quick.

"You have one more chance. Why do I drink?"

He swore. "Then you'll shut up?"

"Promise."

He was staring at her through the rearview mirror. "Because you're a chicken. Too fucking scared to face the world."

"We have a winner!" Viv said.

He turned back to his device. Viv turned back to her bottle.

Sometime later, she woke up to Stu going, "Hey . . . Hey!"

She opened one eye and clambered up onto her elbows.

"I see where you get your self-control issues." He handed her her phone. "Your mother's been texting nonstop."

"Shit." Viv grabbed the front seat and pulled herself up to check the dashboard: 11:28. If she wasn't home soon, Allie would be setting the cops on Ross.

She checked her texts—then laughed. "Stu, you're the best."

He'd answered her mother. His spelling was a little shaky, but it would pass.

"And you're a drunk, so what can I do?"

She got out her garlic. "Home, James," she said. She was going to hate herself tomorrow.

Davida

4 days after the party
4:05 p.m.

I give the parcel a shake. Maybe Dad ordered something for me on-line. Sometimes he has trouble sleeping then three days later weird packages start arriving for everyone. He bought a years' supply of iron pills for me once and a clock on wheels that races around the room when the alarm goes off.

Or maybe it's from my mother. Who knows where her head's at these days? Could be anything. Clothes that would have fit me at six. Religious paraphernalia. A live asp.

I brace myself and tear the brown paper off the box.

I open the flaps and dig through the Styrofoam peanuts.

I pull out a squirrel.

A taxidermied squirrel.

Viv

Viv's name that day was Becca. She was seventeen, lived at home. Her father (Aaron) was a manager at an insurance company. Her mother (Tonya) ran a small upholstery business. They were religious. Becca, however, seriously doubted there was a God, at least one who gave the smallest shit about her. She was presenting with a sore stomach, but her parents suspected she had a drinking problem. When asked, Becca was supposed to claim she never touched alcohol, despite stinking of it. The med students were expected to see past the bellyache and realize Becca had bigger issues.

A little close for comfort, Viv thought, *but whatever.*

The first three simulations went fine. The students all caught a whiff of booze (supposedly on Viv's clothes) and thought, *Ah-ha! Tummy troubles = thinly veiled cry for help.* They palpated her abdomen while discreetly prying into her deep-seated emotional issues. The appointments ended with them offering compassionate psychological advice, as outlined in chapter twenty-two of the textbook.

Before leaving, med student numero three smiled and said, "It's all about attitude, Becca. So much of what we worry about turns out to be nothing in the end."

Easy-peasy, Viv thought. As soon as the door closed behind him, Viv gave her attitude a boost from her water bottle. They'd all basically said the same thing, a nicer version of what Stu regularly told her: "You don't need a drink. You need a boot in the arse."

Wrong, Viv thought. A boot in the arse wouldn't have given her two blissful hours of total blackout in the back of his cab after the debacle at Ernestina's.

Viv took another sip of the Goose and the next doc walked in.

"You again!" Dr. Hotness said, splurching hand sanitizer through his fingers.

Jack had only been gone a couple days and here she was, grinning like a fool at some random guy. Not her fault. Alcohol is a disinhibitor. Said so in her script.

"Pardon?" she said. "I've never been here before."

"Oh. Sorry." His back was to the camera. He went *oops* with his mouth and his eyes laughed. "Mistook you for someone else. Same yellow hair."

He checked his clipboard then looked up, a doctor-smile on his face. "Rebecca."

"Becca."

"Okay. Becca. I'm George Pineo, a first-year medical student here. What brings you in today?"

"My stomach. It's like . . ." Viv squeezed her hands into fists.

"Cramps?"

"Sort of, but not like my, um, period. More like all the time."

"How long has this been going on?"

"Since, maybe, Christmas?"

"Ooh. Long time to have a tummy ache." He asked her all the when/where/how-bad/how-often type questions. Then he got out his little flashlight, brushed her hair off her forehead and looked into her eyes.

His fingers pulling them open, one at a time. Her head tilted back, like a baby bird about to be fed.

"How's everything else going?" His face was so close she could feel his breath. "Got a summer job?"

"Part-time at the mall."

"You like it?" He put down the flashlight and stepped back.

"It's okay."

"And your social life?"

I haven't a friend in the world.

That's what hit her. It was ridiculous. She had Tim and Davida. They'd laughed their heads off at the taxidermy show. Jack loved her. She knew a million people and they'd all say, *Yeah, let's do something.* Stu always came when she called. So why did it feel true too?

The sadness was suddenly overwhelming. George's expression softened. She was sure he could see it on her face, but that was okay. Becca was supposed to be sad.

"Good," she said.

"And your family life?"

A bubble rose in her throat. She had to swallow repeatedly to keep it down. "All right."

"Having some trouble there, are you?"

The way he was looking at her. She stared at her hands.

He said, "Being a teenager is tough. Parents don't always understand the pressure. Kids are left feeling they have to solve their problems on their own."

Dr. Hotness had no idea what her problems were. This was just an act.

"Why don't we get a look at this stomach of yours?" he said.

He took her elbow and helped her on to the examination table. She lay flat on her back, not quite sure what to do with her arms and legs. They seemed too straight, like she was dead or scared stiff.

He said, "Any allergies? . . . Okay. Eating all right? Good. Any recreational drug use? Uh-huh . . . What about alcohol?"

"No."

"None?"

"Never."

Viv shook her head and tears rolled into her ears. It happened so fast.

George casually handed her a tissue then placed his hand on her arm. It was warm and solid.

He said, "It's not unusual for kids with difficult problems to find ways to mask them. Alcohol can provide short-term relief but never a long-term solution. It gives you the illusion your issues have gone away, but you sober up and they're still there, so you drink again. It's a vicious cycle. Enough to give anyone a stomachache." There was a smile in his voice.

He put on his stethoscope, lifted her shirt to her ribs and listened to the sounds her body made. The little metal thing on the end was cold. "Sorry," he said when she flinched. He unbuttoned her pants and started to lower her fly.

The door banged open. Someone went, "Whoa! Stop!" Viv bolted up. George swung around, like he was ready to fight off the intruder.

Dr. Keppo was standing there, his palms out flat in front of him.

George's face went from angry to confused. "Is there a, um—"

"A small procedural issue, Mr. Pineo. Any idea what that might be?"

George looked at him blankly for a few seconds then slapped his mouth. "The zipper."

Dr. Keppo wrinkled his lips and nodded. "A young woman alone in a doctor's office. A male doctor, undoing her trousers. You can see how that could make her feel vulnerable—even if it was completely innocent, which I'm sure it was."

George shook his head, shell-shocked.

Viv shimmied down off the table. "He was just examining me. I didn't mind. I mean, I didn't think he was . . . you know."

She realized her pants were open and her underwear showing. Her sad old yellow ones, with the torn waistband. She pulled her fly up so fast it nipped her skin. A memory, then, of Jack's dad coming home early from church and poking his head into the bedroom, seconds after they'd gotten dressed. That same feeling of being caught.

"I appreciate that, Vivienne, and I'm sure the future Dr. Pineo does too." Dr. Keppo had a kid's smile, sparkly and real. "But here's the thing. *You* might not mind, but the next person very well could, especially if she's been traumatized in the past. That's why boundaries are so important. Even the slightest whiff of impropriety could be devastating for the patient—and the healthcare provider."

"I'm really sorry." George was pale and damp-looking, as if someone had carved his perfect face out of congealed bacon fat. "I know better. I would never—"

"Hey." Dr. Keppo gave his shoulder a squeeze. "A learning experience. That's what the SP program is all about." He turned to Viv. "No harm done?"

"None."

"Great. And great until then, too, George. You instantly formed a warm rapport with your patient. Based on what you saw before you were so rudely interrupted, what would your diagnosis be?"

"She's definitely been drinking." They both laughed, which Viv hoped was a good sign. "I'd want to get to the bottom of that. See if it's just adolescent experimentation or something more serious."

"Excellent." Dr. Keppo checked his watch then said, "I'd like to see if George has any other concerns, but you're free to go now, Vivienne. Great work today. You're a natural, kiddo!"

Excerpt from police interview with George Pineo, 4 days after the party

Lt. Alan (Pidge) Eisenhauer: So it was a mistake, pure and simple. That's what you're saying?

George Pineo: Simple but, um, maybe not totally pure. I didn't do it *on purpose*, but I don't know . . . Viv's a pretty girl. I guess it, um, threw me. Dr. Keppo's always talking about "appropriate behavior," so I thought he was really going to rip into me.

Eisenhauer: And did he?

Pineo: No. It probably helped that Viv wasn't upset. He just talked to me about how physicians touch their patients' bodies in really intimate ways. How it's a sacred trust, so we have to be careful not to even *appear* to break it.

Eisenhauer: Meaning?

Pineo: Patients can misread intentions. A doctor can do something totally innocent—make a comment, perform some normal procedure—but there are patients who'll see it as proof the doctor was abusing them or had "feelings" for them. That's why you have to do everything by the book. You don't want to give anyone any ammunition to shoot you with.

Eisenhauer: That's how he left it?

Pineo: I think his exact words were, "Respect boundaries, follow procedures and don't let your hormones do your thinking for you, my friend."

Eisenhauer: And did you?

Pineo: More or less.

Viv

Viv left the examination room feeling jittery, upside-down. She wasn't sure what was doing it, George's hands or her thoughts, but she needed a drink. She nodded at some kids in the hall then took a gulp from her water bottle, and another, just in case.

Booze was magic. It really was. By the time she got to the lunchroom, she felt fine. Tim and Davida were at the snack table with their backs to her, arms touching, heads together, laughing about something. They turned around, still killing themselves, and saw Viv. Davida blushed as if Viv had caught them necking. Tim jerked his head to a table like *sit with us*. Viv waved back *no*. She could tell they wanted to be alone, and that made her happy.

But now they were both waving at her to *come, come, quit being such a jerk*. She gestured *okay* and then grabbed a tuna sandwich. Tuna was as good as garlic when it came to camouflage.

She slipped in beside Davida, her mouth full. "How'd it go this morning?"

"A-one," Tim said. "I'm experiencing my first schizophrenic episode and you know me. Nothing I like better than a break with reality."

Viv took another bite. "You didn't make the med student cry again, did you?"

He mouthed *oops*.

She turned to Davida, "You?"

"I was a 'well teen,' so just normal stuff—pulse, reflexes, abdominal examination . . ."

"Oh my God. Speaking of which . . ." Viv bounced in her seat. "You know George Pineo? . . . Med student?" Blank stares. "Gorgeous?"

"You're not going to talk about Dr. Hotness too, are you?" Tim stuck his neck out and dropped his jaw. "If heterosexual guys were panting like that over some female med student, you'd all go nuts. We'd get castrated or hung in the town square or publicly stoned or something."

"I only called him gorgeous so you'd know who I meant. I wasn't panting over him. At least not much." Viv gave a little moan and a shiver. "Anyhoo . . . I was doing an alcoholic teen . . ."

"Hence the stench." Tim made a gag face.

Davida said, "Shh. I want to hear."

"As I was saying . . . George was about to examine me, so I'm lying on the table and he lifts my shirt just to, like, here. No biggie. Then instead of asking me to do it myself or explain what's up, he reaches down and unzips my pants."

"Were you going, 'Oh my God, this date's moving awfully fast?'" Tim fanned his face.

"Didn't have time. Dr. Keppo literally flew into the room."

"*Literally* flew," Tim said. "Wow. The man really is too good to be true, isn't he?"

Viv ignored him and licked tuna off her lip. "George looked like he was going to die. Seriously. Like he got caught fondling me or something."

"Poor guy," Davida said.

"How do you know he didn't do it on purpose?"

Davida and Viv both threw food at Tim.

"What? Geez. I'm on your side. Standing up for women."

"Are not," Viv said. "You're just trying to sound 'sensitive.' As if some med student's going to molest me with his supervisor watching on closed-circuit TV."

"Maybe all that apparent testosterone was making him do crazy things."

"Oh, right. Too much male hormone. The dreaded Zanger Syndrome. I forgot about that."

Davida and Tim laughed but avoided looking at each other. Viv's plan was clearly working. She could hardly wait to tell Jack.

"BTdubs," Tim said, no doubt to break the tension, "any interest in ax-throwing tomorrow?"

Viv rocked her head back and forth, considering, then went, "Aargh. Sorry, can't. I'm busy."

"With what?" Tim removed a slice of pickle from his sub and took a bite. "Starting a global charity? Applying to Ivy League schools? The usual Viv stuff?"

"Close. Going to the bridal salon to try on dresses."

He slapped his hand on his chest with his fingers splayed. "Jack popped the big question?"

"You mean as in 'Fries or onion rings?' No. This is for my *father's* wedding. I'm the—wait for it—maid of honor." Viv mimed a scream.

"That bad?" Tim said.

"Hard to warm up to the floozy who ruined my parents' marriage. Worried it's going to be a little awk-ward, know what I mean?"

Everything Katie had ever said to her came with a quiver of exclamation points, a bouquet of hearts-and-flowers emojis. It was exhausting. Normally, Viv could deflect to her dad, but bridal salon? No grooms allowed. She was going to have to do this alone. The thought was excruciating.

Viv closed her eyes and shuddered. She opened them and there, across the table, was the solution. "Hey. Davida. How'd you like to go with me?"

Tim went, "Why, there's an invitation you can't pass up!"

"I'm asking Davida . . ."

Davida poked at the lettuce strips in her chicken pita and blushed. "I'm usually the one making things *more* awkward."

"Perfect! Think how smooth I'll look in comparison."

"I'm kind of not the bridal salon type."

"Oh, and I am? Come. Please?" Viv whined. "It'll be fun. They have prom dresses too. We could, you know, pop some E and try on prom dresses! The really ugly ones. Take a bunch of selfies. Sneer at the pretention. Come on! I'm begging you. Please?"

Tim looked at Davida and said, "I'm dying to see you in a fit-and-flare."

She laughed. "Guess I better go then."

Viv felt herself relax, felt herself smile. It was like the first gulp of Grey Goose after a long, hard day.

Davida

The North American red squirrel. More brown than red, really, but that's its name. It's the one you see everywhere, all twitchy and scamper-y and kind of adorable. I even know the genus. *Tamiasciurus hudsonicus.* (All that *Planet Earth* has finally paid off.)

I push the box aside and set the specimen down on the kitchen table. It's about six inches tall. It's standing up on its hind legs, its big, black, anime eyes wide open. In its paws, there's a tiny white envelope with my name written on it in green ink.

Viv

"Sorry. Sorry!" Viv barreled into the salon, waving her hands and grimacing goofily. She'd forgotten to mention Katie was always late.

Davida was waiting under a giant black-and-white photo of a bride gazing across a fjord, her veil unfurling behind her in the wind. Davida looked so out of place in her jeans and sneakers that Viv blurted, "Sorry," again. This was going to be painful. "Been waiting long?"

Davida shook her head and smiled.

Katie looked at Viv like *what's going on?* Viv hadn't told her she'd invited a buffer. She couldn't help but enjoy Katie's disappointment.

She introduced Katie to Davida and tried to introduce Lulu too, but the little girl had somehow disappeared. They found her on her tip-toes, stealing a fistful of brightly wrapped chocolates from a fishbowl on the reception desk.

"Now, now." Katie bustled over and pried them out of her hand. "You don't need candies. You already had your dessert."

"No, I didn't." Lulu wasn't happy. "I had a peach and that's a fruit and I don't like fruit."

"Yes, you do-ooh." Katie pasted on a smile and crinkled her eyebrows. She dropped the chocolates back in the bowl.

Viv mentally rolled her eyes. As if anyone was judging Katie because her kid actually ate like a kid.

What they *would* judge her on was that dress. It was skin-tight and sleeveless and, with the heels and gold cuff, exactly what you'd expect someone's trophy wife to wear. Viv could imagine what Davida was thinking about her father right then.

She could imagine what everyone at the wedding would be thinking about him.

Lucky guy.

Letch.

Fool.

She was going to hate it. Every second.

The smiling. The vows. (*If they write their own*, she thought, *I'll puke.*) The kiss. (*I'll puke for sure.*) She didn't know how she was going to make it through.

Champagne. That's how. Had to toast the bride, didn't she?

She'd kill for a drink right now.

"This must be the Braithwaite party." A middle-aged lady in a slim black dress and stylish pumps glided into the lobby.

Katie positively twinkled. "That's us!"

Not yet, Viv thought.

Maybe never, she hoped.

"Well, then, may I show you some dresses?"

"Please! We're so excited, aren't we?" Katie smiled and nodded at all of them, even Davida, as if she were part of the wedding party and had been forever, and Viv saw herself for the bitch that she was.

The lady—Reena—led them into the showroom. Everything was white and drape-y.

"Oh my God. It's like a toilet-paper commercial in here," Viv whispered to Davida.

A bride-to-be was standing on a little pedestal looking into a three-sided mirror. The dress she was trying on was way too small. The sides were so far apart in the back they had to be clamped on to her bra with big plastic clips.

Lulu wagged her finger and said, "You're too fat for that dress." The bride and her entourage burst out laughing. Katie gasped in horror.

"No! You're utterly gorgeous. I'd kill for those curves!" She dragged Lulu off before she could stick her foot in it again.

Viv filed that little story away to tell Jack next time he called from training camp.

"Nothing's written in stone yet, of course," Katie said to Viv when she'd recovered, "but I was thinking a robin's-egg blue / French blue, something in that family. I thought it would be lovely with your blond hair and pale skin, but also with Lulu's darker coloring. What do you think?"

Viv thought Katie was more a beigey-blush type, but Viv wasn't. Those non-colors made her look dead.

Viv realized that was the only reason Katie was suggesting blue.

She's being nice, asshole.

"That would be awesome, wouldn't it, Lu?" Viv said then added another "Lu" because Katie didn't like it shortened. Her own mother hated it when people called her Viv.

"Phew!" Katie touched her throat. "I was so worried. I was in last week and got the ladies to put a few dresses aside, just to narrow it down. Didn't want us getting overwhelmed. So. Shall we get started?"

Reena showed them to separate rooms, one for Lulu and Katie, one for Viv.

Davida said, "I'll wait outside," but Viv dragged her in. The room was small and white with a big mirror and two curlicue dining chairs that looked old but weren't. Five dresses hung on hangers from coat hooks.

"Vintage seventies with a twist" was more Viv's go-to look, but she saw the dresses and melted. She took one by the hips and stepped back to inspect it. A long straight sheath of shimmery silk, narrow straps, slit up the back.

"Wow."

Davida puckered her lips and nodded. "Try it on."

"This one first, or the one with the low neck?"

"Depends. You want to start with the best or check out the 'maybes' first?"

"Duh." Viv was already taking her clothes off. "Life's too short for messing with the 'maybes.'"

That sounded like a meme. A poster in the guidance counselor's office or a Lululemon store. It made her think of her mother. Allie had gotten up that day, but just barely and only because Christie was sending a yoga instructor over for an at-home class.

Viv was down to her thong when the door burst open and Lulu barged in. She was wearing a baby-blue party dress with a high waist and a puffy skirt.

"Look at me, Vivi! I'm so pretty. I'm like a princess. I'm like Elsa only littler. I'm—hey!"

She stopped dancing around and squinted at Viv. "What's that?"

"What's what?"

"That!" Lulu poked Viv's ass with a sticky finger. Viv looked over her shoulder to see.

"Oh, that. It's a piece of pizza."

"A piece of pizza! On your"—Lulu put her hand beside her mouth and whispered—"bottom?"

"Silly, eh? I drew it on with a pen. It'll come off. See?" Viv licked her finger and rubbed.

"No, it didn't. It's still there. That's why you're only allowed to draw on paper. I got in trouble when I drew on Ross's car seat. Mommy said you're only allowed to draw where you're *supposed* to draw—"

Viv shook like she was scared. "Promise not to tell her! I don't want to get in trouble!"

Lulu nodded seriously. "That's okay, Vivi. I won't tell."

Viv high-fived her. "You and me, kid! Against the—"

The door creaked open a crack and Katie peered in. Viv whipped the dress up in front of her. "Sorry, Vivienne. I didn't know where she'd gotten to. Lulu, out!"

"That's okay." Viv's smile was too wide and too fake, but she couldn't fix it. "I don't mind."

Katie grabbed Lulu, blew Viv a kiss and left.

Viv slumped against the wall. "You think Katie saw my tattoo?"

"That's a tattoo?" Davida took another look at the tiny image on Viv's butt.

"Yes. You think she saw it?"

"No."

"Sure?"

"Absolutely. She was trying *really* hard not to look at any of the naked parts."

"Oh, thank God. My parents would kill me if they found out. They're convinced tattoo parlors are crawling with HIV and hepatitis and, I don't know, Ebola or something. It's seriously the only thing they've ever agreed on."

"It's a piece of pizza?" Davida sort of laughed. "It's so small it's hard to tell."

Viv turned around to show her in the mirror. "Yeah, see? It's a piece of pizza shaped like a heart. The circles are pepperoni."

"Why pizza?"

"Jack and I had it on our first date. His dad drove us to Mother's Pizzeria then sat in the car while we ate." Viv rolled her eyes. "*Very* romantic, but hey, we were fourteen."

She wriggled into the dress. "This spring, we wanted to get our names tattooed before Jack left for rugby camp, but the tattoo artist was like no. You're too young. Love doesn't last. Blah, blah, blah. Major downer. It was almost funny. Jack went, 'Can we get pepperoni pizza then? We know we'll always love that.' It was a joke. We were like hahaha, but then hey, why not? So I drew this and we got the guy to put it somewhere no one would see it. Jack's parents would be even more pissed off than mine if they found out. You're the only other person who's ever seen it—so don't make me have to kill you."

"Hey, my lips are sealed. Lulu's the one you have to worry about."

"Nah." Viv swiped the air. "The kid's a goldfish. She's forgotten already."

There was a knock at the door. "Vivienne? Your stepmother would love to see the first dress whenever you're ready."

"Thanks, Reena. Almost done!" She turned to Davida and mouthed, *Stepmother*? She was *never* going to call Katie her stepmother.

She pulled on a pair of strappy five-inch heels left out for her then twisted her hair into a bun. A little messy but whatever. "One maid of honor, coming right up."

She lifted her dress at the knees and walked into the showroom. She felt like a princess too, although more Meghan than Elsa. She stepped onto the pedestal. Everyone turned. The room gasped. Katie and Reena took in the long view then moved in for a close-up.

"Love the up-do," Katie said, "but for the big day, maybe a bit sleeker?" She raised her eyebrows, looking for Viv's answer.

"Absolutely."

"Now let's see this dress." Katie stood behind her so she could study Viv's reflection in the mirror.

"The color, the neckline, the length—all fabulous. But I'm thinking it could be a little more form-fitting here." She put her hands on Viv's waist. The dress—and Viv—took shape. Reena cinched it in place with plastic clips.

Katie went, "What do you think, Davida?" She even got her name right.

"Lethal," which made Viv laugh. So un-Davida.

"Exactly. Her father's going to have my head." Katie looked thrilled. "One little thing . . . See the back?" Viv turned and looked over her shoulder into the mirror. "What if instead of going up to your shoulder blades, we had it come down in a nice low V." Katie drew the outline on Viv's back with her finger. "Could you do that?" she said to Reena.

"Sure. I can show you what it might look like." She unzipped the dress to the waist, turned the sides under and readjusted the clips. "How's that?"

"A little lower," Katie said. "Wouldn't you say, Vivienne?"

"A little." Jack was going to die.

She turned to face the mirror. Reena had a pincushion strapped to her wrist and was pinning the alterations into place. Viv was just thinking how her mother would never agree to a back that low and realizing, happily, that—right now, at least—Allie's opinion didn't matter, when she looked in the mirror and there she was, her mother, striding into the showroom, a big ugly smile stretched across her face.

The receptionist said to Katie, "The rest of your party is here, Mrs. Braithwaite," and in that second, Viv knew everything was going to go spectacularly wrong.

Davida

4 days after the party
4:07 p.m.

I know it's only going to make me feel worse, but I peel the envelope off the squirrel's paws and open it anyway.

It's so tiny. Postage stamp tiny. Inside is a very thin, almost see-through sheet of paper that's been folded neatly in four. The words are really small but easy to read because Tim's handwriting's so good.

D—Things aren't what they seem. I took an oath so that's all I can say.
Don't hate me.
   XO T

Viv

24 days before the party
4:08 p.m.

"The rest of my party's here?" Katie looked past Viv to see what the receptionist was talking about.

"Yes." Allie's voice was scarily pleasant. "I'm crashing your party, just like you crashed mine." She was wearing leggings and a T-shirt that Viv realized used to be her father's. Her mother—the mother she once knew—would never have appeared in public like that.

"Allie." Katie was visibly shaking. "What are you—"

"Don't you fucking Allie me! I'm Mrs. Braithwaite."

"Mum." The pins in the dress pricked Viv's side when she tried to move. "This isn't—"

"And you!" Allie roared at her. "You *knew* they were getting married? You felt no need to inform me? You thought it better I find out from some yoga teacher who's popped by to help me *relax*?" She put on a high-pitched voice. "*Your name's Braithwaite? Really? A client of mine is marrying a Ross Braithwaite. Any relation?*"

"Mum. Sorry. I—"

"Don't you see what's going on? This . . . *woman* isn't your friend. She doesn't *like* you. She'd love to get rid of you. You're ruining her plans! All that money your father has to pay to support you right through graduate school? Without *you*, that would be hers! She'd be living the life if you hadn't screwed it up."

The whole time Allie was talking, Viv was going, "Mum! . . . Mum. Stop. Please. Go home. Please."

Lulu pulled on Katie's arm. "Why is that lady screaming at Vivi? That lady's not nice."

Reena ran out of the room. Some customers laughed. Others stood frozen, their hands over their mouths. Bitches in white dresses had their phones out, recording it all.

"Please. Mum," Viv whispered. "Wait in the lobby. I'll be right there."

Allie stopped yelling. There was a moment when Viv thought it was all going to be fine, but no. Allie grabbed her by the shoulder strap and screamed, "Get that dress off!"

Viv grabbed the strap too, to keep it from tearing, but her mother just kept yanking. "Take it off! Take. It. Off!"

Someone said, "Ladies. Please," and stepped between them. It was the curvaceous bride, clipped into a different dress and wearing a veil now too. "How about you let go and we can talk this out?" She pressed one hand flat on Allie's chest and the other flat on Viv's.

Allie said, "Mind your fucking business," and pushed her. The bride went, "Hey, now," still pretty reasonable, but when Allie slapped her face, she slapped back. Suddenly, they were going at it, Viv tossed around between them like a rag doll.

It went on and on like that until there was a screech of fabric and Viv's shoulder strap came off in Allie's hand. Allie's arm flew up. She screamed and fell flat on her back, taking the bride down with her. For half a second, Viv stood alone, wobbling on the pedestal, and then, because of the shock or maybe the five-inch heels, she lost her balance too and landed on Allie. She tried to get up, but Allie—sobbing now—pinned her in the saddest hug ever. The bride yanked her dress out from under them and crawled away.

Two beefy security guards marched in. They picked Viv and her mother up in a single bundle then the dark-haired guard peeled Allie off.

"You okay?" He was surprisingly gentle. "Can I call someone for you? A friend?" Allie bowed her head and let him lead her away.

The other guard—younger, bearded, bald—took Viv's elbow. His badge said his name was Cory. "You okay to stand, sugar?" When she didn't say anything, he helped her to a tufted velvet chair, sat her down and took off her shoes. "Better?"

Viv shook her head.

"Don't worry," he whispered. "That was nothin'. We've had bridesmaids going after each other, mothers-of-the-bride getting into it with mothers-of-the-groom. A grandmother once too. Fiesty."

Viv tried to smile but barely managed to bend her lips.

"Good thing you're not wearing mascara. Half the time after these things there's makeup all over the carpet. I told Mrs. Rivera white isn't a good idea for a place like this but"—he shrugged—"it's all about the illusion, right?"

"Where's my stepmother?" There. She'd said it. Didn't mean to, but she had.

"They hustled her out the back. The little one didn't need to see this."

"What about the other girl? My friend."

"I'm here." Davida was leaning against a rack of gowns on the other side of the room. Her skin had gone as white as raw fish. The loud noise, no doubt.

"I'm sorry." Viv stood up to go to her, but Davida was already walking over.

"No," she said. "They did this, not you."

"Too true." Cory gave Viv's shoulder a jiggle. Davida put her hand on Viv's arm and rubbed it up and down. They stood like that for a while in a weird, awkward, semi-group hug.

"I told you this would be fun," Viv said, sort of laughing.

"That's the spirit!" Cory said.

"Want to go home?" Davida said.

Viv nodded. "But, um, by myself. That okay? I kinda want to be by myself."

Davida gave a sad smile and nodded. "Call if you need me," she said then lifted her hand in a little wave and left.

Viv turned to Cory. "You know where my mother is?"

He checked his phone. "Other guard's taking her home. Says her sister's meeting them. What about you? Can I drop you off?"

"No, but thanks. You've been really nice."

"I just do what I can."

In the changing room, Viv texted Stu.

She left the dress on the chair. It was too hard to hang up with the shoulder strap missing.

Excerpt from police interview with Stu Fenske, 4 days after the party

Lt. Alan (Pidge) Eisenhauer: So you picked her up at the bridal salon?

Stu Fenske: Yeah.

Eisenhauer: And how was she?

Fenske: How do you think? Not quite suicidal but close. Guzzled half a bottle pretty fast then passed out. The video had already popped up on my feed so I called dispatch and clocked out. I figured it was better if she just slept this one off.

Davida

I throw the squirrel into the compost but first I pull out its eyes. I tell myself it's because they're glass so they aren't biodegradable, but that's not true. I do it because I want to hurt something.

Some*one*.

I rip off its tail too and bang its little head against the bin until the stuffing comes out. Someone knocked my insides out too. Now it's my turn.

I lean against the bin and catch my breath. It's sunny and warm. There's a breeze shuffling through the leaves of the big tree in our backyard. I hear birds singing. Chickadees, I'm pretty sure.

This isn't me. This isn't the type of thing I do. I drop the squirrel into the compost. Its head comes off and rolls up against an apple core. This is the type of thing my mother would do. It scares me.

Muriel, the old lady across the street, opens her screen door and calls out, "Are you all right, honey?"

I turn around and go, "Yup. I'm fine." I even smile. "Something was just stuck to the . . ." I let my voice trail off because the less I say about abusing small animals the better, especially to Muriel, since she gets me to look after her Yorkie when she visits her daughter and I'm going to need the money, now that I'm quitting the SP program. (I just realized that.) She gives me a flappy wave and goes back inside.

I look at the squirrel, all splayed out and dismembered and pitiful. I take a picture and send it to Tim. Meet me at the breakwater in 15 minutes

I shouldn't have done that, but it's too late now.

Viv

The next morning came. Viv huddled under her duvet, her head pound-
ing, her body aching. No way she could go to work. She kept her eyes
closed tight and patted the bedside table until she found her phone. She'd
leave a message saying she was sick then she could just lay there until . . .

Until what?

She put her phone back down. *Seriously—until what?*

During World War I, soldiers actually drowned in the mud. They
weren't shot or gassed or blown to bits. (That was for the lucky ones.)
The shit in the trenches just consumed them. Viv had learned that in
European History.

That's what this felt like. She was drowning in her parents' shit.

She had to get up.

She staggered into her bathroom, her brain hard and chipped and
rattling in her skull. She turned the tap to cold and stayed in the shower
until she was blue and shivering. She gargled mouthwash, sprayed on
cologne, squeezed mentholated ointment on her arms and shoulders—
covered her stink any way she could—then went downstairs.

"Hey, Sleepyhead." Christie smiled at her. She and Allie were sitting in
the kitchen nook overlooking the garden, sun streaming in, Bach tinkling

in the background. Christie was dressed in high-end street-casual. Allie was wrapped in an ancient housecoat, hair in a limp ponytail, gray roots showing. She didn't look up. Christie must have given her a little something from her doctor bag.

I'll have what she's having. It was Viv's favorite line from *When Harry Met Sally*, although not as funny here.

"Scrambled eggs?" Christie checked the bowl on the table. "They're a little cold, but won't take a second to whip up some more."

Viv somehow managed not to barf. "No, thanks. I'm late for SP." She grabbed a bagel off the counter and blew them kisses. "Gotta go."

She clamped the bagel between her teeth, hopped on her bike and burned off down the street. For a moment, it felt like she'd escaped, but she wasn't stupid. There was no escape. Her mother would apologize, explain, break into another rage, die some more. Her father would calmly begin legal proceedings and finish off the job he'd started. Lulu would grow up into a confused and angry adolescent.

Viv took a gulp from her water bottle and picked up speed. She shouldn't be on the road in this condition. She turned left at the next light and detoured through the park. She tried to review her lines for that day's simulation: *My name is Anna. Good at school. No previous behavioral problems. Mother died suddenly of undiagnosed heart condition. Now I'm grieving and my grades are suffering.*

Viv thought: *Would I be grieving?*

Or would I finally be free?

Free of these people. Free of the need to pretend that everything was just goddamn perfect.

She rode the rest of the way to the med school in shame.

The morning simulations went fine, thanks in part to regular hits of Grey Goose and garlic chasers. The student doctors "listened actively." Some reached out to touch her "therapeutically." One—a stiff guy with a pointy face and too much hair product—even got a little teary-eyed. Either they were really good at their job, Viv thought, or she was really good at hers.

She turned her phone back on at break. A bunch of texts from Jack. She held her breath and scrolled through them.

Working my ass off but loving it

Roommates named Pierce english super funny you'd love him

Sorry to disappoint you but everyone here really supportive

She exhaled, relieved. He obviously didn't know about the video. She texted back all the things he wanted to hear then hit the washroom.

She pushed open the cubicle door and remembered Eva Federov's feet and her sobs and her pathetic attempt to hide them both.

Then she remembered the commotion the year earlier, the sick *thrill* that had gone through the SP program when Eva's dad died. (Everybody loves a tragedy.) He'd gotten all dressed up in his chef's outfit—puffy hat and everything—and hanged himself from a tree outside the restaurant where he'd worked. It was all over the news. Viv felt bad realizing it had taken YouTube's runaway hit "JILTED WIFE GOES ON BRIDAL SALON RAMPAGE" for her to feel true empathy for Eva.

She sat on the toilet and raised a toast to the poor kid. Better late than never.

As Viv was on her way out, Charlotte and Erica barged into the washroom, squealing and laughing and hanging off each other.

"Oh, ah. Hey!" Erica said, and just the way the two of them froze, Viv knew exactly what they'd found so funny.

"Oh, hey, yourselves! How'd your sessions go?" A little vodka and she could do chipper as well as anyone. "That yellow looks gorgeous on you!"

Erica recovered enough to laugh. "Yeah. Jaundice. Pretty good, huh? Mandy even dyed my eyeballs." She pulled down her bottom lid to show off the urine-sample whites of her eyes.

Viv went, "Eww," faux-horrified, then Charlotte leapt in with some story about the huge zits Mandy had made out of Elmer's glue and pasted all over her face last year. Charlotte thought she'd peeled them all off before going out with her new crush, but she'd gotten home later and noticed this giant pustule on her forehead. The guy must have noticed it too because he ghosted her. Viv smiled and laughed and did the whole "you're so funny" thing until she'd established that she was perfectly okay and could safely say, "Better run. Need to eat before the next session starts." She left them in the washroom to dissect her behavior.

She was halfway down the hall when Dr. Hotness charged around the corner, white coat unbuttoned and flapping. He'd seen her too but flicked his head away as if he hadn't.

Then he flicked it back and walked straight up to her.

"Vivienne," he said.

"You again."

He laughed but only as a placeholder. "Any chance we could chat sometime?" He was standing weirdly far away from her and semi-whispering.

"Is it, um, something bad? Did I—"

"No. I mean, not really. But we should talk."

Viv noticed Davida walking down the hall toward them. Viv smiled and gestured in the direction of the lunchroom, meaning she'd meet her there. Davida stopped and bent her head like *what's up?* Viv turned her face away from Dr. Hotness and made her mouth into a happy little *O*, as if she didn't want to drag herself away from this thrilling conversation. Davida looked at them for a second then nodded and headed to the lunchroom.

As soon as she'd gone, Viv turned back to Dr. Hotness, her face serious again. "Tell me now." She didn't need any more bullshit.

George stared at his shoes for a second. "The other day. I wanted to make sure I didn't, um, traumatize you when I, you know . . . The zipper? Your pants?"

Viv hadn't taken a breath in quite a while, so maybe it was just oxygen deprivation, but she burst out laughing.

"Trust me. Takes *way* more than that to traumatize me." She was thinking about "JILTED WIFE," but then realized he wouldn't know that. "It was just a mistake! No harm, no foul."

"Sure?"

"Yes. Totally. Forget it."

He put his hands together in that Hollywood-humble-thanks way and left.

The lunchroom was buzzing when Viv walked in, buzzing louder when people noticed her. They'd all seen the video, that was obvious. She pulled herself up straight and headed to the food table. She wanted ice cream or butterscotch pudding—something sweet and loving like that—then she wanted to go.

Davida saw her and no doubt saw what was going on too. She came right over. "You get my texts? I tried to call. You okay?"

"Yassss." *Never let them see you sweat.* That was her father's mantra. Ditto for tears. She laughed.

Davida didn't. "C'mon. Tim's saving us seats."

"Nah! Don't want to horn in." There was one pudding left. Vanilla. Not as good as butterscotch, but Viv took it.

"You're not. C'mon."

"Can't. Got stuff to do. If I'm lucky, I may even run into Dr. Hotness again . . ."

Davida frowned like *really?* but Viv just winked and left. She smiled her way out of the room then tossed the pudding into the garbage and pulled out her water bottle.

The vodka felt cold and hot and like the answer to all her problems until she slapped the cap back down and looked around and she was still standing in the hall alone and her mother was still on YouTube and her father was still getting married and Jack was still away and somewhere poor Lulu was no doubt still crying.

She took another swig. It made her legs wobbly and her eyelids heavy, but it didn't turn her brain off. She leaned against the wall, like anyone would who was a bit tired, say, or lazy, or depressed about some normal teenage thing. The wall was solid and so was the floor, but Viv felt like she was on a boat in a storm. She spread her feet for balance and dug around in her backpack until she found some garlic. Two cloves. She peeled one, put it in her mouth, chewed. She hadn't got all the papery stuff off and some got stuck under her tongue. She put her finger into her mouth to get it and almost gagged herself.

Barfing here. That's all she needed. She turned and staggered toward the washroom, the boat really knocked around by the waves now, and there was Dr. Keppo, striding down the hall, smiling. The lines spreading across his face reminded Viv of ripples in cake batter. Happy lines. She smiled back. He stopped and looked at her.

"Viv?" he said. "You okay?"

She pulled her shoulders back, indignant, all ready to deny anything he accused her of, then something changed.

"No, Dr. Keppo," she said. "I am not."

Excerpt from police interview with Charlotte Ito, 4 days after the party

---

Lt. Alan (Pidge) Eisenhauer: Did you ever see any sign of Vivienne using drugs?

Charlotte Ito: No. I *heard* about it. This girl Makayla said Viv took Ecstasy, but other kids said Viv was just joking about that.

Eisenhauer: What do you think?

Ito: I don't know her very well, but my friend Erica and I ran into her in the washroom right after that video of her mother came out? If it was my mother doing that, I'd have freaked, but Viv was laughing and joking like nothing happened. We figured she had to be on drugs then. On something, anyway.

Davida

I bike to the breakwater. It's not that far.

His van is right where I thought it would be, on the side of the parking lot that gets a little shade. Tim's sitting on a bench with his back to me, looking at the ocean, the sun shining through the sudsy globe of his ridiculous hair.

I can't believe I ever liked him.

I walk up behind him, super quiet, but he stands before I get there. He shoves his hands in his pockets and says, "Thanks for coming."

"Don't thank me." As if I'm doing this for *him*. "And don't talk to me ever again." That's basically all I came to say.

" . . . Unless you're going to be honest for a *change* and explain what you and Viv were doing in the van."

Why do I care? I don't. I don't know why I said it.

"I can't tell you that."

I laugh (sort of). "You don't need to. I'm not blind. I saw exactly what you were doing."

"I don't think you did actually."

"Well—*actually*—I did. I had a pretty good view and, pathetic as this sounds, I recognized your technique. Or are you saying *I'm* the liar here?"

"No. I'm saying you believe what you saw, but appearances can be deceiving."

"Oh, really? Like it *appeared* you actually liked me? That kind of deceiving?" I turn to go before I make a fool of myself. "Just forget it."

"Sorry, sorry. Stop. I'll tell you. What I can."

I turn toward him.

He says, "I love you."

I want to hit him. I clamp my hands on either side of my head and silent-scream. I say, "I'm leaving."

"Are you hurt?" he says.

Of course I'm hurt. What kind of question is that? Then I see he's looking at the burn on my arm.

I sneer, "It's *moulage*." I love making him sound stupid.

"Wow." As if he's impressed. He moves in for a closer look.

"Get away from me." I can't trust myself.

He puts up his palms. "Sorry, sorry!"

I'm overreacting. I make my body relax.

"I'll tell you what I can," he says.

"Okay, what?" I cross my arms.

"Viv's life wasn't what it seemed."

"Oh, really? I never would have known." He's told me exactly nothing. He looks away. I tap my foot.

"I took an oath." He's kind of pleading. His eyes are turned down at the sides and he's grimacing like he's got a bad splinter or something.

"I *hate* you." I wanted to stay calm.

"Sorry. I know you do. But this is one promise I can't break. It's really important to me. And so are you."

"If you've got something to say, you better say it now, because I'm leaving." I don't move.

"I have to ask you one question first."

"Oh my God. I can't believe you."

"Just one."

I sigh. "Okay, *one*."

"Do you think Viv loves Jack?"

It feels like a trick.

"Sorry," he says after a while. "Just answer that. Please? Yes or no?"

The look on Viv's face when she said Jack's name, when she saw his number light up her phone, when she told me about the tattoo.

"I thought she did."

"But now you don't?"

I shrug. I also remember how she looked when she talked about Dr. Hotness.

"Seriously?" he says. "I'm asking for real. You think that's an act?"

"Why?"

"Did you delete the videos we took of the three of us together?"

I'm not going to lie so I don't answer. "You said you had one question."

He smiles as if I made a joke. "Watch them when you go home. Please? Something was happening to Viv. Something she didn't know was happening. She loves Jack. A lot. You know she does."

"And you somehow managed to get video of this thing that was happening to her?" I hope he knows how ridiculous that sounds.

"No. But there are clues there about what was going on. She hadn't even seen them herself yet, but they're there."

He loves being so mysterious. "Just tell me what they are."

"I can't. I shouldn't even have said that much." He hooks one hand around the back of his neck and looks away.

"What if I don't see them?" I say.

"You will. Jack did."

Something about his face when he said it. I go, "Is that why they had that fight when he came back from rugby camp?"

"Yeah, but he got it all wrong. She—" Tim suddenly swings around and heads toward his van.

"She what?"

He doesn't stop.

"Where are you going?" *I'm* the one who walks away here.

"I can't say anything else." He unlocks the van and gets in.

"Yeah? Well, I have a question for you." I'm kind of screaming at him.

"Okay." He holds the door open with his right hand and turns to see me.

"Do you think she took the pill on purpose?"

He looks at me funny. "Yeah." Like he can't believe I'd even ask. "Of course she did."

Tim

Standing that close to Davida again, seeing how upset I'd made her was pure agony. All I wanted to do was tell her the truth. It would have been such a shitty thing to do to Viv but, boy, would it have felt good.

I hate being honorable.

I didn't mean to ask Davida to look at the videos. It was just a desperate last-ditch attempt to keep her from leaving—but now I think might work. She's an observant person. She knows Viv loves Jack. She knows she'd never cheat on him. She'll put two and two together and see what a mess Viv's life had become.

Or maybe she'll watch the videos and all she'll see is how much fun we used to have. See how much *everything* we used to have.

That might be enough to make her believe me.

Viv

Dr. Keppo's office was crowded, but not messy. The walls were covered with diplomas and certificates and photos of him shaking hands with important people. The shelves were crammed with books, some standing, others shoved on top. A coffee table was almost invisible under neat piles of papers. He pointed to the couch and smiled. "Have a seat."

"Thanks." Viv batted the door closed behind her.

"Sorry." He opened it. "Regulations. Three people in the room or doors open."

She looked at him, looked into the hall, thought of everyone who could come by, all the stories they could tell, all the truth that could get out.

"No," she whispered. "Someone. Could. Hear." She went to slap the door closed but he caught her arm.

"Who?" He chuckled. "Other than my office, the whole floor's under renovation. There's no one here. Someone does come by, though, we can stop, recommence when you're comfortable." He helped her into the seat. "You okay with that?"

No, not really, but her head was lolling and the room was swaying, so she didn't argue. Besides, on the elevator up, he'd asked if she'd been drinking and she'd said yes, so the worst was over.

He arranged himself into the leather armchair across from her. He didn't look angry or disappointed or disgusted. Just his usual self, all sort of serene. She'd once told Tim that Dr. Keppo reminded her of a Buddhist monk in dad clothes and it was true. Such a dad.

He picked up a pad of paper from the coffee table and got a pencil out of his pocket.

"You're taking notes?" Viv didn't like that.

"No. Just doodling. Helps me think. Not to mention relax." That twinkly, little-kid smile of his. "You should try it sometime."

"You're not going to, going to . . ." She rolled her hand, trying to think of the word.

He put his pencil down. "You're worried about something."

She nodded then wished she hadn't. It made her queasy.

"What?" he said.

She closed her eyes. It was better that way. "I don't want people to know."

"I'm a doctor, don't forget. Anything you say to me is confidential. Your secrets are safe. *Capiche?*"

"*Capiche.*" The word tickled her lips.

He started doodling. "I used to be a drinker," he said.

"What?" She opened her eyes for that.

"Drunk every day. Shit-faced, as they say."

"Noooo."

He shrugged as if he didn't like to brag. "You're not the only one with secrets."

"When?"

"A little older than you. I was the first person in my family to go to university. My parents were so proud. I'd always been the smart kid, the one who was going to make a difference. Then I got to med school and realized there was a very real chance I was going to flunk out. So I worked really hard and passed—but then next term would start and there'd be another credit I might not make. Or a month's rent I might not scrape up. Somehow, I always made it through, but the stress was killing me."

He drummed his pencil on his knee and smiled. "So I drank. On the sly. I was old enough to drink legally but the way my mind worked, I figured I had enough strikes against me. Poor. Immigrant. Bald." He rubbed his head and laughed. "I didn't need anyone finding out I was a drunk too. I'd have a social beer with friends to cover my tracks then I'd sneak a bottle of medical alcohol home in my backpack. That stuff is lethal. I'd usually water it down with orange juice or pop, but not all the time. Big bio-chem exam coming up?" He tipped his hand back in front of his mouth. "Straight down the hatch."

He began to draw again. "So what drives you to drink?"

Viv put her head in her hands and whimpered out a laugh. "Where do I start?"

"The bridal shop video?" he said.

She looked up. "You saw it."

"Tough stuff." He scrunched up his lips and shook his head. "Other people were probably surprised by your mother's behavior, but I bet you weren't. Am I right?"

Viv thought, *I'm going to cry. I'm going to cry. I'm going to cry.*

She didn't.

"That's very stressful for you. And her too. She no doubt hates herself for what she's doing but can't make herself stop. Our parents aren't superhuman. They screw up all the time. It's one of the hardest lessons we have to learn."

Viv nodded.

"You're an only child?"

"A stepsister. Lulu."

"Can you confide in her?"

Viv flopped her arms out. "She's fi-ive, Dr. Keppo!" That seemed hilarious until she saw the look on his face. She hated pity.

"Who do you have to talk to then?"

She pushed her tongue up hard against the roof of her mouth.

"No one?" he said when the silence got too long. "No friends?"

Stu, she thought, but she wasn't ratting him out.

"I've got a boyfriend." She wasn't totally pathetic.

"Good." He settled back in his chair.

"But I'd never tell him."

"Why?"

She looked up as if she was thinking, but she was really just trying to keep the tears from spilling over.

"Can I put some tea on for you?"

"Okay." She didn't love tea, but it might sober her up.

Dr. Keppo dropped the pad of paper on the coffee table. It was covered in cartoony drawings. A bottle. A backpack. A little bald character scratching his head. He filled the kettle at the sink in the back of the room and plugged it in.

"Herbal okay?"

"Yeah."

"So . . ." He rummaged around for stuff in the cupboard. The door hid his face from her. "Your boyfriend. What keeps you from telling him?"

"Jack?" She snorted. It hurt her nose. "He wouldn't understand."

"How do you know?"

"I just do." She wanted to leave it at that, but the quiet got weird. "I used to tell him stuff and everything but you know . . . He's nice. What can you do?"

"That sounds like a good thing." Dr. Keppo closed the cupboard door and looked at her.

"No. No, no, no." She let her head fall forward. He didn't get it.

"Why?"

"Everyone in Jack's whole family is all perfect and loving and, you know, *'Oh, can I help you?' 'No, let me. No, let me. After you. Why, thanks!'*" She sighed as if she'd had enough of these stupid people.

"Supportive. Even better." He spooned loose tea into one of the mugs. "Could you talk to his parents?"

"No!" Larry and Carleen were even worse than Jack.

Dr. Keppo laughed. "That bad?"

"Yes." She tried to sound light, not turn this into some big tragedy even if it was. "They'd be, like, horrified."

"You'd be surprised. They're grown-ups. They—"

"They go to church!"

"So?"

"My parents hump the help! Go, like, apeshit in bridal salons!" That made her laugh. "So, ah, no, Dr. Keppo. I cannot talk to Jack's parents. It's like, you know, climate change or something."

"Climate change?"

"Yes!" It had made sense when she said it, but now she couldn't remember why. She pulled her eyebrows together into a thinking face, but nothing happened.

"You mean something you can't control?" The kettle whistled.

She pointed at him. "Bingo!" She hadn't thought of that, but it was a good point.

He clinked around with mugs and spoons while she thought.

"And . . . and it's not my fault. Someone else made this giant fuck-ing mess but I'm the one it's going to kill."

She looked at him to see if he understood. His eyes kind of melted. She turned away.

"And *meanwhile* . . . while I'm trying not to get fucking *incinerated*, I'm supposed to be working, and applying for scholarships, and 'beef-ing up my résumé,' and keeping in shape, and cleaning my room and, of course, having fun! Because—yay! I'm a teenager and these are the best fucking years of my life!!!! Fuck." She slapped her hands over her face. "Sorry. Sorry about the swearing. I am so drunk."

"Well, if there was ever a time to swear, it's now." He handed her a cup of tea. "This'll help. I have it made specially. My own blend."

She held it with two hands and leaned into it. It smelled apple-y. She'd said too much.

Dr. Keppo sat back in his chair. He made a big, happy, closed-eyed *ah*, the way they do in commercials. "Nothing like a nice cuppa tea. All I drink now."

Viv took a sip. It was very hot. She couldn't really taste it.

"How . . . ," she said. "How did you, like . . ."

"Quit? Wasn't easy. I got caught and got an ultimatum. Several, in fact. From Laura." He pointed to the framed family photos on the window ledge. "She's my wife now but wasn't then. I'd dry out for a while then fall off the wagon, she'd threaten to leave, I'd dry out, fall off the wagon, etcetera, etcetera." He wobbled his head like it was a joke. "I knew I'd lose her if I didn't figure out why I needed to hurt myself. I found a psychiatrist, a bit older than me but a hell of a lot wiser. I spent many hours in a room just like this, talking things through. That too hot for you?"

Viv blew on her tea, took another sip and shook her head.

"You sure? I can add a little cold water. I like mine scalding."

"I'm sure." She took a bigger drink just to prove it. "It's delicious."

"I know. Anyway. Where was I? Oh, yes. Elwin. Great guy. Very proper but, you know"—he pointed two fingers at his eyes—"very focused, intuitive. He used to say, 'Choose life, Ivan.' He convinced me that was my only choice . . . Oh, sorry, hold on. My phone's been vibrating like mad here. Never a good sign."

He read his text, replied, scrolled through some stuff, texted again. Viv drank her tea. He frowned. "You got somewhere you have to be today?"

"I have some sessions."

"No, you don't. I just took the liberty of texting Janice and cancel-ing your afternoon. Probably not a good idea showing up in your cur-rent state."

The blood ran out of her face.

"Don't worry. I just said you weren't feeling well. So, no rush then?"

"No rush."

"Great. I have to run downstairs for ten minutes. I've cleared an hour for you. Can we continue this when I come back?"

Viv sucked on her lip and gave the tiniest nod. Her head was spin-ning. She felt like shit. *I am shit*, she thought.

He put his hand on her shoulder as he got up. "This'll be okay. You'll see."

He closed the door behind him. Viv texted her pool supervisor and gave her notice. How could she be a lifeguard when she couldn't even save herself? She texted the person in charge of the environmental street fair and said she wouldn't be able to help anymore. As if she ever had.

She let herself cry for a while. Then she told herself to smarten up and she drank some more tea.

Excerpt from police interview with Janice Drysdale, 4 days after the party

---

Lt. Alan (Pidge) Eisenhauer: So, far as you knew, Vivienne seemed to be doing fine? No signs of any problems?

Janice Drysdale: . . .

Eisenhauer: You're hesitating.

Drysdale: You've probably spoken with med school security so know she'd been seeing Dr. Keppo for help . . .

Eisenhauer: No, we didn't.

Drysdale: Oh, I thought you would have . . . I was actually surprised myself when I found out. Vivienne always had such a good head on her shoulders. Very socially connected. Not the vulnerable type at all.

Eisenhauer: Any idea what type of help she was after?

Drysdale: Gee. I don't know. Half the time with these young girls, it's something silly. They've fallen in love or think they have. A lot of drama at that age . . . Ha. Listen to me! As if I haven't done some crazy things for love myself.

Eisenhauer: You think that was it? Romantic problems?

Drysdale: Well, I know her boyfriend was away. And I saw her more than once with one of our better-looking med students . . .

Eisenhauer: George Pineo?

Drysdale: I shouldn't be spreading rumors . . . Oh, and there was that video too.

Eisenhauer: Video?

Drysdale: Of her mother? At the bridal salon? Vivienne was probably upset about that. That makes the most sense, come to think of it.

Eisenhauer: I'll try reaching Dr. Keppo. See what he can tell me.

Drysdale: He's very busy at the moment, but I'll see if I can track him down for you. I'm not sure he'd be much help, though, given the restrictions of doctor-patient confidentiality.

Viv

Someone was shaking her shoulder. "Vivienne . . . Vivienne." She didn't recognize the voice.

Or did she?

She forced herself to swim up to the surface and open her eyes. The ceiling light was blinding. She moaned and rolled onto her side. She saw skinny legs in purple cords.

Janice.

"Oh, sorry." Viv bounced up. Her brain seesawed wildly.

"You're awake." Janice was smiling.

Viv rubbed her forehead, hiding her face until she could pull herself together. "I was asleep?"

"You must have been exhausted. Dr. Keppo came back but you were out cold and he had to leave. He asked me to wake you before I left." She beetled over to his desk. "Take your time. I'll be here for a while." She started straightening papers and standing the photos up on the window ledge.

Viv said, "I should get going. I've got, um, things to do." *Like die, for instance.*

She stood up. The room spun. She sat back down and pretended to

197

look in her backpack for something. She noticed the top two buttons of her shirt had come undone. She could feel spit crusted in the corner of her mouth. Her pants were twisted, one sandal off. Her shirt was stained with tea. She was a mess.

She tidied herself up and got out her phone. Seven o'clock. She'd been asleep for hours.

She was out of control.

"Can I drive you somewhere?" Janice was rinsing teacups. The roar of water, the crash of china against the counter. Did she have to be so loud?

"No, thanks." Viv got up, more slowly this time. "Can you apologize to Dr. Keppo for me? I didn't sleep last night. I must have passed out."

"Of course. You're sure about the drive?"

"Totally." She was out the door before Janice could say anything else.

Viv headed down the hall. The place was deserted. She peeked in an open door. The room was empty except for a ladder, a couple of big red toolboxes and a power saw. The next office was in the same shape. Viv didn't remember seeing any of this on the way to Dr. Keppo's office, but she'd been pretty drunk. She felt like she still was.

She eventually found some elevators, but the sign above them said STAFF ONLY.

She took one anyway. She hit the bottom button. The elevator lurched up, plunged down and opened with a clang. It was a miracle she didn't hurl.

She flattened her hands against the doors to keep them from closing and looked around. Everything was concrete and darkish and damp-smelling. It took her a moment to realize she'd pressed the wrong button. She was in the basement. There was a red exit sign on the far wall. She headed toward it.

She texted Stu. He texted back. Diliver pizza cant talk

Last thing she wanted right then was to talk. She answered, Just take me home

He texted back, 12 mints

She pushed open the steel door and threw her arm over her face. The brightness of the evening sun stung like allergy drops. It took her a few seconds before she could open her eyes.

The parking area was cracked and buckled and covered in cigarette butts. The light over the door was smashed. It was definitely the ass-end of campus. She'd have to find her way to the entrance for Stu to pick her up.

She was walking past two rusty green dumpsters when a bright white puff of smoke billowed up over them. She turned to see where it was coming from.

A guy was standing in the narrow alley between the dumpsters and the wall.

"George?" It took her a second to recognize him without his white doctor coat. He was wearing ratty jeans and an untucked short-sleeved shirt. "What are you doing here?"

"Ooh." He smiled awkwardly. "Caught me." He opened his hand to show a Juul. "Figured my secret was safe here, but guess not. What are *you* doing here?"

"Um . . . I took the staff elevator by mistake and ended up, ah, wherever this is. I have to get to the front. Got a cab coming."

"I'll walk you."

"No. That's okay. Enjoy your filthy habit."

"Can't. You ruined it for me." He tossed the Juul overhand into the dumpster. "C'mon. I'll walk you."

"You're just hurrying me out of here so you can come back and get it."

He took her arm and started walking. "I've met you, like, three times? How'd you figure me out so fast?" That smile of his. His hand around her wrist. He was flirting with her.

"Takes one to know one," she said stupidly.

"You hooked on watermelon-mint too?"

"No. Gross."

"Exactly. That's why I get it. I keep hoping if it's gross enough I'll stop vaping but—" He made a face. "Addiction. You know."

She shook her head. *Who me?*

"But you've had something too." He leaned his face into her hair and sniffed. Viv froze. Alcohol. He could smell alcohol on her. "Something apple-y."

She relaxed. "Oh. Yeah. Tea. I had tea with Dr. Keppo just now. Spilled some on my shirt."

George laughed. "I *thought* I recognized that smell." He leaned in again for another sniff. "It's nice. Dr. K and his cuppas."

Viv was not going to let herself enjoy this. She took her hand away and tried to chuckle. "Yeah . . . Um. I should get going. Don't want to keep my cab waiting."

"Right." The smile drained from George's face. "And I should get back to the books."

They stepped away from each other then Viv squealed, "Ow!" Her head cranked back toward him.

George went, "What?! What? You okay?" He looked around, flustered, until he noticed her hair caught on his shirt.

"Sorry." She put her hand on her head to stop it from pulling and stepped toward him again. "Me and my rat's nest."

"I'll get it," he said. She stood there with her face awkwardly turned up toward his as he painstakingly tried to untangle her hair from his button.

He laughed. "I think I just made it worse."

"Not possible."

"Oh my God. This is like some alien life form. How did it latch on so fast?"

"Just pull it out." She was still dizzy and this wasn't helping.

"I'm not going to pull your hair out."

"I got lots."

"Obviously."

"Just do it." *Please.*

"No."

"Why?"

"The Hippocratic Oath." He wagged his finger at her. "First, do no harm . . . Gimme a sec. I'll get it."

Viv put her hand against his side to steady herself. No way this would take a sec. She was worried she was going to be sick.

She heard a car honk insistently in the distance. *Stu.* That was all she needed.

"Oh, for God's sake." She grabbed the hair and yanked it out herself, leaving a ragged yellow fringe around his button.

George looked down and went, "Wow. I can't believe you did that."

She shrugged. "A little souvenir for you of our precious time together."

"I'll cherish it always."

Viv put her hand on her chest as if she was so touched then she ran off to catch Stu before he gave up on her.

Excerpt from police interview with Stu Fenske, 4 days after the party

Lt. Alan (Pidge) Eisenhauer: You think something changed around this time?

Stu Fenske: Hoped it would. I picked her up at the med school a few days after the video came out and she was, like, *I'm never going to drink again.* Typical drunk-talk, but it sounded like she meant it. On the way home, she made me promise I'd never ever no matter what buy her another bottle. Like I was the one pushing it on her or something.

Eisenhauer: Any idea what prompted her to want to stop drinking then?

Fenske: No clue. Normally, I couldn't shut her up, but she was pretty quiet that night. She got the promise out of me then just stared out the window until I dropped her off.

Eisenhauer: Did you ever break your promise?

Fenske: No. And that really pissed her off too.

Viv

Tim was the one who'd heard about the Knights of the Round Table re-enactment and suggested they go. It was being held in a seedy hotel out past the airport. It sounded like just their thing.

Viv and Davida took the shuttle and got there early because they had to pick out costumes. Tim was working for his dad that day so would be late, but that was okay. He already had his own costume. (The girls cracked up when they heard that. *Of course* he would.)

The shuttle dropped them on the highway just outside the hotel. The Satisfaction Inn had seen better times. Both *a*'s in the sign were burnt out and the front window was cracked, but the parking lot was full.

The hotel clerk was changing the dinner special on a plastic display board when Viv asked where the re-enactment was. "The Opulence Ballroom," he said, without looking up. "Second floor. Near the vending machines."

"Sounds *real* opulent," Viv whispered to Davida, but happily. She loved the hotel's quirky charm.

A large carpeted divider sectioned the wardrobe department off from the rest of the ballroom. Outfits were organized on portable clothing racks by size and type. Overeager volunteers helped the girls find what they needed then sent them to makeshift dressing rooms in the back.

It was weird for Viv putting on another gown in another dressing room. She couldn't look at herself in the mirror without remembering her mother storming into the bridal salon, face like a war mask. It made Viv wish she had her water bottle with her, but she'd sworn off booze. For real, this time. Dr. Keppo was right. She had to learn to deal with this stuff straight up. She turned away from her reflection and pulled on her dress.

Ruby-red velvet or, at least, velvet-ish. Too hot for July but gorgeous in a slutty-Halloween kind of way. Skin-tight bodice, flowing skirt, fitted sleeves ending in a wide, pointed bell. Viv let her hair spill down her front, long and loose. She figured that's how they would have worn it back then. She tied a rope belt low around her hips and put a wreath of plastic flowers on her head.

She stepped out of the dressing room. Davida was waiting for her in a matching green velvet gown, the bodice so hard and flat that her breasts bubbled up over the top like snowballs.

Viv whistled. "You're going to give Tim a heart attack in that thing."

"Yeah, right," Davida said, but even her boobs blushed.

They curtsied at each other then sashayed into the main part of the ballroom. It was like walking into the grocery store and seeing all the customers dressed in medieval gear. That's how random it was. Old people, young people, tattooed people, people who'd look more comfortable in athleisure wear or business suits. King Arthur might even have preferred to be naked, Viv thought, seeing him on his wooden throne up front. Something about his big belly, skinny legs and too-dark tan just said *nudist* to her. She knew the banquet waiters had to be laughing at them. There was something kind of pathetic about being in a rented hall in a rented costume, pretending you're ancient royalty.

The girls were listening to a bunch of severely middle-aged knaves playing lutes when Tim showed up.

"You'll never guess who I just saw." He waited two beats. "Eva Federov."

"Here?" Viv was surprised. The Satisfaction Inn was way in the boonies.

"No. In town. I had to stop for gas. I was filling up and noticed something move next to the station. I look over and there's Eva, climbing into a dumpster."

"You sure?"

"Yeah. I called her name and she looked right at me but then she just slammed the lid shut."

"With her inside?" Viv kind of laughed in horror.

"Yeah."

"What did you do?"

"What could I do? There were cars lined up behind me for the pump and I could hardly, like, crawl in after her."

"Not in your spiffy new ensemble, you couldn't." Viv leaned down and straightened Tim's tights, which were twisted around his skinny ankles. His ensemble really was quite spiffy. A blue tunic she would have worn herself, a low-slung leather belt and a hood sort of like a skin diver would wear, only knit out of metal. He looked pretty cute.

"Why would she be in a dumpster?" Davida said.

Viv wanted to say something along the lines of "there's no 'why' with Eva. That's just the way she is." But it sounded mean, and probably was.

Tim piped up, "She could be a freegan," and Viv was off the hook.

"A what?" Davida asked, smiling.

"A freegan. People who *choose* to forage in dumpsters to reduce food waste. I'm kind of interested in it myself."

Viv laughed. "That's not normal. You do realize that, don't you?"

Tim shrugged. "'If you're always trying to be normal, you'll never know how amazing you can be.' Maya Angelou."

Now Davida shrugged. "I dunno. It might also be pretty amazing to be normal. I'd like to try it someday."

Tim laughed. His arm moved up as if he was going to hug her then hovered at shoulder height for a second before he dropped it to his side and looked away.

Viv squeed internally. Her plan was working. "Let's get this show on the road," she said.

They wandered around the room for a while saying things like "pray tell" and "whither" and drinking mead that tasted suspiciously like flat cream soda. Then King Arthur invited everyone present—including damsels—to take the oaths of the Knights of the Round Table.

The oaths were apparently famous. Some people knew all the words by heart, but servants handed out printed sheets for those who didn't. There weren't quite enough to go around, so Tim held the paper and Viv and Davida huddled in close on either side.

"Hear ye," King Arthur began. "By these twelve trusts shall my knights be known. Rise and make thy pledge."

Viv struggled not to laugh. It was all so ridiculous—the polyester costumes, the king's sad attempt at an English accent, the faux-heroic pledges—but she droned along with everyone else.

"To never do outrage nor murder, and always flee treason."

"To ride abroad redressing wrongs."

She barely understood what she was saying, but somewhere along the line, the words started to get to her.

"To never lie."

"To defend the defenseless."

She felt her eyes fill up with tears, her chest tighten. There was suddenly nothing ridiculous about this at all.

Viv realized the oaths were having the same effect on Tim and Davida. They'd moved closer together. Their faces had gone serious. When they got to the part where they all swore as Knights of the Round Table "to seek after wonders," Viv noticed Davida take his hand.

Tim turned and smiled at her. He didn't let go.

Davida

4 days after the party
5:30 p.m.

I bike back home so fast you'd swear Tim was chasing me.

No one's here. It's Dad's rowing night and I think Steve might be on a date. I go to my room. I haven't watched the videos once since I caught Tim and Viv in the van. I was being strong. Now I have to be even stronger and watch them.

I open my laptop. It crosses my mind that Tim might just be trying to manipulate me again. First him sending me the squirrel; then him reminding me of the oaths we took; now the heartwarming montage. I've got to be careful. He's good at this. I've seen his psychotic patient. I've seen his overbearing bully. Maybe this is just his heartbroken teenage guy.

But then I remember his face, the way he looked at me just now at the breakwater, and I don't believe it.

Or maybe I do.

I don't know.

Viv

8 days before the party
6 a.m.

Viv was lying in bed, all bundled up and blissed out under her puffy white duvet, phone clamped to her ear. Her eyes were shut, but she could feel the sun. Jack was talking. It was early, just after six, but he had practice all day so this was the only time that worked.

"You're not listening." He was in the dormitory washroom so he wouldn't wake his roommate. His voice sounded round and echoey.

"Am too."

"Then what did I just say?"

She pictured him in his gray boxers, sitting on the cold tile floor, one arm hanging off his bent knee, laughing at her. She paused too long.

He went, "Ha! I knew it. You have no idea. It's like you're drunk or something."

He was so wrong. Ending up passed-out drunk in Dr. Keppo's office had been her rock bottom. She hadn't had a drink since. The first day, she didn't even want one. That's how shitty she felt. And not just shame. Physically shitty. Everything hurt—her head, her elbows, her toes, her hips. Brutal. She promised herself she'd never do that again.

Then another day passed and another and she went to the Knights of the Round Table re-enactment with Tim and Davida and she had 100-percent sober-fun and she realized *I don't need booze. I can do this*.

Her mind was as clear as a bell that morning, just a little slow so early. "I'm tired! I went for a long run last night with Mum then stayed up writing that podcast."

"Allie's running again?"

"Like a fiend."

"Wow."

"Yeah. The comeback queen." Jack hadn't been in a total bubble after all. He'd found out about the "JILTED WIFE" video a few days earlier, from his own mother. He'd called Viv right away and threatened to come home, but she'd held him off. Meanwhile, Allie had miraculously improved. "Running every day. Meditating. Going to lunch with her BFF coven. No doubt just putting hexes on Dad but, hey, at least she's getting out."

Jack snickered. "I like Allie. She's intense but . . . you know me, I like intense people . . . Oh. Hey. What's up?"

Someone was in the washroom with him. Jack mumbled *love-you-gotta-go* and hung up.

Just as well. Viv wanted another quick read-through of her podcast pitch before she sent it off. She'd ended up doing a thing on Caterina Sforza, this Renaissance noblewoman Tim told her about at the re-enactment. Caterina was battling with these men who threatened to kill her children if she didn't surrender her castle, but she was like, who cares? She flashed her lady parts at them and said, "I have what it takes to make others." Totally badass. Viv loved her. She wanted the podcast to be a kind of funny-serious commentary on why we're only taught history about men. Heaven forbid we gals get uppity ideas!

When she'd finally sat down to write it, the script didn't take that long.

Likewise, the reference letter for the scholarship. She just came right out and asked her dad's friend for one. He'd sent it back the next day, no problem. Why had she tortured herself about this stuff?

She got in the shower. It didn't feel like punishment anymore. No gagging. No stench of old booze. No desperately hoping the sound of running water would cover her sobs. She decided to figure out something fun to wear then whip herself up some huevos rancheros.

She put on the green paisley elephant pants Christie'd bought her in Italy, a white sleeveless turtleneck and giant red flower earrings her grandmother had worn in the so-called Swinging Sixties. She bounced down the stairs. She felt about twelve.

"Hi, sweetheart." Her mother was standing at the counter in a fitted gray suit, ivory blouse and fabulous heels.

"What are you all dolled up for?" Viv rummaged around in the fridge for eggs. "Job interview or something?"

"No, not a job interview." Allie took a delicate bite of toast, careful not to get crumbs on her jacket.

"I said, 'or something'?" Viv found the eggs and started looking for a pan. "Spill."

Allie nodded as if her mouth was too full to talk.

Viv leaned one hand on the counter and gave her the eye. Allie was hiding something.

She patted her chest and swallowed. "Just a legal thing with your father. Apparently, some loose ends to tie up." She was smiling but her face was oddly immobile.

"You okay?"

"Yes!" Allie flapped her hand. "I imagine it's just a few *t*'s to cross." She dropped her crust on the plate. "Better fly."

"Put some toast on for me first, would you?"

Allie went, "Aargh, lazy girl," but did. They were both still playing at being their old selves. Fake it 'til you make it. "Dinner tonight?" She put her plate in the dishwasher. "I could pick up that Portuguese chicken you like."

"Actually, I was thinking of seeing some friends . . ." Viv cracked two eggs into the pan.

"Who?"

"Tim Zanger. A kid from the SP program. And Davida. She was at"—*Don't say the bridal salon! Don't say the bridal salon!*—"camp with me. Remember?"

"Davida? No. Now there's a name." Allie touched up her lipstick in the hall mirror. "Well, ask them too. I never get to meet your friends. I promise to be in bed by eight, so I won't cramp your style."

"Can I text you about it later?" That would give Viv time to come up with an excuse.

Allie stiffened, dropped her lipstick in her purse. "Sure. If you've got other things to do, I'll—"

"No. No." Viv disgusted herself. She could be such a dick. "I just meant timewise. Tim sometimes has to work for his dad."

Allie perked up. "I'll get two chickens and we can warm them up whenever he arrives then."

"Awesome."

"I'd turn those eggs down if I were you," she said on her way out the door.

Viv texted Davida and Tim. Dinner tonight with my mother attendance mandatory 6 pm here

It'll be fine, she thought, and buttered her toast.

Viv got home eight hours later. Allie's heels were in the hall, one tipped on its side as if it had fainted or died.

Those were expensive shoes. Allie wouldn't just leave them in the hall. Normal-Allie wouldn't just leave *anything* in the hall.

"Mum?" Viv hung her backpack on the hook. "I'm home!" No answer.

Maybe she'd just been late for Pilates. Maybe she'd gotten in after her meeting, desperate to pee, meant to put them back and forgot.

Chill, Viv told herself. *It's nothing.*

She tiptoed up the stairs, her hand on the rail, her head tilted in the hopes of hearing something other than this creepy quiet.

"Mum?"

Allie's door was open a crack. She peeked in. The bed looked unmade—that was odd too—then Viv noticed an arm, a gray linen sleeve, sticking out from under the cream duvet.

She's dead. That was her first thought. Viv's insides boiled up, her outsides froze.

Then the arm moved. Allie sucked in her breath and rolled over. She was alive but out of it.

Viv crept back downstairs and called Christie. "What's going on? Why's she in bed with her clothes on?"

Christie sighed. "Probably best if you talk to your father. He's not speaking to me anymore. I've given her a sedative. She'll be all right for a couple of hours. I have a patient now, but I'll come right after that."

Viv called her dad. "What happened?"

"Sweetheart."

"What the hell happened?"

"Just about to step into a meeting. Perhaps we could—"

"Tell me now."

No answer.

"Now!" She pictured his head jerking away from the phone.

"Relax. We're just concerned about your mother's mental health. She needs help."

"She's getting it. She's getting better."

"Unfortunately, she's not out of the woods yet."

"She was fine this morning. Fine until she talked to you. What happened?"

"Nothing *happened.*"

"Okay. What did you say to her then?"

He took a breath, like he was filling his lungs before a dive. "Why don't you meet me for dinner?"

"Tell. Me. Now."

Another breath, then, "We know how hard this is on you."

"Yeah, well, it's no picnic for her either."

"No. It isn't. But I can't help her. I can only help you now." There was a long pause. "That's why we want you to live with us. I know the guest room isn't really your style, but after the wedding in September, you and Katie can redecorate to your—"

"Is that why she's upset?"

"Your welfare is what's—"

"No. Forget it. I'm not going to."

"I'm sorry, Vivienne. I phrased that wrong. You *will* be living with us after the wedding. You need a stable environment and your mother needs time to reflect and heal. This is non-negotiable."

Excerpt from police interview with Dr. Christina LeBlanc, 4 days after the party

Dr. Christie LeBlanc: Can I straighten up one thing before I go?

Lt. Alan (Pidge) Eisenhauer: Absolutely.

LeBlanc: I hope I didn't make it sound like this whole mess was Allie's fault. Their marriage stunk and I'm glad Ross left but that doesn't mean he couldn't have done it better. Had a little mercy. Pulling that custody shit on her? Threatening to take away the last good thing in her life? That was just cruel. I didn't know if I'd ever get her calmed down. Allie's a good mother—the best—and Ross knows it. He just wanted to push her over the edge. The worse she looked, the better he looked in comparison. He's as much to blame as she is. More, if you ask me.

Eisenhauer: Understood. I've been doing this job for a while so I know. There's nobody worse than two people who used to love each other.

Viv

8 days before the party
5 p.m.

Something turned off in her head.

Viv hung up on her father, walked into the dining room and opened the liquor cabinet. She dusted the cap off with her sleeve then drank her mother's vodka right from the bottle. It didn't help. Viv had watered it down too much, back in the days before she'd found Stu.

So she went for the gin, the bourbon, the vermouth—just an inch, an inch and a half, not so much that her mother, or more likely Christie, would notice. She kept going until she got to the crème de menthe. Then she asked herself *why? Why am I wasting my time with this stuff?* She texted Stu.

Pick me up at home

10 mints he said.

I'm paying by cash

No

Yes I'm paying by cash

No

Yes this is an emergency

10 mints

Still nine minutes left, so she worked her way around the liquor cabinet again. By the time she got back to the crème de menthe, she was almost happy. This was her favorite level of drunkenness, when it took her whole body, her whole brain, just to screw the cap back on the bottle. Nothing else mattered.

She put everything back in the cabinet nice and neat-ish. When she looked up, Stu's cab was out front. She had one second of thinking she probably shouldn't leave her mother like this—but, hell. Sometimes you just gotta do what you gotta do.

"Am I glad to see you!" She slid into the back seat.

Stu squinted at her in the rearview mirror. "What did you do, asshole?"

"Moi?!?" Viv found that hilarious.

"You fucking moron. Where'd you get the booze?"

"Jealous? You're not my only dealer, you know." That was funny too. She looked out the window. "Hey, speaking of morons . . . you're going the wrong way. The warehouse is that-a-way. And step on it. It's cocktail hour!"

"Not today it ain't."

"What are you talking about?" Something about the way he said it made her nervous. "Where's my bottle?"

"What bottle?"

He was just bugging her. It was probably rolling around on the passenger side. She lunged over the seat to look.

He swatted her back. "Sit the fuck down. I mean it."

"Where's the booze, Stu?"

"There's no booze."

"I *asked* you to buy me booze."

"Yeah, but you made me *promise* not to. A promise is a promise."

"That was before. I was drunk. I. *Need*. My. Vodka." Where the hell was he going?

"Never means never."

216

She was getting scared. He'd turned south. "Where are you taking me?"

"Where I should have taken you ages ago."

He stopped at the light. She tried to open the door, but it was locked.

"Childproof," he said, "and, of course, asshole-proof."

"Where are you taking me?" She kicked the back of the seat.

He kept driving. She kicked it again.

"I trusted you! Why are you doing this?!"

"Because I've had enough of this shit."

She cried and screamed but it didn't matter. A few minutes later, he pulled into the med school parking lot. "Keppo's waiting for you."

"What?"

"Keppo. I called him."

"How do you even *know* him?!"

"Because you never shut your fucking mouth. Now get out."

Viv had never hated anyone so much in her life. She pounded his headrest with her palm. "I'm not paying you for this."

He shrugged. "I'd pay to get rid of you."

She slammed the door and got out, but if he thought she was going to talk to Keppo, he was crazy. She headed toward the street. One leg felt shorter than the other. Stu crawled along behind her. She turned and went the other way.

He leaned out the window. "I ain't leaving until you walk in that door. That's another promise."

She gave him the finger.

"And, unlike some people, *I* keep my promises."

She gave him both fingers, but she knew he meant it. That's the only reason she went in. So he'd piss off.

Tim

It feels like ages since I asked Davida to look at the videos and I still haven't heard from her.

That's not necessarily a bad thing. I've got to keep telling myself that. Sometimes something looks like it's going to be a disaster then it turns out okay. Even better than okay.

For instance, that night we were supposed to go to dinner at Viv's. Things were pretty rocky there for a while too.

I parked the van in front of Viv's place then Davida and I walked up the driveway, holding hands. Before we even made it to the door, though, we heard the screaming. I thought it was just the television, pretty loud but whatever. I kept thinking that, despite the fact that I could clearly see Viv's mother in the window. Her cheek was flat up against the glass and her mouth was wide open and her hands were over her head like she was being frisked or something. Another lady tried to get her to sit down but she kept slapping her away.

I stood there watching it with this stunned dolphin smile on my face until Davida went, "Let's go, let's go," and I kind of came to. Generally speaking, I'm pretty hopeless in an emotional crisis but she was shaking so bad I had to do something. I practically carried her to the van.

We drove to the breakwater and parked there. Seeing Viv's mother screaming like that reminded Davida of what had happened when she was little with her own mother. She told me everything. I didn't know until then why she'd gotten all woozy that first day at the SP program.

This wasn't our first time at the breakwater. Davida and I had gone there after the Round Table re-enactment and that had been great. By which I mean GREAT. But this was different. This time we talked. She told me about her crazy family. I told her about mine. We talked for hours. It was as if it was just the two of us and that's all that mattered. I feel bad saying this, but if we hadn't seen all that stuff with Viv's mom, that might never have happened. It's like her tragedy brought us together or something.

So I guess it's fair that now it's Viv's tragedy tearing us apart.

Viv

The security guard looked up from Words With Friends on his phone and said, "Can I help you?"

Viv had planned to leave as soon as Stu's cab pulled away but now she had another idea. Maybe this guy could help. He was young, cool. She had money. He'd get booze for her.

"Yeah . . ." She giggled. "I was wondering if . . ." She took a step toward him, then two little steps to the left to keep from falling. She didn't quite know how to ask.

"You Vivienne?" he said.

"I am!" She was surprised he knew her. She staggered toward him, still smiling, hoping to get close enough to read the name on his shirt so she could pretend she knew him too.

"Dr. Keppo's waiting for you." He walked over to the elevator and tapped his pass card on the up button.

"Dr. Keppo?" Viv was confused for a moment then she remembered. *Stu.*

Stupid fucking Stu.

She hurried over to the guard. If she was going to ask, she had to do it fast. "Um, hey . . . don't suppose you—"

"Here you go." He held the elevator open until she got in. "Have a good night."

"Know what would make it better?" she said, but the door was already closing.

"Shit." She banged her fist against the guardrail.

"Shit," she said again as the elevator started moving. She saw her face reflected endlessly in the mirrored walls. The half-open eyes. The matted hair. The green dribble of crème de menthe down her front. She lifted her shirt, licked it off and watched as many, many Vivs licked and staggered and mumbled. She couldn't get away from the image. The truth of it.

She could kill Stu. This was his fault.

And her father's.

The security guard's.

She hated them all. She was going home.

Maybe not home. But somewhere.

She hit *L* for lobby, then hit it again. She banged away at the button, but the elevator kept going up until it made a cheery *ping* and the door opened at six. Dr. Keppo was standing there.

"Ms. Braithwaite!" Like she'd just arrived at his party. "Need a hand?"

"No." What did he think she was? An invalid? A drunk? "I'm fine."

"Good to hear." He swung his arm to the side. "Right this way."

"I can't stay long. I've got to be . . ." Where? Where was she supposed to be? ". . . someplace."

"Stay as long as you want." He was walking too fast. She dragged one hand against the wall to keep from wobbling. "I'm just catching up on some paperwork while it's quiet," he said.

A machine screeched nearby—a saw or something. Down the hall, three guys in hard hats pointed at a hole in the ceiling and hollered over the noise.

"Quiet?" Viv laughed. She might have had a bit too much to drink, but she knew that wasn't quiet. She knew a lot of things. People should leave her alone.

Dr. Keppo laughed too. "I barely hear it anymore. The guys usually work until about nine on the reno. Less disruptive for the students. Not going to bother you, is it?" He pushed open the door to his office and gestured Viv in.

The couch looked so good. She'd sit down, but just for a second, then she'd bolt.

"Stu tells me you're having some problems."

"Stu." She gagged.

"He's only trying to help."

"Ha. Yeah. So's Dad."

Dr. Keppo looked at her, his fingers tapping his hips, then sat down. "Have problems at home escalated?"

The shriek of the saw sounded like demons in some bad video game. "Can we close the door?" she said.

"Sorry. It'll stop soon enough . . . Tell me what's happening."

His hands cupped the armrests of his chair. He smiled at her, but not as if he was happy or this was funny or because he should. He was smiling because this was going to be okay. She could see that. He was going to make it okay.

She picked at her fingernails. Her brain felt like it was underwater. She wanted to catch the thing she should say to him, but it kept bobbing away from her.

"While you're thinking, can I put on some tea?"

She nodded.

"Same as last time okay?"

"Sure."

She heard the water run, cupboards open and close, the kettle whistle, dishes clink. She sat on the couch getting smaller and smaller until she realized if she didn't say something she'd disappear entirely.

"You'll feel better with something in your system." Dr. Keppo held out a tray. "Try the cookies. Excellent for dunking."

He put the tray on the coffee table and sat down. For a while, they both drank their tea in silence. He was right about the cookies. She had five, one after the other after the other, and then she was ready.

"I've been drinking again," she said.

He took a sip. "I noticed."

"It's that obvious?"

He made fun of the way she said *obvious*.

"It's a hard word!" They both laughed. Weird, but they were kind of friends.

He picked up a pencil and a pad of paper. "What prompted this exactly? Any idea?"

Viv clamped her lips together, but he kept beaming warm, loving rays at her.

"Dad's making me live with him."

"And you don't want to?"

She shook her head.

"You're happy to stay with your mother?"

As if happy was an option. "No, but I don't want to . . . like, *kill* her."

"Kill her how?"

"Leaving. That would kill her."

"She may be stronger than you think."

Viv went, "Ha!" with such force the room spun.

"You okay?" he said.

"No." She was careful not to move her head. "I can't take it."

"What?"

"My parents. The shit they do to each other. The mess they make of everything . . ." She took a drink of tea to hide behind the cup until she calmed down. "Sorry. I . . . I shouldn't blame them." She didn't mean that. It was totally their fault.

"No, but we all do. I did. 'My parents' expectations were too high.' 'My mother potty-trained me too early.' 'They don't understand me.' No one's parents are perfect."

He scribbled something then turned the paper toward her. He'd drawn a howling baby falling backwards into a giant toilet.

She smiled, but just to be polite.

"Look." He tossed the pad on the coffee table. "Your parents are behaving very badly. You have to remember though—they're just your parents. They're not you. Not your destiny. They're going through a rough patch, but people come out of rough patches way worse than this. There's hope. There really is. In the meantime, you need support. I know some very good addiction counselors. Would you like me to set you up with one?"

"Yeah. I want—" She held her breath to keep from crying. She held it until her chest hurt. "I want to stop this."

"Excellent." He patted her knee. "I'll make some calls. If you'd like, you can keep coming to me until you see the specialist. I'm always happy to help."

She squeaked out "Thanks," then tears started gushing. She didn't know if they were from shame or relief, but they wouldn't stop.

"You okay?"

"I'm . . . I'm just so tired."

"Go home. Sleep it off. I'll call as soon as I've got you an appointment."

"I can't go home." The thought terrified her. "My mother. She's, like, she's having a total breakdown, and if I went to Dad's he'd know, and Jack's away so . . ."

"Anywhere else you can go?"

She shook her head. "Can I lie down here? Please. Just for an hour or two? Then I'll be fine."

"Vivienne. I'm sorry, but I can't have someone in your state sleeping in my office."

"I did last time!"

"You didn't ask last time."

"I don't have anywhere to go." She could barely get it out.

He rapped his knuckles on his armrest and stared out the window.

After a while he said, "Stay here." He pointed at her, smiling. "And stay awake."

He left the room. Viv could barely keep her eyes open but she checked her phone. A text from Jack she couldn't bear to read. A text from Tim saying he and Davida couldn't make it to dinner at her place after all. *Thank God*, she thought. She'd forgotten all about them.

A couple minutes later, Dr. Keppo was back. "C'mon then."

He led her down the hall, past the staff elevators. He unlocked a door and pushed it open. "The old staff lounge," he said. It was a big room full of mismatched gray couches, torn pleather armchairs and a musty smell. "They haven't started renovating it yet. You can stay here. I'll alert the security guard so you don't scare him on his rounds. I've got about an hour or so of administrative stuff to get through. How about I wake you before I go?"

"Thanks." She wanted to hug him but didn't. "Thank you so much."

He waved her away. "There's a washroom at the back if you need it. Here's a cushion and a blanket." Dust billowed up when he plunked them down on the couch. "Now, please let your mother know where you are so she doesn't worry. When I leave, you can lock the door from the inside."

Viv said *yes, yes, yes* but she was asleep before she managed to do anything he'd asked.

Davida

4 days after the party
5:45 p.m.

I start scrolling through my videos. Us at the taxidermy show laughing about the angry moose, pouting over the baby chicks, looking up the warthog's nose, other random stuff. Viv adjusting Tim's tights at the Knights of the Round Table, me in that dress. Us dancing.

Then a short clip of Tim at the breakwater after the re-enactment. He's still wearing his costume, although the hood's down and his belt is off. He says, "Look. Look," and points at the sky. There's a cloud, a storm cloud I guess, all gray and puffy and outlined in gold, as if God is suddenly going to start talking to us in this big holy voice or something. The cloud was way more spectacular than it appears in the video but I remember. Tim turns back to me with this huge smile on his face and says, "To seek after wonders. Am I right?" My heart almost stops.

I can't think about that now. I can't think about us at the breakwater. Us in the van. Them in the van. None of that stuff. It'll just make me sad and mad and crazy and I've got things to do. I've got to figure this out.

Viv

And then someone was shaking her. "Viv. Vivienne. Hey. C'mon." She was cold and her brain hurt. He took her shoulders and helped her up, wiped her hair off her face, held her head between two hands until she opened her eyes.

It wasn't Dr. Keppo. She jumped back in shock.

It was George. His eyes searching her face. His smile, all worried and hopeful and perfect. It was like a close-up in a Hallmark movie, like something she'd invented.

She threw her arms around him. Things had been so terrible and now they weren't. She nuzzled her face into his neck and kissed him.

"Whoa. Hey!" He pushed her back. "Vivienne. It's me. George. From the—"

"I know who it is!" Her voice was sort of swoopy and laughing. She leaned into him. She'd have kissed him again, but he was holding her shoulders too far back.

"Viv. Stop."

It was his tone, almost angry—the tone someone would use on a puppy who'd been chewing the furniture. She was suddenly horribly awake. She slapped her hands over her face.

"Oh my God. Sorry."

"It's all right. Relax." George slipped his hands under her armpits and propped her up on the bench. "You're a little confused. That's all."

She looked around.

It was night.

Night?

She realized she was outside.

The parking lot. The trees over there. The Bunker.

She was behind the med school.

How did she get here? She kept her hand over her mouth so George couldn't see how freaked she was.

"I was studying late and came out for a vape," he was saying. "I saw your hair hanging off the bench and thought, this can't be good. You were out of it."

"I, uh, must have fallen asleep."

"Ha! Passed out, more like."

She looked at him, looked for an excuse, then thought, *He's not an idiot.* She tried for a mischievous smile. "Accurate."

"Who were you drinking with?"

"Just, ah, some friends."

"Where are they?" George said.

"You didn't see them?"

He turned his head this way and that, as if the answer was obvious. The back of the building with its dented steel door. The dark, empty campus. "Can't believe they'd just leave you here. Something could have happened to you."

"They wouldn't. They must be around somewhere. Guess I overdid it. I'm not much of a drinker."

She didn't like the way he was looking at her, as if he was seeing more than she wanted him to, so she lied again. "They took pictures of me like this, I'll kill them. That's the type of thing they'd think was funny."

She got out her phone as if she was checking.

It was after eleven. She'd been out for hours.

There were a bunch of texts from Dr. Keppo.

Came by the lounge but you'd gone. Text me so I know you got home all right.

Where are you?

Please text.

Are you all right?

Sorry **she answered.** Should have told you I was leaving. Home safe and sound. Thanks for putting up with me ☺

"They're at a party," she ad-libbed. "I'll meet them there."

She stood up, wobbly as a newborn giraffe. George reached out to steady her but didn't get a good grip. She fell, pulling them both down. Her back was flat on the bench, her legs hanging off at an angle. He wasn't quite on top of her but almost. He hovered over her for a second then pushed himself up. "How much did you have?" He was laughing but appalled. She could tell.

"Don't ask."

"You can't go anywhere like this."

"I just lost my balance."

"Viv. C'mon. You're pissed. I'll drive you home."

She opened her mouth to say no, but he put up his palm. "Sit there. I'll bring the car around. In the meantime . . ." He wiggled a finger at her. "Might want to fix yourself up."

She looked where he was pointing. Her fly was wide open. She scrunched her eyes closed. He laughed and left.

She must have peed and not done her pants back up. She remembered Dr. Keppo saying there was a washroom in the lounge, but she didn't remember using it. Did she just squat out back somewhere? She pictured herself, bare-assed, one hand on a tree for balance, shaking the last drips off, just like she'd done all those times behind Stu's cab, but she didn't remember doing that either.

She gazed at the back of the med school and tried to piece things together. That's when she noticed someone was there. Just a dark figure at first, a mid-sized human blob—then the blob moved under the light and turned into a girl.

Eva.

Eva Federov, staring straight at her. She lifted her hand, shook her finger at Viv, then disappeared back into the darkness.

If she'd been sober, Viv might have gone after her, at least said, "Hey." But she was drunk. She did up her fly, checked the buttons on her shirt, slicked the hair off her forehead.

And worried about Eva.

Something about what she'd just done seemed so—it took Viv a second to get the word—*deliberate*. Eva wanted Viv to *know* she'd been watching. That's what it felt like.

Viv stared at the black shadow near the door.

How long had Eva been there? What had she seen?

Viv peeing?

Passed out?

George shaking her, Viv throwing herself at him, the two of them falling? Even from where Eva was, Viv knew she must have looked baked.

So? What was Eva going to do? Viv thought of the weird look on Eva's face and decided she was probably baked too.

A crappy subcompact crunched along the gravel. Rusted-out hood. Too many bumper stickers. Sideview mirror held on with duct tape. George pushed the passenger door open from the inside. Her legs felt weak but Viv made it to the car more or less in a straight line.

"You okay?" he asked. He really was gorgeous.

"Yup. But something weird just happened." She was only saying that to distract him, or maybe herself. "You know Eva, one of the SPs?"

"The one who had the incident a while ago?"

"What do you mean 'incident'?"

"The, um . . ."

"Screaming in the hall?"

"Yeah."

"That wasn't part of the simulation?"

"No. Um." He adjusted the rearview mirror. "No."

"What was it then?"

"Ah. Well. Not that."

Viv looked at him.

"Doctor-patient privilege," he said. "Well, at least med-student-patient privilege. I shouldn't be talking about this."

Viv shrugged. "Anyway . . . she's standing right there."

"Where?"

She pointed to the back door.

"I don't see anything."

"Probably hiding again. She did this weird ghost-girl thing. Came out under the light and stared at me then poof! Gone. All, like, sinister."

"Is she okay?"

"Don't know. She didn't seem to be crying or bleeding or anything."

George said, "Wait here." He walked to the door, shook the handle, went around the side of the building. Viv heard him call Eva's name. He was gone a good five minutes.

"No sign of her," he said, climbing into the car. "Hope she's all right."

"Me too." Viv didn't actually care. She was more concerned about herself and where *she'd* disappeared to for all those hours.

"You hungry?" he asked.

"Starved." She realized this was true.

"Habanero's okay?"

"One of my favorites."

Habanero's was just a takeout counter in an ugly industrial strip, but the food was legendary. When George went in to order, she texted her mother to say she'd be late, although she doubted Allie was in any shape to notice. George came back with two fat chicken fajitas and a pile of napkins. Viv sat cross-legged on the seat, her back against the door, and gorged. After a while, just for conversation, she asked where he was from.

"Here." He wiped orange grease off his bottom lip with his thumb. "Like right here." He tilted his head toward the block of brick apartment buildings across the road.

"That's where you live?"

"Where I grew up. Mom and me in our cozy basement junior studio." He smiled. "My ticket to med school."

Viv raised her eyebrows as if she didn't see the connection. Her mouth was too full to ask.

"Dr. Keppo likes to recruit 'underprivileged youth' into the SP program as a way of getting them interested in healthcare professions. I was just doing it for the money, but he took me aside, said I had what it took to become a doctor. I'd never considered it—wasn't even the wildest possibility—but he made it happen. Pushed me when I needed pushing. Gave me a couch to crash on when Mom wasn't holding things together. No doubt made sure some money came her way too. I really owe the guy . . . You know him very well?"

Viv chewed, wondered what to say.

George was waiting for an answer. He wouldn't tell. Doctor-patient privilege.

"Yeah." She wrapped up the rest of her fajita and put it back in the bag. "That's where I was tonight. With him."

"Drinking?"

"No." She laughed. "The drinking I did by myself. He was, um, counseling me, I guess."

"Why?"

"Because my life is shit."

"Yours?" Like that was so impossible. "How?"

She told him everything. All the gory details. Her mum, her dad, Katie, the bridal salon, the custody stuff, the total collapse of her little civilization, her chats with Dr. Keppo. George listened, asked questions, said the right things.

An hour later, he drove her home. She'd felt he'd understood her, maybe even liked her, but then they turned onto her street with the big trees, the perfect lawns, the massive houses. She was just a spoiled brat. He must have realized that.

"Thanks for the ride," she said, staring straight ahead.

"No problem."

"And the chat."

"Ditto."

"And rescuing me," she said.

He leaned against his door and scoffed. "I didn't rescue you."

"You did. And sorry, too, for—like—*accosting* you. I don't know what got into me."

"Forget it. Seriously. I mean, hey, now we're even."

It took Viv a second to get it. That SP session. When he'd undone her pants. She laughed. "One-all," she said.

"Exactly."

They bumped fists. She got out of the car and closed the door.

"Viv." He leaned across the seat. "Can I tell you something?"

She rested her elbows on the open window. "Sure."

"You were drunk. I'm almost a doctor. Otherwise, I absolutely would have kissed you back."

He let that sink in, then he drove off.

Excerpt from police interview with George Pineo, 4 days after the party

Lt. Alan (Pidge) Eisenhauer: That's all you said?

George Pineo: All? That's bad enough. I'm in med school. I'm six years older than her. I'm in a "position of power." I can't let myself think like that. I can't let *her* think like that. Dr. Keppo's right. This is dangerous territory. Girls like her are vulnerable. I've got to stop letting my dick do my thinking.

Eisenhauer: Good plan.

Viv

Viv had arranged to meet Tim and Davida in the SP lounge but, by some miracle and a crazy-assed bus driver, she'd gotten to the med school early. It was a perfect day—hot and breezy—so she sat out front on a bench until they arrived. The sun felt like fresh bread or love or something good like that.

It hadn't even been a week since Dr. Hotness found her, but she felt stronger. She still kept vodka in her water bottle but only to prove to herself she didn't need it. She was working on her scholarship application, helping around the house, watching hours of mindless Netflix and not giving herself a hard time for doing it. She popped by Dr. Keppo's office occasionally when she was at the med school but just to chat. She liked the guy.

Her parents were better behaved now too. After the blow-up in the lawyer's office, they'd retreated to their separate corners. Christie had taken a leave of absence and moved in with Allie and Viv. She'd gotten a mutual friend to convince Ross to drop the custody dispute. Allie was meditating again, eating again, smiling again.

Viv felt almost free. She exercised, did her SP sessions, hung out with Davida and Tim. Their shy, goofy sweetness worked better than booze for keeping her spirits up.

And now, today—finally—Jack was coming home. She'd get some shy, goofy sweetness of her own.

She took out her phone and scrolled through her feeds. A few weeks earlier, she'd have been terrified, but the gossip mill moves fast. "JILTED WIFE" was almost forgotten. The vultures were circling new victims. She didn't even bother finding out who. Instead, she checked out the Barking Robot site. She still hadn't heard back about the podcast pitch. She couldn't decide if that was a good thing or a bad thing.

Or maybe just a thing. Life was full of things.

She was enjoying that thought when a shadow fell across the screen. She turned around, expecting to catch Tim or Davida mid-prank.

It was Eva looming over her.

The sun was directly behind her. Viv had to shield her eyes, raising her arm as if to protect herself from assault. Eva's face was blank, her lips pushed together in a hard, thin line. She was wearing way too many clothes for such a hot day, standing way too close for someone Viv barely knew.

"Oh, hey." Viv tried to sound cheery.

"I saw you," she said.

"Oh? Ah. Where?"

"Here."

"You mean, last week? I was wondering if that was you." Clearly a lie.

"You were out of it. He was all over you." Eva's cheek twitched as if she was about to cry or explode.

"No. Ha-ha-ha-ha-ha. It wasn't that. I was just feeling a little, ha-ha, light-headed. I'd been exercising. He—"

"No." She stabbed a finger at Viv. "You were totally out of it."

"No. Really. I was just—"

Eva was right in her face, quiet but sputtering, little blobs of goo at the corners of her mouth. "You don't know who you're playing with. You want to get hurt? You—"

Someone called Eva's name. She stopped talking but didn't turn to see who it was.

Viv went, "I think Janice wants you," so relieved to see her running down the med school steps toward them. "She's—"

"Stay away from him." Eva got closer, spoke faster. "I mean it. Stay away from him or you'll be sorry. Understand?"

Viv nodded, scared not to.

"And don't tell her what I said."

"Who?"

"Her!" she whispered, jerking her head toward Janice. "She won't help you."

Janice came up behind them, laughing, out of breath, her hand on her throat, a black crescent forming in the armpit of her purple shirt. She waved at Viv then turned to Eva. "I thought I'd lost you! I was looking everywhere. Want to have our chat now?"

"Why would I want to *chat* if no one listens to me?"

"Let's talk in my office, shall we?"

"See?" Eva said to Viv, but left with Janice anyway.

Viv's skin erupted in goosebumps.

He was all over you. The words flashed in her head.

She leaned her elbow on the back of the bench and watched Janice lead Eva into the med school. Her arm was around Eva's shoulders, their heads together. Eva was talking. Viv turned back.

Is that what she was telling Janice? That George had been all over Viv? She wiped her face, tried to breathe.

George would be in deep shit. Taking advantage of a girl, a drunk girl, a drunk almost-patient. It would be a disaster.

Viv was sure she was going to throw up then things swam back into perspective.

I'll just say it didn't happen. And anyway, who's she going to tell?

Not Janice, Viv realized. Eva herself had just told Viv not to tell Janice. *So who else? Dr. Keppo?*

Viv let out a dribbly laugh. He knew about the drinking. He no doubt knew what Eva was like too. Everyone did. No one believed her.

In one of their meetings, Dr. Keppo had talked to her about "mental hygiene" and this is exactly what he meant. Keeping her thoughts in check. Managing the situation instead of letting it escalate in her mind. She remembered the doodle he'd drawn for her of a crazy-haired character being carried into the air by her giant inflated head.

She looked up. The sun was still shining, just like he said it would. She checked the time. Almost nine. She turned and saw Tim and Davida heading toward the med school, holding hands. It was as if birds started twittering again.

She went, "Hey!" and took off after them.

There must have been a bump in the sidewalk because, next thing, Viv was bouncing off the cement. Arms out, neck back, squawking like a chicken. Pathetic.

Tim and Davida ran to help.

"Oh my God. Jim Carrey or what?" Tim was laughing his face off. "That was hilarious, by which I mean are you okay?"

She punched him in the shin then rolled onto her back, her arms folded across her chest. "Ow. Ow. Ow." She must have landed right on her boobs.

"I take that as a no."

They helped her onto her feet, slapped the grass clippings off her clothes, and got her moving. Got her laughing. She could just picture how ridiculous she looked. She wished they'd caught it on video.

They headed into the med school, Viv leaning on their shoulders, limping but happy.

Janice stopped them in the lobby as they walked by. "Mind if I steal Viv for a moment?" Her smile was weird. "Just a little something I need to talk to her about."

Excerpt from police interview with Janice Drysdale, 4 days after the party

Lt. Alan (Pidge) Eisenhauer: You mentioned George Pineo earlier. You think something might have been going on between him and Vivienne?

Janice Drysdale: I . . . ah . . . really couldn't say. I mean, I'd certainly *seen* them together but, you know, the med school is a sociable place. You bump into people, chat. Totally normal.

Eisenhauer: That was all?

Drysdale: I did see them one other time.

Eisenhauer: When?

Drysdale: I was tidying up in the Bunker one night—

Eisenhauer: The Bunker?

Drysdale: The building where the staff offices are.

Eisenhauer: Gotcha.

Drysdale: It was late. I glanced out the window and saw Vivienne and George on a bench out back. I was a little surprised. We have a strict no-dating policy between SPs and med students. What was happening between them might not have been a "date" but . . .

Eisenhauer: But?

Drysdale: Nothing really. Dr. Keppo just doesn't like to encourage that sort of thing. I'm a bit more relaxed. They're young. What's a little harmless flirtation?

Viv

"You look like hell." Mandy tucked in her chin and gave Viv the once-over.

"Would you quit saying that? Every time I come here . . ." Viv flopped into the makeup chair, her arms sprawled over the sides.

"Yeah, well. Look at yourself." Mandy pointed her contour brush at the mirror.

Viv went, "What?" but she could see. Dirt on her face, grass in her hair and a tear in her shirt from where she'd hit the sidewalk. Her insides were in even worse shape.

Mandy clicked her tongue. "I suppose I should find it refreshing you don't care about these things, but geez, girl. There's not caring and then there's coming in looking like you got mugged."

"All part of my devil-may-care charm. And just so you know, I fell on the way here. *Crushed* my boobs." Viv cradled them in her hands. They were still throbbing. "Thanks so much for your concern."

Mandy gave Viv a "poor baby" pout, snapped the cloak around her neck then checked the cheat sheet. Nelly Moreau, the patient Viv was playing, was cyanotic from deoxygenated hemoglobin, so her lips and skin were blue. It would look good with her eyes.

"How're things?" Mandy said. "Anything new?"

Viv didn't want to get into it. "That's what I should be asking you. You're the gossip queen."

"True . . ." Mandy wagged her head proudly. "Whaddya want to know?"

"What's up with Eva?" Viv figured there was no harm asking. She'd just come from speaking with Janice, who'd told her a bit about what was going on, but only enough to make Viv suspect there was more she wasn't saying.

"Federov?" Mandy dabbed Viv's forehead with bluish-gray powder.

"Yeah. I saw her this morning. She's all wound up about something."

"Well, her dad died."

"That was last year."

"So? Not something you necessarily bounce back from."

"I know. I don't mean to sound, like, callous . . . but I don't think that's it. Something else was bugging her. Some guy? . . ." Viv didn't want to say too much in case she was wrong.

Mandy hesitated. "You didn't hear this from me, okay?" She changed sponges and started on Viv's nose and under her eyes. "Word is she's obsessed with someone at the med school. Like *pathologically* obsessed—and, as usual, poor Jan's stuck dealing with it."

"Any idea who?"

"Several possibilities, but no."

"George Pineo maybe?"

"Dr. Hotness? Wouldn't be surprised. You girls are *all* obsessed with him, but I can't say for sure. My informant was very vague about the whole thing . . ."

Viv nodded, casually she hoped. What Mandy said pretty much jibed with what Janice had told her. Eva was off her meds and experiencing "a break with reality." That's all she'd say, other than not to let Eva bother her. It was "the mental illness talking." People were trying to help her. Viv shouldn't worry.

241

"Okay. Your turn." Mandy used her long matte-gray nails to pick an eyelash off Viv's cheek. "What's up with you?"

Viv almost said, "Nothing," then remembered with a laugh. "Jack's coming home tonight."

"Oooh, baby. How excited are *you*?"

"I believe the correct medical term is *hypomanic*—"

"You're always hypomanic, girl." Mandy stepped back to give Viv a final look-see then undid her cape. "Since this is a special occasion, how about you drop in when you're through today? I'll make you up good. Maybe a cat's eye? . . . Dark lip? . . ."

Viv stretched her mouth into a silent *wow*. "Really?"

"Yes. Let's show that boy what you can look like when you actually try."

Excerpt from police interview with Mandy Chan, 4 days after the party

Lt. Alan (Pidge) Eisenhauer: How well do you know Vivienne?

Mandy Chan: Pretty well. It's like the hairdresser thing. Moulage can be complicated. A broken bone, a bad laceration—you're looking at an hour. The SPs sit in my chair and jabber away the whole time. Viv and I always had a lot of fun.

Eisenhauer: When did you see her last?

Chan: A couple of days before it happened.

Eisenhauer: You remember what you talked about?

Chan: Her boyfriend coming back. She was really excited.

Eisenhauer: What do you know about him?

Chan: Jack? Rugby player. He's funny. Sweet. She's crazy about him. That's about all. Never met the guy myself.

Eisenhauer: She seem worried that day? Agitated?

Chan: No. Her usual self.

Eisenhauer: You talk about anything else?

Chan: Um . . . We talked about another SP?

Eisenhauer: Who?

Chan: Eva Federov.

Eisenhauer: She's been mentioned before. We're trying to track her down. Why'd she come up?

Chan: This was before she went missing.

Eisenhauer: She's missing?

Chan: Well, "*missing*." People haven't seen her in a while. Friends have posted stuff on social media asking for information but, knowing Eva, she could have just taken off for a while. She's a bit of a flake.

Eisenhauer: Why were you talking about her?

Chan: Viv bumped into her somewhere and said she was acting strange. Wanted to know what was up. I'd heard rumors Eva was obsessing over some guy at the med school. Didn't know who. Probably shouldn't have told Viv about it, but what can I say? I'm a gossip.

Eisenhauer: We like gossips. Good source of information.

Chan: Yeah. Or stories . . .

Eisenhauer: So what stories have you heard then? We're specifically interested in where Viv might have gotten the drugs. Any chance Eva was the connection?

Chan: I can't see it.

Eisenhauer: Why?

Chan: Okay. You're going to see what a terrible person I am, but here goes. I love Viv. Eva, not so much. She's too over-the-top, even for me—and I spent seven years doing makeup for the Drag Queen Prom.

Eisenhauer: What do you mean, over-the-top?

Chan: Look. There's exaggeration and there's fabrication. I like people who exaggerate. Take the truth and just make it big enough for the rest of us to see. Fabrication is kind of the opposite. Making something up and pretending it's true. You ask me, that's what Eva does. I'm not talking about when her dad died. I'm sure her grief was real. It's the other stuff. A couple of years ago, it was some boy who dumped her. Then she claimed a bunch of girls bullied her. Then someone else ignored her or tormented her or whatevered her. Everything's always a major trauma with that kid. She needs a lot of attention and I think she'd do whatever she needed to get it. No wonder she loved being an SP. I mean, getting to be sick and have people fawn over you? Talk about her dream job.

Eisenhauer: Okay, but why would her, ah, *neediness* mean she's not connected to the drugs?

Chan: I just think if Eva were into that stuff, she'd want us to know about it.

Eisenhauer: You ever see signs of drug deals going down at the school?

Chan: No. I've been there fifteen years now. In and out all the time. Popping in at midnight to check on a mold for the next day or doing some prep work after I get my kid down. I've seen a lot of weird stuff over the years, but drugs? Never.

Eisenhauer: Anyone else you can think of who's got their nose to the ground there? Someone who might know what goes on after hours?

Chan: You talked to Janice Drysdale?

Eisenhauer: Yeah. We have . . . Why are you laughing?

Chan: Oh, just, you know, *Janice*. She's certainly got her nose to the ground. I'm not sure she'd tell you everything she knew though.

Eisenhauer: Now, you've got my attention.

Viv

2 days before the party
10:30 a.m.

Viv left the moulage station and did her morning sessions in a happy, fluttery, pre-Jack state that made diagnosing any sort of illness a challenge for the med students. At noon, she met Tim and Davida in the lunchroom. They were snuggled together on the same side of the table, giggling accident victims with matching contusions.

"Why, if it ain't my favorite casualties." Viv slid in across from them. The dark purple moulage made Davida's eyes super green. Viv could see Tim appreciated it. *She* appreciated it. She appreciated everything. The lukewarm apple juice. The last maple cookie. The sun toasting the back of the orange plastic chair. Life was good and about to get better.

They talked about their sessions then moved on to Ariana Cohen's party coming up that weekend. Tim was just saying he'd get the Zanger & Sons service van so they could "arrive in style" when Viv remembered something.

"Gah!" She slapped the table. "Sorry. Sorry. I forgot. I'm doing some wedding shit with Katie. Sampling cake or something. I can't miss it."

Tim had finished his sandwich and was slipping the cast back on his wrist for the afternoon session. He went, "Ohh . . . ," like *too bad*, but didn't fight it. Last thing anyone wanted was another Braithwaite family meltdown.

"I'll be through by eight." Viv was pretty sure she could slip out by then without setting Katie off. "Jack and I'll meet you at the party."

Davida said, "Or . . . we could do something else?"

They glared at her cartoonishly until she went, "Okay. Okay," her face pink and splotchy. "I'll go."

"Da-vid-ahhh . . ." Viv squinted at her.

"I said I'd go!" She was laughing, but Viv still made her spit-promise. Davida had been trying to weasel out of the party since the first day they'd met.

After lunch, more sessions, then Viv headed back to Mandy's for her makeover.

A voice came over the PA system: "Would Vivienne Braithwaite please come to the office? Viv Braithwaite."

Her first thought was *Mum*. She checked her phone. No texts, no missed calls, no suspicious "nothing to worry about" messages from Christie.

Then: *Eva*. Had she ratted Viv out after all?

Then: *Dad*. Ever since that custody thing—no, ever since she'd found out about Katie two years earlier—Viv had lived with a constant underground buzz of anxiety. She never knew what he was up to.

She was trying to calm her breathing when Davida scurried up. "You hear you're wanted in the office?"

Viv grabbed her arm. "Come with me." That was all she could get out.

She was expecting cops, her parents, Janice—angry faces of some kind—but the receptionist just smiled and said, "Special delivery." She handed Viv a Mother's Pizza box.

Inside was a sixteen-inch pepperoni pizza shaped like a heart.

And jumping up behind it was Jack, so happy to see her, so thrilled to have pulled this off.

Davida

4 days after the party
6 p.m.

I pull myself together and start at the beginning again.

I click on the video from the taxidermy show. The ant in the wart-hog's nostril. Tim and me cooing over the baby ducklings. All of us laughing about the weasel looking like Janice Drysdale. Viv pretending to dance with the giant bear at the entrance. The security guard asking her to stop.

I sit cross-legged on my kiddie-pink coverlet and watch them all again, just to be sure I didn't miss any clues.

Nothing.

What is Tim talking about?

I move on to the videos from the Round Table re-enactment.

Jack was away at rugby camp by that point and the three of us were hanging out a lot. Viv came up with this idea she called "The John Green Challenge." No doing ordinary stuff—that was the only rule. No watching movies together, playing video games, going out to McDonald's. Everything we did had to have a "quirky charm." Those were her exact words. The way she looked across the table at Tim when she said it. The invisible waves that sort of snapped and buzzed between them. I should have known something was up, but I didn't.

I just thought it was one of their inside jokes. Tim and Viv had known each other a lot longer than I had.

Tim had been to re-enactments before and claimed they "positively reeked of quirky charm" so we went and he was right. It was fun.

There's tons of footage of Viv and me dressed as damsels, posing in this skeezy hotel ballroom. I can hear Tim's voice in the background, shouting out suggestions. Vogue, gangsta, medieval virgin. They had to prod me into doing it, but I was laughing too.

I'm embarrassed now to see how much cleavage I was showing. I remember, before Tim got there, Viv saying I'd give him a heart attack in that dress. I'd turned, looked at myself in the changing room mirror and seen a whole different person. The type of person who could do that to someone. The type of person Tim would want.

I wasn't the only person he wanted, but I didn't know that then. If I had, I never would have reached out and taken his hand when we were swearing our oaths.

Afterwards, in the van, he told me it felt like electricity when we'd touched. He told me he felt like we were wonders, seeking each other.

I'd thought he meant it.

Now it seems like the only oath he's interested in keeping is the one he made to Viv.

I make myself look at the videos anyway.

Viv

Jack eventually managed to peel her off him. "Not exactly the face I've been dreaming about, but hey. Lots of other reasons I love you."

"Yes, there are," Viv said. She went to hug him again then noticed his shirt. "Ah . . ." She bit her thumb.

"What?" He bent back his arms at the elbows and looked at the smudgy blue streaks of moulage across his chest. "Oh my God," he laughed. "Do I have to wear a hazmat suit around you? Seriously." Jack was always bugging her about how grubby she was. He slapped at the moulage for a while, realized it was useless, then went, "Hungry?"

"Duh." Another thing he always bugged her about. Her appetite.

He said, "What about you, Davida?" Viv had forgotten he knew her from school. Forgotten she was even there. "Up for a little pizza?"

Davida shook her head and tried to back away, but Viv went, "No. Uh-uh." She wanted to show Jack off. She took one of Davida's arms, he took the other and they dragged her outside. By the time they got to the picnic tables, they'd picked up Tim too. (No dragging required.)

Jack dealt out the pizza. Viv leaned against him and thought how solid he was. Physically. Mentally. Probably spiritually, for all she knew. He did what he said he was going to do. No running off with younger women. No busting up bridal salons. No drunkenly kissing random medical students. He was a brick.

She smiled at Davida and rolled her eyes heavenward, a GIF of bliss. Davida smiled back.

"Kinda crowding me there, Vivisection," he said.

"Oops, sorry." She eased up a little, but not so much she couldn't feel his body heat. He went to take a bite then pulled back, a long blond hair draped across his pizza.

He showed it to Tim and Davida. "The one thing I didn't miss. This—and, like, the garlic breath."

They both made gagging noises.

"I love you too, guys," Viv said, cheeks bulging with pizza, meaning every word.

Jack swept her hair behind her shoulder to keep it off his food.

"Hey." He put a finger on her neck. "How'd you get a hickey? I've been away for weeks."

"Hickey? What are you talking about?" She wiped it off. "It's moulage, darling. See?"

"Your moulage is blue. This is green. And it's still there," he said.

"No, it's not."

"Am I right?" He turned her head to the side. "Davida? Tim?"

Davida went, "Hmmm," not taking a side. Tim flipped his glasses onto his head, leaned across the picnic table and inspected Viv at close range.

"Yup. Still there."

Viv palmed his face. "Yeah. Right. It'll come off. Give me some water."

Next thing she knew, Jack was licking her neck and she was laughing and the two of them were falling, limbo-like, off the bench.

Davida stepped back out of her seat. "I think we'll get going." Tim grabbed another slice and got up too.

Viv and Jack were saying, "No, no, stay!" and trying to get up but they were bent over so far and tangled in her hair and still laughing and not willing to let go of each other. By the time they'd pulled themselves together, Tim and Davida had disappeared.

"That's bad," Jack said. "They're going to think we're animals."

"We kind of are."

"Yeah."

"I'll text and apologize."

"But not now."

"Not now."

He lifted her hair. "It's still there, you know."

"Just needs more spit."

"I know where to find some."

"Yeah?"

"Geoff's brother's gone again." He jingled a set of keys at her.

"You think of everything."

"No. One thing."

They packed up the rest of the pizza and left. They figured they'd have more of an appetite later.

Tim

What's taking Davida so long? I'm getting nervous. There weren't that many videos.

Maybe she's not even looking at them. Maybe she's like *screw you. You had your chance.*

Or maybe she watched them all and saw something I didn't notice and now she's even madder at me than before.

No. I'm being an idioot. I didn't do anything wrong. There's nothing to see.

I just got goosebumps.

I suddenly realize how Viv must have felt. She didn't think she'd done anything wrong either and then boom. There it was. Plain as day.

Viv

2 days before the party
Almost midnight

Viv was in her bathroom, one ear pressed against her shoulder, scrubbing at her neck. The color wasn't coming off. Didn't matter what she did.

She threw the face cloth into the sink then stood there, panting, her hands gripping the sides, her head down.

She twisted her hair into a coil and checked the other side. There was one there too, down low and to the back. It was yellower, older. Definitely not moulage.

She slipped off her jumpsuit. She'd left the apartment so fast she'd put it on inside out. She hadn't even bothered putting her bra back on. She pushed her right boob flat so she could see what Jack had been talking about. More bruises. On the underside. Gray and yellow. He hadn't said anything about the left side—he didn't have a chance—but she checked there too. The same. How could she have missed them? Viv was so pale they stood out like polka dots.

Maybe I'm sick. Maybe it's my iron. Viv kept forgetting to take her pills.

Maybe I just bumped into something and don't remember what. Yesterday when I fell. She remembered bouncing off the pavement in front of the med school.

No. They'd still be purple.

What about those times I blacked out? She imagined all the falls she must have taken, blind drunk, getting from the lounge to the bench out back.

She pulled off her underwear and stood naked and shivering in front of the mirror. Her nipples were hard little pebbles. Her boobs ached. She turned around. More marks.

She stood on her tiptoes and hitched up the skin of her ass.

This was no disease. These weren't bruises from a fall. Five yellowy-green marks in an almost perfect circle around her tattoo. She had no idea how she got them.

She stood there in front of the mirror, just staring at herself—the drunk, the slut—until some time later her phone buzzed.

Viv I'm sorry pick up

Pick up please I hate it when we fight

I shouldn't have accused you

Viv I love you PLEASE PICK UP

I'm sorry I was exhausted I got up at four to catch the early plane to surprise you I shouldn't have said it I know you'd never cheat on me

Well, that's where he was wrong, wasn't he?

Viv clearly would cheat on him. Leave her alone with a good-looking guy and bingo. She was all over him.

Or was George all over me?

That's what Eva had said.

What happened before I came to?

Viv didn't know. All she knew was that Jack didn't deserve this.

She texted back. Leave me alone

Davida

My eyes are stinging from staring at the screen—and from crying, too, even though I practically bit my lip off trying not to. These videos are killing me.

The one of the sunset? That's the worst. Tim took it the day Jack came back. He and Viv obviously wanted time alone, so Tim and I went back to the breakwater.

"Went to the breakwater."

That's what I'd told Dad. What a joke. "The sunset was insane," I said the next morning. I showed him the video, as if I had to prove it or something. (That's what liars do. Produce proof when no one asks.) He didn't notice it was taken through the back windows. We never even got out of the van.

Or the next night either. (I can't remember if there was a sunset.) Tim brought these Dutch doughnuts he calls *oliebollen* and tulips and a blow-up mattress too. Our own little "heaven on wheels." That's what he called it. Corny, but I didn't care.

I was totally happy. I'd never experienced anything like it. It's not as if I was *unhappy* before. I was fine. I mean, no complaints. This was different though. This was like opening your door one morning and stepping out into Paris or Disneyland or the Brazilian rainforest or something. It was amazing.

Was amazing, as in *used* to be.

Now it's poison. It's ruined everything.

Dad and Steve only ever really talked to me and my half-brothers once about Mom. They sat us down and said, "Okay, ask whatever you want." I was pretty little. I can't remember what I asked. Max and Bennett were starting high school. It was different for them. They were older when Mom left and had more memories. They wanted to know why Dad and Steve weren't mad. "You can't wallow in the past." That's what Dad said. (That was the first time I'd heard the word *wallow*. I thought it was a color. It still is, in my head. A muddy green. The color of misery.) "You can't regret stuff," he said. "You have to accept it and move on." I don't remember what else he said. I just remember they let us order in Chinese.

I'm just going to look at the videos once more then I'm going to move on. If Dad and Steve can put entire marriages behind them, I can forget thirty-six days.

This time, I start with the Knights of the Round Table. I fast-forward through any parts Viv isn't in. I stop at the bit where she and Tim are dancing.

The dress looks really good on her. It would probably look good on anyone, the way it pushes up your boobs. That's all I'm thinking, but then I notice them.

My heart thumps.

Tim spins Viv around and she flings back her hair and there they are.

I rewind, start at the beginning, stop when I get to that spot again and zoom in.

Hickeys.

Great big hickeys.

Viv

1 day before the party
11:40 a.m.

She'd tried calling Stu after the fight with Jack, but he didn't answer so she'd snuck downstairs and guzzled the last of her mother's crème de menthe. It was a disgusting way to kill the pain, but it was what she needed. A punishment to fit the crime.

She was paying for it now. The morning sun streamed through her window like acid. She was too sick to groan. She pulled the sheet over her face.

Like I'm a corpse, she thought. She wished.

She stuck her hand out from under the sheets, found her phone, then slid it onto the bed and up to her face. Thirty-two texts from Jack. She deleted them.

A text from Katie about the cake sampling on Saturday. Viv sent a thumbs-up, too wrecked to invent an excuse. She'd do that later.

An email from Barking Robot. They loved her pitch. Would she be open to revisions?

Yes, she'd be open to revisions. She'd like to revise her whole fucking life, thank you very much.

Her mother tapped on her door and peeked in. "Honey?"

Viv flinched.

"Sorry, sweetheart. Still have that headache? I'm about to meet a friend for lunch but I could cancel if you—"

"I'm fine."

"I could stay."

"No. I'm getting up. I gotta go to the med school and . . ."

"Now don't overdo things. I know you're probably just sneaking out to see Jack but . . ."

"Mum! Go. Please. Sorry. Just go."

The door clicked closed. Allie slunk off. Viv felt like shit.

She'd only said that thing about med school to make her mother think she was busy—to make her mother leave—but maybe that was exactly what she should be doing. Talking to Dr. Keppo. He'd help.

She texted him. He answered immediately. Booked solid until five. Can it wait until then?

Fuck.

Sure. Thanks!

She flopped onto her back. How was she going to survive until then? She couldn't go out. People would ask where Jack was. Why they weren't together. Why they weren't all over each other after a whole twenty-five days apart.

She had to just lie there at the mercy of her thoughts. The same four or five thoughts in a vicious loop.

How long was I out before George woke me up?

Why was she even asking?

It's not as if George would have done anything to her. She'd practically offered herself to him on a platter and he'd said no. (Even now, even knowing much worse things had clearly happened, it still embarrassed her.)

He was all over you. Eva saying that, the look on her face, how angry she was.

259

So? It was dark and Eva's crazy.

But what if she wasn't? What if she'd actually seen something, seen *him* doing something? Maybe he was one of those guys who seemed nice but was actually a perv.

She pictured George's face, how concerned he was, how kind.

No way.

He wasn't a perv.

Plus, he was in med school. They don't let in pervs.

That left Stu.

Stu. Viv hated herself for even going there—but she had to.

How many times had she been passed out in the back of his cab, him covering up for her, texting her mother to say she'd be late? Him—an adult—buying her booze, letting her get that pissed? How many times?

Too many to count.

She could totally understand why some people would think Stu was guilty.

But she didn't.

She *couldn't.*

Because if it really was Stu who'd done this to her—Stu who'd cleaned up her puke, put up with her bullshit—she would totally give up on the world. Even in her current state, she wasn't quite ready to do that.

All she knew was that she'd been sexually assaulted.

Viv felt sure of it and, suddenly, enraged too, that someone would have done something to her when she was in that state. Treated her like a piece of meat. Abused her. She was all ready to call 911, but then it hit her. The questions she'd have to answer. The cop going, "You can't remember? Nothing? How come? Had you been drinking? Were you high? How could you not remember?"

And then of course her parents would get involved—as if things weren't bad enough, as if that wouldn't push her mother off the fucking edge—and all for what? They'd never find out who did this to her.

Davida

4 days after the party
6:51 p.m.

Hickeys.

On her neck and, later, peeking out the top of her dress when she did this wild hip-flying thumka to the lute music. I can hear myself laughing in the background. Choking, I'm laughing so hard. It almost sounds like I'm crying.

I go through the videos again. Now that I know what I'm looking for, I see them all the time. I check my photos too. The selfie of us in our Guinevere dresses, her reaching across the lunchroom table to steal the last of Tim's samosa, sitting on the bench out back getting some sun. I see them there too.

Hickeys.

Real ones.

I slam my laptop closed.

I remember her telling Jack they were moulage. That was the day he came back. Her trying to rub them off. Him licking her neck. Us leaving.

Us going to the breakwater.

I'm so mad. I can't believe Tim would do this to me. I text him.

I want to talk to you come here now

Viv

Her mother would be home soon, asking questions about why she hadn't left yet, worried about her so-called headache, wondering where Jack was. Viv couldn't face that.

She threw on jeans and a turtleneck to cover the "bruises." (That's how she tried to think of them.) She put her hair in two thick braids down the front for added camouflage.

Now she just needed a place to hide for three hours.

Shops, malls, parks were all too dangerous but there was the library, the old one with the lousy AC. No one she knew went there. She locked her bike out front, found a spot in the periodical room, grabbed some back issues of *People* and tried to disappear into the mindless black hole of celeb diets and *Who wore it best?*

At four-thirty, she left for the med school. She was there by ten to five. She'd never been early for anything in her life.

There was a light on in Janice's office but the door was closed. Viv was super quiet, but it didn't matter.

"I thought I heard someone!" She turned around to see Janice poking her head into the hall.

Viv swore silently then put on a smile. "Just me!"

Janice let her reading glasses fall on the chain around her neck. "What are you doing here? I don't think we have any simulations this evening." She leaned back to check the schedule on her wall, even though they both knew she was never wrong.

"No. I . . . I'm here to meet Dr. Keppo."

"He's gone for the day."

Viv must have done something with her face because Janice said, "Oh, sorry, honey. Anything I can help you with?"

"No. It's nothing."

"Not to me it isn't." Janice was so obviously *thrilled* to help that Viv felt obliged to let her.

Another lie to come up with. "I . . . I just wanted to talk to him about, you know, maybe at some point, applying to med school and what I could do to . . ."

"In that case, I certainly *am* the person to talk to! Come in. Come in!"

She waved Viv into a seat by her desk. She opened a metal cabinet, ran her finger along the files and pulled one out. "I've been meaning to update our website, but until then, my good old hand-typed notes! . . . Okay. So, here's a document outlining undergraduate courses to consider. You've got another year of high school, right? Still, not a bad thing to keep in mind . . . And these are some volunteer opportunities. Old age homes, blood drives, that type of thing. Oh. And this one." She stacked another paper on the desk between them.

"A Spring Break camp for high school students interested in medicine. The kids who took it last year raved about it."

"Awesome." Viv tried to sound sincere.

Janice tapped the papers into a nice, neat bundle and passed them to her. "Need anything else?"

Dr. Keppo. "No."

"Well, if you think of anything, just ask. In fact . . . why don't I give you my cellphone number? Easiest way to reach me."

"That's okay. You don't—"

"No, no! Give me your phone and I'll punch it in."

Viv put in her password and handed the phone to Janice.

Janice opened an address book on her desk and flipped through the pages. "I really should have my number memorized but I hardly ever use it . . . Still a landline person myself. I just picked up this little throwaway phone for my SPs." She smiled at Viv. "In case they ever need me."

She found her number and painstakingly typed it into Viv's phone with one finger. "I'm such a terrible texter. Don't know how you kids do it . . . There you go. I put it in under my initials. J.E.D. Janice Elizabeth Drysdale. Will you be able to remember that?"

"Yeah. Thanks."

"Do look into that camp. It would be just your thing." Janice swept a little dust off her desk with her fingertips. "By the way, did Eva get in touch again?"

"No. How's she doing?" Viv was actually interested. Eva was the only person she knew whose life may have been worse than hers.

Janice smiled a perfect U. "Better. We were worried for a while. I used to be youth advocate at the police station so I've seen just about everything teens can go through. Personal problems. Addiction. Legal issues—*lots* of those. But poor Eva—with no help on the home front? She had her hands full. Thankfully, she seems to have come out the other end. I'm just glad I could be of some help." Another perfect U. "Anything else I can do you for?"

There was a moment when Viv teetered. Janice was right there. She'd helped Eva. She'd worked with the police. She was a nurse.

But no. Viv didn't want Janice. She wanted Dr. Keppo. "This is good." She waved the pile of handouts. "Thanks."

"My pleasure!"

Viv smiled and left. The hall was deserted. The only sound was the sticky flap of her flip-flops on the long tile floor.

She needed Stu, she realized.

She needed him, like, *now*, but she couldn't call from her cellphone. He'd see her number and wouldn't pick up.

She squinted down the hall. There was a phone at the reception desk. He wouldn't recognize that number. The security guard was gone. She walked a little faster, but not so fast as to make Janice suspicious.

She'd picked up the phone and was just wondering which button to push for an outside call when she heard a man humming.

"Working switchboard now, are we, Viv?"

She looked up to see Dr. Keppo, with a big mug of tea and that LED smile of his.

Excerpt from police interview with Mandy Chan, 4 days after the party

Lt. Alan (Pidge) Eisenhauer: What do you mean Janice wouldn't tell us everything she knew?

Mandy Chan: I dunno. This isn't about her "withholding information from the police" or anything. Janice just kinda sees the world through rose-colored glasses. Or at least sees the med school that way. "The best in the country." "The finest doctors." "An outstanding SP program." Everything is perfect, right? And Dr. Keppo . . . Don't get her started. Something bad could happen smack-dab in front of her and Janice wouldn't see a thing if she didn't want to.

Eisenhauer: So this is more about denial?

Chan: *Big* time. Frankly, denial's probably the only thing that makes life bearable for her.

Eisenhauer: Things are that bad?

Chan: Yeah. Every so often, I'll do Jan's makeup. Just for fun. Give her a little boost. She'll sit in my chair, smiling away while she tells me the saddest stuff ever. I mean, her life! I'd curl up and die . . . She spends every waking moment at the school. No outside interests. No friends, that I can tell. No kids. She lived with her mother until last year when her mother died of some horrible disease. That's the only time I knew Janice to take time off. She stayed by her mother's bedside day and night, topping up her painkillers, changing her diapers, cleaning up her vomit. That was her holiday.

Eisenhauer: What kind of painkillers?

Chan: No idea.

Eisenhauer: Okay. Go on.

Chan: Then her mother died. So now what does Janice have? A mangy cat, the SP program and Dr. Keppo—who, since you asked, she's in love with.

Eisenhauer: She told you that?

Chan: Didn't have to. I'm not blind.

Eisenhauer: Is it reciprocated?

Chan: Ha! Keppo barely knows she exists—except when he needs her to do something for him. If there's a crime here, that's it. How he treats her. She's run ragged and he gets all the glory. But that's beside the point. Bottom line: I doubt Janice can help you.

Viv

She dropped the phone and ran to him, speaking as fast as she could, half-whispering, not wanting to give anything away, not wanting Janice to hear. "I need to talk. Right now. Something happened. I—" but it was too late. Viv heard the squelch of sensible shoes coming up behind her.

"Dr. Keppo!" Why couldn't Janice mind her own business? "I thought you'd left. What brings you back?"

"This young lady." He put his hand on Viv's shoulder. "We have a five o'clock appointment. I just nipped over to Vandal's for a doughnut. You know me and low blood sugar . . ."

Janice clicked her tongue. "A doctor. Eating like that! Dr. Keppo, you promised you'd go home for a real meal tonight. Laura's going to be—"

"Who'd want a real meal when you could have a maple-bacon cruller?" He winked at Viv. "Now I understand you have some questions—"

"Vivienne was just looking for advice about med school. I gave her the handouts, so I think that's taken care of. Which reminds me . . . Is your son still interested in updating the website? I've got—"

"Sorry, Jan. Can we put that thought on hold? There's something else Viv and I need to discuss. You still be here in an hour?"

Viv saw frustration, maybe even anger, flit across Janice's face, then disappear. "Absolutely! Plenty to do until then. The lunchroom is empty. You could chat there."

"Perfecto!"

As soon as they were out of earshot, Dr. Keppo said, "I gather you're not here about pre-med courses."

Viv wanted to answer but the tears snuck up on her.

"Maybe you'd like a little more privacy than the lunchroom offers." She nodded.

"Good," he said. "Because I'd like more tea—and I don't mean the crappy no-name stuff they pawn off down here. My office okay?"

On the way to the elevators he talked about artisanal doughnuts and bacon and what was happening with the building renovations. Viv knew he meant well but his cheeriness felt wrong, like someone throwing confetti at a funeral.

Before they'd even pushed the button, the elevator opened. A couple of med students stepped out. The girl said, "Dr. Keppo! I got the residency I wanted!"

He held the door with his foot and raised both fists in the air. "Yay! They'd have been crazy to pass you up."

"Yeah, at least based on that reference letter you wrote me . . ."

"The truth, the whole truth and nothing but the truth, so help me God."

"I owe you one."

He laughed. "Whatevs . . ."

He and Viv stepped into the elevator. The door closed and they started moving. "Bella's going to make a wonderful pediatrician."

Viv couldn't even smile.

"She struggled too. A lot of people do, Vivienne. Half the faculty here have some unexplained gaps in their résumés. Goes with the territory."

"Not like this."

He gave a small nod.

The elevator opened. She followed him down the empty hall to his office.

"At least it's quiet tonight," he said. "Some permit problem so the renovations are on hold for a while. Nice, isn't it?" He smiled. She couldn't.

He unlocked the door.

"Sit. Make yourself comfortable." He took the papers she was carrying and plopped them on the coffee table. "These the handouts from Janice? Don't lose them. They're excellent."

Viv had no interest in med school. Any school. Anything. She pressed her fingers hard against her mouth to stop her lips from quivering.

Dr. Keppo put his hands on his hips and looked at her. "What is it?"

No answer.

"I'm going to close the door, okay? Just in case someone comes by. I think you have something important to tell me."

She couldn't even nod.

The door clicked. He sat down across from her, his hands clasped between his knees. "You're safe here. Tell me."

"I think I've been sexually assaulted."

Tim

4 days after the party
6:52 pm

Davida just texted. She wants to talk. I'm a natural optimist so part of me wants to believe she's finally come to her senses and realized she can't live a second more without me, but I know that's not it. She didn't use the pissed-off emoji, but it was implied.

Viv

1 day before the party
5:20 p.m.

He slumped when she said it. "You think?" His eyes were so sad. "You mean you don't *know* if what happened was sexual assault, or you don't *remember* what happened?"

"I don't remember."

"Nothing?"

"Nothing."

"Were you drinking?"

"Yes."

"When did it happen?"

She shook her head, looked away. "I don't know."

"Don't know?"

"Um. There are a number of times it could have happened."

"You blacked out more than once?"

"Yes."

"How often?"

The time Janice woke me up. The time I ended up behind the med school. All the times in the back of Stu's cab. All the times before I met him.

"I'm not sure. A lot."

"Vivienne." He reached across and squeezed her fingers. "I'm so sorry. I had no idea your drinking was that out of control."

She took her hand away and put it over her mouth.

"Would you like some water? Or tea maybe?"

"No." She'd only knock it over. She made herself breathe. In. Out. In. Out.

"So," he said after a while. "If you can't remember, what makes you think there was an assault?"

She lifted her hair and turned her neck toward him. "These."

He crouched beside her, touching them gently, first one side then the other. "Bruises. Are you thinking someone held you by the neck? If so, these wouldn't be the standard markings for that."

"No. I think they're . . ." She was embarrassed not to know the correct word. "They're hickeys." A hickey didn't sound like assault, but it was. She knew it was.

He frowned and studied them through the bottom of his glasses. "Could be. Any others?"

"Yes."

"Where?"

"My, um, breasts. My . . ." Buttocks? She'd never said the word out loud. " . . . My butt. Do you want to see?"

"No, I believe you. Anything else? Any scratches? Any unusual aches and pains? What about your hands?" He flipped his over and back as if she didn't know what hands were. "Notice any broken nails or scratches, as if you may have tried to fend the attacker off?"

"The only thing I noticed is sore breasts, but that's probably just my period."

"You're on it now?"

"No. It's coming. I think. I don't really keep track."

He patted her leg and went back to his chair. "You remember nothing about the assault? Nothing that would give us any clue as to who did it or when?"

Stu? George? There were big black holes in her memory. It could have been anyone.

"I was totally out of it." The words squeaked out, deprived of oxygen.

Dr. Keppo let her pull herself together then said, "Your boyfriend. I don't mean to be indelicate, but you're sure these aren't the result of some consensual play and you're only spotting them now?"

"I'm sure. Jack was away."

"Oh, right. I forgot."

"He, ah . . ."

"Yes?"

"He was the one who noticed them. He thinks I cheated on him."

Dr. Keppo smiled sadly. "Maybe it's time you told him about the drinking. Wouldn't it be better if he thought you had an alcohol problem than if he thought you were sleeping with other people?"

Other *people*. Not just one. Many.

Viv shook her head. She was not telling Jack. Perfect Jack. Never.

"Sorry, but I really need a cup of tea." Dr. Keppo got up. "You want one?"

"I don't know what I want. I don't know what to do."

"I wish I could help you, Vivienne." He filled the kettle. "But here's the thing. Those bruises are quite old. It's too late for a rape kit. It wouldn't pick up any useful information, especially if you've had sexual relations with your boyfriend in the meantime."

He looked at her. That was a question.

"I did."

"So where does that leave us?" He dumped the old tea out of his mug. "Unfortunately, failing a sudden recovered memory, there's not much that can be done about this assault. What we *can* do is make sure it doesn't happen again. Would it be appropriate for me to speak with your parents?"

"No! Please. They're . . . Like, their lives are just . . ."

He lifted his hand. "Say no more. I've got a call in to an excellent addiction specialist. We chatted about your situation a while ago, but he had a long waiting list. Tomorrow morning, I'll see if he can push you ahead . . . I don't—"

There was a knock. He put his finger to his lips and walked toward the door. "Yes?"

Janice bustled in. "Sorry, Dr. Keppo, Vivienne."

"Now's not the best time."

"Apologies, but this can't really wait. It's, ah . . ." She whispered something to him.

Dr. Keppo's face went serious. "Give me two minutes."

"Thank you." Janice backed out and closed the door.

"I hate to do this, Vivienne"—he shrugged—"but I have to go. This thing with Eva is—"

"There's something the matter with Eva? Janice just said she—"

"Don't you worry about it. Trust me, there's no better person in a crisis than Janice, so Eva will be fine, but I do have to see what's up. You'll be okay? This might take a while."

"I'll go home."

"Sure? The kettle's on . . ."

"Yeah, I'm sure. There's something I have to do."

"Okay then." He side-hugged her. His armpit was damp, but he smelled nice. "Your secret's safe. We'll get you through this. You're a great girl. You've got a brilliant future ahead of you." He gave Viv a little shake then scooped the med school handouts off the coffee table. "Here. These should inspire you. Follow Janice's instructions to a tee and you won't have time for a drink. Now come on. I'll walk you to the elevator."

HAVE YOU SEEN THIS GIRL?

Eva Ivana Federov

Age 18

5 feet, 9 inches
140 pounds
Blue eyes
Light brown hair

Last seen on Thursday, July 17 near MacKinnon School
of Medicine wearing a brown leather bomber-style jacket,
jeans and a black or navy turtleneck.

If you have any information regarding Eva's whereabouts,
please contact findeva@easymail.com.

Please share this post!

Viv

Day of the party
3 a.m.

On the way back from Dr. Keppo's, Viv had snuck into a seedy drug mart and bought a pregnancy test. Her boobs were killing her. She had no idea when the sexual assault had happened or how many there'd been but she'd done the math. Her period should have started.

Her mother and Christie were at a movie that night. Viv made sure the light was out in her room by the time they got back.

The instructions said the test worked best with the first pee of the morning. That's when the hormones were most concentrated.

Was 3 a.m. morning?

Close enough. It was useless trying to sleep.

She didn't turn on the light until she was in her bathroom and the door was closed. She got the pregnancy test out of the tampon box where she'd hidden it. She sat on the toilet, lifted her nightshirt and put the wand between her legs. Four hickeys were lined up like buttons, just above her pubic hair.

Why would someone do that? That's not what someone does in the throes of passion.

It's like they wanted to brand me.

"They."

What the hell?

Viv meant *he*.

Or did she?

How would she know? Could have been he, she, they, it. An alien. An animal. A succubus. She disgusted herself.

Viv suddenly realized there could be pictures out there. Videos of her doing stuff. Having stuff done to her. How long before Jack stumbled on them? Or her mother? Her father? Christie? Katie? The world? She suddenly understood the meaning of the word "viral."

Normally when she was nervous she needed to pee all the time, but now she couldn't squeeze out a drop. She turned the tap on to a trickle. That was how her mother used to make her pee when she was small. She held the wand between her legs until she felt a dribble hit. She counted to ten.

Now she just had to wait five minutes.

A lifetime.

She snuck downstairs and filled her water bottle with whatever was left in her mother's liquor cabinet. She figured she might need it.

Davida

I take Steve's hoodie off the hook by the door then sit on the front steps and wait for the van.

The van.

Just the word kills me. My head fills up with stuff I don't want to think about.

The breakwater.

Tim making it all cozy.

A love nest. (Our joke.)

And then, my phone.

My stupid phone ruining everything.

I keep thinking: had I just checked my pocket before I'd gone home that night, just left the ringer on, just waited and picked it up later, none of this would have happened.

Wrong.

It would have happened. I just wouldn't have known about it. If I didn't know, I wouldn't care, and I'd be fine with that. Sad but true. Instead, I get it shoved in my face, all because of my stupid phone.

I pull my knees up inside Steve's hoodie and put my arms around them. I try not to think about what happened but I do.

Tim and I went to the breakwater the night before the party. We'd been spending more time alone, just the two of us, because Jack was back and Viv—*I thought*—wanted to be with him. It wasn't the first time we'd gone to the breakwater, but this was different. I woke up the next morning all happy and, I don't know, *new*, I guess, wanting to tell Tim, talk to him, hear his voice again, but I couldn't find my phone. I looked everywhere.

I went downstairs for my usual Saturday morning waffles with Dad. I was pouring on the syrup when this memory hit me. Not really a memory, more just a sound. The clang of something hitting the van's metal floor. I laughed.

My phone.

Tim and I hadn't even stopped to find out what had made the noise.

Dad went, "What's so funny?" I said, "Nothing." He didn't ask again. He could see I was happy. That was enough.

After breakfast, I borrowed Dad's phone to call mine, but no one picked up. I couldn't call Tim's because I didn't know his number. He'd told me he was working on the AC at the Wedgewood Motel that day. I checked the phone locator app on my laptop and it pinged near the motel, so I knew it was still in the van.

The crew always takes their lunch at noon. Tim likes to read, but the other guys bug him about it, so sometimes he hides out in the van. I decided to surprise him. I put on the green T-shirt he liked and some lip gloss too. (Viv's lip gloss. She'd worn it to the taxidermy show. When I said it was nice, she went, "Here. It's yours." At the time, I thought that was sweet. Now I think *guilty conscience*.)

I walked to the motel and found the van parked on a side street. I couldn't tell if Tim was inside. The sun had turned the windshield into a big, white, shiny rectangle. Then the wind blew or a cloud moved or something because suddenly I could see right in, clear as day.

What I saw was Viv, with Tim's arms around her and her face tucked up against his ear. I froze. Literally could not move, even though I was sort of thinking *they're just hugging*—they're friends, sometimes friends hug—*and it's going to stop,* but it didn't. It went on and on, her slobbering all over him, his hands all over her back.

I couldn't watch, but I couldn't leave either. I hid behind a car and waited. It was forty minutes before she left, her face bright red, just like mine had been when *I'd* been the one in the van with him. I heard Viv laugh and say, "See you at the party!"

Tim went, "You okay?"

"Yeah," she said. Then, the killer: "I love you, Tim. Seriously. I love you."

I couldn't hear what he said back, but then she went, "You promised. Remember? This is for*ever.*"

I watched her walk away. I watched him watch her. I couldn't believe what I was seeing. Then I could.

Viv was always telling me how great Tim was, so funny, so smart and goofy. She just "loved" him. Her exact words. I used to think she was just trying to get me to go out with him, but no. She meant it.

I remember thinking on the way home that at least I didn't have to go to Ariana's party. I could go back to my boring old life. I was free to stay in my room and cry.

At quarter to seven that night, Tim showed up at our door. I told Steve to tell him to go away.

Tim didn't go to the party either. He sat across the street from our house in his van until eleven, by which time Steve had had enough and told him to move along.

And now here's the van again. Tim opens the door and starts to get out but I wave him back in like I'm swatting flies. He doesn't really think we're going to have a nice friendly chat, does he?

Not a chance.

I'm going to tell him what I have to say, then that's it. I'm done. I mean it this time.

Viv

Eleven hours before the party

Viv woke up the next morning to the sound of her mother laughing. Her first thought: *This will kill her.* Somehow that seemed the most shameful thing of all. That in the end, it would be Viv's fault.

Mum can't ever know. Viv had to fix this.

Her mother laughed again. Who was she talking to? It wasn't Christie. The other voice was low. A man. Viv couldn't make it out.

Who would be here at 9 on a Saturday morning? The last man she'd seen her mother with was her father, but the laughter made that highly unlikely, unless of course Allie had just stabbed Ross in the heart or something.

Viv got dressed—the turtleneck again—and then for added coverage, a jean jacket. She checked herself in the mirror, rotating her head, leaning in close. Nothing showed.

Should I wait until the guy leaves?

Go now, she decided. Allie wouldn't interrogate her with someone there.

She bounded into the kitchen. Her mother was at the counter, frothing milk for cappuccino.

"Just what I wanted!" Viv said, because it was important to appear normal, happy, totally unpregnant.

"It's not for you." Allie sounded disconcertingly impish. "Look who's here!"

Viv turned, slo-mo. Jack was leaning against the island, bright blue T-shirt, perfect arms, perfect teeth. He went, "Vivarium," as if he'd never said all those things to her, as if she'd never said all those things to him.

Allie squiggled a heart into the froth and handed the cup to Jack. "He wanted to surprise you, but you took so long waking up he finally broke down and let me get him something. Want one?"

Viv walked over to the island. Jack leaned in to kiss her. She let him then snatched his cappuccino and downed it. "No need." She grabbed his arm. "Let's get out of here."

He laughed. "Thanks for trying, Allie."

"You're back for supper?" She was laughing too.

Jack raised his eyebrows at Viv. "Ariana's party's tonight, isn't it?"

"Yeah." She told her mother she'd text her later then dragged him out the door.

"Where to?" Jack smiled and opened the car door for her. "What do you feel like?"

Shit, Viv thought. *I feel like shit, and you smiling is only making it worse.*

"There's a place on University," she said.

"Just tell me where!" He backed out of the driveway then looked at her, his pupils dilating.

She turned away.

"I'm sorry for surprising you today, but I'm happy you said yes, so maybe I'm not sorry." He was working hard to be cute.

"I didn't say yes."

"Not technically, but you came. Silence is consent."

Viv thought of herself all those times, blacked out, too drunk to say no. "That's not the way it works."

"How does it work?" He thought this was banter, that they were having fun.

She looked out the passenger window. They drove in silence.

"You're still mad," he said after a while.

She shrugged.

"You have every right to be. It's disgusting what I said. I'm stupid. I'm stupid with love." He smiled at her.

"Eyes on the road."

"I'm craaaaaaaaa-zy," he sang. "I'm crazy for trying, I'm crazy for crying and I'm crazy for loving you." His father had sung that song to his mother on their twentieth anniversary. Viv had loved it then.

"Turn here," she said.

"The med school?" He parked in front of MacKinnon Hall. "They put in a new café? Since when?" He bent over the steering wheel and peered out the windshield, looking for a neon sign or something.

"I told you, Jack. I don't want to see you anymore."

"Viv?"

"Leave me alone. I mean it."

"Viv . . . What's going on? I said I'm sorry. We've been together for three years. I can't make a mistake? One mistake?"

She got out and started walking toward the med school.

He ran after her and grabbed her arm.

"Let go of me."

"I'm not hurting you. Please. I just want to talk. You're being unreasonable."

She yanked her arm away. "No, I'm not. I've wanted out for ages."

That shut him up. He stood with his hands at his sides, palms out, unmoving. Viv thought of the skinless man on the anatomy poster in Dr. Keppo's office. Perfect, but in so much pain.

"You don't mean that," he said.

She kept walking.

For a moment, she thought he'd given up, but then the sound of running, his hand on her shoulder. "Don't do this, please."

She swung around and slapped him. He barely flinched so she hit him again and again and again, her head snapping back with each useless punch. Normally, he'd have been laughing by now, grabbing her wrists, tickling her, because she was a weakling and a klutz. Instead he just stood there and took it.

When she finally stopped, he said, "You done?"

"No."

"Then go on. Do what you have to do." Not cocky or anything. Just *fair's fair.*

"Okay," she said and walked away.

When he went, "What?!?" she said, "This is what I have to do, Jack."

She didn't turn around. She knew he was still standing there, watching her.

Excerpt from police interview with Jack Downey, 4 days after the party

---

Lt. Alan (Pidge) Eisenhauer: The argument you had with Vivienne. What was it about?

Jack Downey: Me being an asshole.

Eisenhauer: Can you be more specific?

Downey: . . . She had bruises on her. Her neck and her, like, chest. She said they were moulage—medical makeup?—but they didn't come off. She's anemic so maybe they were just from low iron. But they looked like hickeys to me, and I said so. She got mad and that got me thinking crazy things.

Eisenhauer: You thought she'd cheated on you?

Downey: Yeah. I said so and she got really mad and told me to leave. The thing is, I don't even care if they were hickeys. I don't care if she slept with ten guys while I was away. I don't care if she was doing drugs. I just want this not to have happened.

Viv

Viv should have called first but didn't. She went straight to Dr. Keppo's office and knocked.

"Come in!"

Janice.

Now what? Walking away would look suspicious. Viv sucked in her breath. She'd just poke in her head then go. "Sorry. Didn't mean to bother you."

Janice was standing behind the desk, her arms full of files. "You're not! Just doing a little tidying."

The floor was covered in bulging garbage bags. The cabinet doors over the sink were open, the counter piled with stuff. "I try to do it while he's out."

"Dr. Keppo's out?" Viv hadn't even considered the possibility.

"At a conference. Not back until tomorrow." Janice plunked the files on the desk and smiled. "Can I help?"

"No, thanks. It's . . . ah . . . something personal."

"Oh dear." Her smile drooped. "Is it urgent?"

"Sort of." The pregnancy test had been negative, but so what? The box warned you could get a false negative if you took the test too soon, and going by the state of her bruises, the assault could have happened pretty recently. Plus, there was nothing false about the way Viv's boobs ached. *So, yeah, sort of urgent.*

"What's wrong, honey?" Janice cleared some books off a chair. "Tell me. I've done enough cleaning today anyway. Sit." She turned her palm out like a restaurant hostess seating a guest.

Viv hesitated—it would be such a relief to tell someone, tell anyone—but no. "It can wait. I'll just catch him later." She faked a smile and hurried out of the room.

And there was George Pineo, just stepping out of the elevator.

Tim

Well, *that* sucked.

Davida kept saying, "Why would you *do* that? Just to torture me?" But I kept my promise. I didn't explain. I just asked what she meant.

Davida literally grabbed her hair and pulled, like this was a cartoon or something. She went, "What do you *think* I mean? Making me look at those videos! Making me *study* them for fucking clues!!!!!" I'd never heard her swear before. I had to put my hands in my pocket to keep from hugging her.

I went, "You really think I was just trying to hurt you?"

She didn't answer. She just said she knew what she saw me do and she knew what she saw in the video and she wasn't stupid. I was making out with Viv and I must have done it lots of times because I'd left big purple hickeys all over her body like I was some horny goddamn bloodsucker or something. (She didn't actually call me a horny goddamn bloodsucker, but seriously. Who else would do that?)

I was trapped. If I didn't fess up, she'd assume it was true. If I did, I was a piece of shit.

I went, "That's not what happened."

"Then what did?"

"I can't tell you."

"How come?"

"I made a promise." More hair-pulling. Then I remembered another promise I'd made—we'd *both* made—so I said, "To defend the defenseless." I wanted her to know this was about doing the right thing, but she just went, "Oh my God! Would you drop the Sir Lancelot shit?"

She glared at me for a long time, all crazy-eyed, then she screamed really quietly and ran into the house.

Viv

9.5 hours before the party

George Pineo. The last person she wanted to see.

"Viv." He didn't look that thrilled to see her either. "What are you doing here?"

"Came to talk to Dr. Keppo." *Just stay calm.*

"Yeah. Me too."

Viv pushed the elevator's down button. "He's out of town. Janice is there, though, if you want to talk to her."

"No." George didn't actually shudder, but almost. "I'll wait."

The elevator opened. Viv stepped in and said, "See ya." She hit L for lobby. The door started to close. George pushed his way in.

"May as well join you."

They rode down several floors in silence then he said, "I actually wanted to talk to you too."

Viv didn't look at him directly, but his face was reflected over and over again in the elevator mirrors. That wasn't a real smile.

"About what?"

The elevator opened on two. A woman in a lab coat got on. She nodded at them then turned to the front. He wasn't going to tell Viv now.

When they got to the lobby, George held the door so the woman could get out first. There were a few people milling around, but not many. He whispered to Viv, "Mind if we talk outside?"

"Why?" She wasn't going to whisper.

"Something I'd rather discuss in private." That fake smile again.

She thought about it for a moment then said, "Okay." She led him to the park bench just outside the med school entrance. It was daylight. Students were coming and going. This was private enough. "What did you want to talk about?" she said.

He moved his mouth from side to side as if he was gargling. "Not sure how to bring this up. That night . . . after we went for fajitas?"

"Yeah?"

"I'd really hate you to mention it to anyone."

She stared at him. What was he saying?

"The, um, kiss. And what I said about it later too. That was inappropriate." He looked away. "I'm just a little antsy about the consent thing."

"I kissed *you*. You're the one who didn't give consent." She didn't know if she was angry or scared. "Why do you suddenly care so much about it?"

"Uh . . . Well . . . Dr. Keppo just sent this memo about boundaries and inappropriate physician-patient contact and stuff like that. I guess there are rumors going around about someone at the med school so maybe I'm being uber-cautious, but I'd really appreciate it if you didn't say anything. There's this attitude like 'if he did that, what else has he done?' Know what I mean? I'm not a doctor yet but still. I can't, um, afford that kind of suspicion. Not now."

Viv said, "How long was I out before you woke me up?"

"What?" His eyes snapped open as if she'd burnt him with a cigarette.

"I was passed out. Did you wake me up right away?"

"What are you talking about?"

"Out back. When you"—she made air quotes—"'rescued' me?"

"I have no idea how long you were out." He was breathing hard.

Viv could see his bottom teeth. "I came outside for a vape. I saw you passed out, no one around, so I woke you up. Immediately."

"That's what you say."

"What does *that* mean?" He moved in close and whispered, "I was trying to *help*. I could have called security, let them deal with you, but I thought, *I know this girl*. She'd be embarrassed. I can't leave her. And now you're what? . . . *Accusing* me of something? I didn't do anything to you!" He jabbed his finger at her. "This is how innocent people's lives get ruined. Someone making totally unfounded allegations."

He was shaking. "And anyway, you were the one who kissed *me*. Remember?"

"It's what I don't remember that scares me." Viv walked away, leaving him there, furious and shaking.

She was too.

"You keep away from him." She'd thought Eva meant it as a threat, that she just wanted him for herself, but maybe it was a warning.

What if Eva wasn't obsessed with him? What if she was *scared* of him?

Viv turned the corner and got out her phone. She scrolled through her contacts. She didn't have anything for Eva, but she found her Facebook page.

Her profile picture was old. Eva still had long hair and was wearing Mickey Mouse ears and bright red lipstick. She had her arm around someone in a Minion mask.

Viv was about to send her a message when she noticed the top post.

"Missing since Thursday . . . If you have any information regarding Eva's whereabouts, please contact . . ."

Viv suddenly went cold. She had to talk to someone.

She called Dr. Keppo's cell but it went direct to voicemail. Stu didn't pick up. Jack was off limits. Her mother was too fragile. She was terrified what her father would do if he found out. Ditto Christie. And she didn't want to horrify innocent little Davida. Who did that leave?

She texted Tim.

Excerpt from police interview with George Pineo, 4 days after the party

Lt. Alan (Pidge) Eisenhauer: When did you last see Vivienne?

George Pineo: That Saturday. Just by accident. Dr. Keppo had sent a memo saying there were rumors about something happening at the med school and reminding us that he had zero tolerance for inappropriate behavior. I didn't think the rumors were about me—I figured he would have told me personally—but I was nervous just the same. I went to his office to tell him about taking Viv to Habanero's that night. Just to get it out there, so it didn't come back to bite me. Dr. Keppo wasn't there but Viv was, so I figured I'd just make sure she was cool with it too. Two minutes later she was accusing me of assaulting her. While she was unconscious! It really scared me. It made me wonder what else she was saying about me.

Tim

I've been sitting here in my room going over what just happened with Davida and I've come to the obvious conclusion: there's no hope. She hates me. So I may as well get this down, once and for all, for my own mental health if nothing else.

Here's Viv's secret.

She texted me Saturday morning to say she needed to talk right away. I was working on the motel project for Pa and my lunch was about to start so I said come on down. I asked what was up, but she said she'd tell me when she got there.

Since Ariana's party was that night, I naturally assumed it was about Davida. I figured Viv had some scheme to make sure Davida didn't flake. She really didn't want to go. She'd been trying to weasel out of the party for ages.

I didn't particularly want to go either but Viv had been really good to us and Davida *did* promise so I thought, *Okay. I'll help*. I was kind of laughing, wondering what plan Viv had cooked up to get her there. I prepared a few kidnapping jokes just in case.

Viv

Tim was sitting in the driver's seat of a bright white Zanger & Sons van, parked around the corner from the Wedgewood Motel. He had a book open on the steering wheel and was eating something large and messy. When he saw Viv coming down the street, he tooted his horn and smiled. He didn't seem to notice she didn't smile back.

"Enter the Zangmobile." He pushed open the passenger door. It smelled a little sweaty inside. Viv remembered some elaborate conspiracy theory he had about aluminum in deodorant. He hardly ever wore it.

"*Olliebolen?*" he said, handing her something doughnutty. "A little stale but whatever. Davida and I didn't get around to finishing them last night." He might have blushed.

Viv shook her head.

"Wow. Vivienne B, not eating? This, my friends, is serious!"

"It is," she said.

Something about her voice. He put the pastry in the cupholder and wiped his hands on his green work shirt.

"What's the matter?"

"I have to tell you something."

"Okay."

"You have to promise you'll never tell anyone. I'm talking Knights-of-the-Round-Table-unbreakable-oath type promise."

"Done," he said. "My lips are sealed."

"No. Say 'I promise.'"

"I promise."

"You have to promise you'll never even tell anyone we talked. Understand? I wasn't here."

"Okay." She kept staring at him until he said, "I promise."

"No one can know." Viv had acted as if George Pineo was an ass-hole, but he'd been right. Stuff she said could ruin an innocent person's life. Viv was only going to tell Tim what she knew for certain, nothing more. "Ever."

"I promise."

"Forever?"

"Jesus Christ, Viv. I promise! You're freaking me out. Are you in trouble? Did something happen?"

She opened her mouth to answer but only a sob came out.

"Viv . . ." He froze for a second, not sure what to do, then he wiped his hands on his shirt again and pulled her into a hug.

Tim

Viv drank, that's what she said. As in, a lot. As in, by herself. As in, anything she could get her hands on. I must have been pretty stunned because I had no frigging idea.

I'd just sort of processed that info when she said somebody had sexually assaulted her. She said that's where the hickeys came from. She had them all over her body.

I asked who did it, but she didn't know. She'd passed out. She couldn't remember a thing. She didn't even know WHEN it happened because she'd passed out lots of times. There were some people she suspected but she wouldn't say who, even when I begged her. She didn't want the wrong guy getting in trouble.

Then she told me she might be pregnant.

I was like, "What do you mean 'might'?" and she said it was too early to tell. She was going to try the test again in a couple of days.

It took forever to get all that out. Viv was crying really hard and whispering right into my ear even though there was no one around to hear. My collar was soaked.

I said we had to go to the police. She shook her head really hard.

"Why?" I said.

Because she had no proof, she said.

I told her that's what police are for, but she was like no, no, no. They'd tell her parents, then her mother would have a nervous breakdown and her father would go out and shoot someone—maybe even me because, knowing her dad, she said, he'd shoot any guy who'd been near her in the last four months. That's just the type of guy he is, she said.

So I said tell Jack, but she wouldn't because she said he'd hate her. I tried to say that wasn't true, but she just cried even harder.

I wish we could have talked longer but by then my lunch was up and my father would be losing it. The motel project had to be done by Monday.

She said not to worry. She felt better just getting it off her chest. She had to do the wedding cake thing with her stepmother but then she'd meet us at the party. I was like, "You still want to go to the party?!?" But she did. Not going after making such a big deal about it would just look suspicious. We kissed goodbye—like on the cheek—and she left.

"I love you," she said. Then, "You promised. Remember? This is for*ever*." That's the last thing she said to me.

That's why I had to keep lying to Davida.

Viv

She felt better. Not great, but better. Crying helped, as did telling the truth, or at least what she remembered. She called Dr. Keppo on her way back from Tim's and got his voicemail again. She left a message saying she needed to see him as soon as possible. She told herself to stop thinking about stuff until then. He'd know what to do.

She went home and had a nap. She got up with just enough time to fix her hair and throw on clean clothes before Katie texted I'm here! just before five.

Christie was at a concert with friends, so Allie was eating alone in front of the TV. She paused *Call the Midwife* and said, "Where are you off to?"

Viv had hoped to avoid this. "Meeting Katie and Lulu."

"Oh." Allie took a slow sip of wine then smiled. "That should be fun."

Viv shrugged like *maybe*.

"While I remember . . ." Allie walked over to her desk. "You left these papers in the hall. They're addressed to Dr. Keppo. Why would you have them?"

Viv leafed through the papers. Letters of reference. A referral for a kidney patient. Something about the renovations. She had no idea how they got there until she noticed the med school handouts Janice had given her. "Must have accidentally picked them up when I was in his office the other day. I'm seeing him soon. I'll give them to him then."

"Well, put them in your backpack now so you don't forget. They may be important."

Viv thought, *I really have to do it right this second? With Katie waiting?*

But Allie was trying so hard, and Viv was leaving her with a wilted salad and Netflix to go out with the person who'd destroyed her life, so she went, "Good idea." She stuffed the papers into her backpack, kissed her mother goodbye and left.

The cake sampling was at Sinful Sarah's Patisserie. Sarah herself went through the choices with them.

Chocolate—too expected.

Coconut—a lot of people don't like coconut (i.e., Lulu).

Vanilla—

"Vanilla seems like a bad start to a marriage," Katie said then cringed. Had she just accidentally blurted out a sex joke? Viv almost said, "Don't worry. I may be pregnant by an unknown assailant. Can't shock me!" She'd reached that point.

They decided on lemon.

Now for icing. (Ganache or buttercream? A hint of lavender? All over or just on top?)

Lemon buttercream with raspberry filling. *Good. Done.*

Wrong. What about decoration? (Describe your personal style. Traditional? Rustic chic?)

Viv smiled and laughed and resisted the powerful urge to say *Who the fuck cares?*

Lulu was clearly losing patience too. She was fidgeting and going out of her way to irritate Katie. (Viv remembered Allie once referring to her as Lululucifer. Nasty but not entirely untrue.)

Sarah said, "Let me clear some of these options away so we can discuss plating."

"There's more?" Lulu slumped and kicked the bottom of the table.

"How'd you like to draw?" Viv asked her. "You're really good at drawing and I need a new picture for my room."

Lulu narrowed her eyes. She knew she was being manipulated. "I don't have any paper."

"I do!" Viv took Janice's med school handouts out of her backpack. She was never going to use them. "Here." She flipped them over to the blank side. "And, look, I've got markers too."

Lulu beamed when she realized they were fluorescent. Katie beamed back. Score one for Viv.

"Guaranteed ten to twelve minutes of silence," Katie whispered to her.

"Whoa. That's like a week in people-years."

They watched Lulu, tongue out, coloring maniacally, adorably, until Katie couldn't resist anymore. She leaned down and kissed her head. Lulu's marker skidded across the page. "Mommy! You ruined my picture!"

"What are you talking about?" Viv picked it up. "I love how you drew my hair! That's not ruined."

"Yes, it is. Now I have to do a whole other one!"

"Lucky you!" Viv slid a couple more sheets toward her.

Lulu was just about to start drawing when Viv realized she'd given her one of Dr. Keppo's letters by mistake.

"Whoops! Not that one." She pulled the page away. "That one belongs to someone else."

"No, it doesn't. It's yours!" Lulu took it back. "Wanna know how I know?"

"I do."

She kneeled on her chair and whispered in Viv's ear. "There's a picture of your pizza." She leaned back, big smile on her face.

"What are you up to?" Katie said, grinning.

"It's a secret," Lulu said. "Close your eyes." Katie did.

Lulu showed Viv the letter. It was addressed to Dr. Ivan Keppo, thanking him for his help at the recent Conference on Community-Based Medicine. There were drawings in the margin. Viv recognized his style. Right near the bottom, just across from where Dr. Catherine Nguyen signed her name, was a doodle of a pizza slice.

A pizza slice shaped like a heart.

With three round circles inside representing pepperoni.

If it weren't for the fact that it was done in blue ballpoint instead of red ink, it would look exactly like her tattoo.

Viv didn't understand. Her heart stopped beating, her blood stopped pumping, while her brain went to work.

"I'm right, aren't I?" Lulu whispered.

"You are," Viv whispered back. "Can I keep it?"

"Can I draw on another paper then?"

"Yes."

"Can I open my eyes now?" Katie sounded playful.

Lulu waited until Viv hid the letter in her backpack and went, "Yup!"

Sarah came back with plating options. Viv asked where the washroom was, grabbed her backpack and headed to the rear of the patisserie.

She sat in the stall, shaking. She had to pull herself together. She didn't have long. Katie would wonder what was taking her. She got out her phone.

She googled the number for the police, hit the first four digits, then stopped.

Dr. Keppo.

Head of the medical school. Honorary this and honorary that. Everybody's hero, best friend.

They'd never believe her. They'd make it sound like she was lying. They'd call her parents.

She hung up.

She stared at the cubicle door. Someone had scratched *Live your best life* in the metal. Someone else had scratched *Eat shit.*

She needed help. She had to do something.

She called Tim. It rang and rang and rang.

She didn't know who else to call.

And then she did. The perfect person. Someone who'd worked with troubled youth. With the legal system. A medical person. Someone who'd know what to do.

It took Viv a while to find the number because she'd forgotten it wasn't under Drysdale. It was under her initials. JED.

Janice picked up right away.

Excerpt from police interview wth Janice Drysdale, 5 days after the party

Lt. Alan (Pidge) Eisenhauer: You're back. Quite a different story now, isn't it?

Janice Drysdale: Yes.

Eisenhauer: Why don't you start by telling me about the oxycodone?

Drysdale: It was left over from when Mother had bone cancer. I had a supply on hand to administer when the pain broke through, thank goodness. We hear so much about opioid abuse these days, but people forget what a godsend opioids can be. Thanks to oxy, Mother's last weeks were by and large quite comfortable.

Eisenhauer: So Vivienne called and asked to meet you?

Drysdale: Yes. Called my burner.

Eisenhauer: You mean your prepaid phone?

Drysdale: Yes. I heard about them on *Law & Order*. Do you ever watch that show? Sometimes, during those long nights nursing Mother, the only thing keeping me awake was *Law & Order* reruns. The detectives on the show could never trace the calls because the criminals all had burners. It dawned on me that one might come in handy for issues with the SPs. When it rang that evening, I knew it had to be Vivienne. Eva used to have the number, but Vivienne was the only person to have it then. Dr. Keppo—in confidence, of course—had discussed her situation with me, so I was prepared.

Viv

"Oh my God. I'm so sorry! A friend just called. She's having a crisis. I gotta run."

"Really?" Katie's smile went flat and square. "You have to go? Now?" Viv felt bad about hurting her feelings with such an obvious lie.

"Yeah. Sorry. There's this thing we're working on and I promised I'd . . ."

"I'll just pack up. Won't take a sec . . ."

"No. You've got plating to figure out." Viv kissed her. "This was fun. Thanks." Then she said, "Love you," which was a first. Viv wasn't sure she meant it, but Katie's eyes filled with tears, so she really hoped she did.

"And love you too, little monkey." Viv blew a raspberry on Lulu's neck then left while she was still laughing.

As soon as she'd hung up with Janice, Viv had texted Stu. He'd actually texted back. His car was waiting out front now. She climbed in, so happy, so relieved to be safe with him again—but it wasn't Stu in the driver's seat.

"Benji," the man said when he saw her confusion. He was a skinny guy with a Yosemite Sam tattoo on the back of his bald head. "Filling in for Stu tonight. He's got an exam or something. Where to?"

Viv checked her phone for the name of the place Janice had given her.

"You know where Bon Pho's is?"

"Nope."

"It's a Thai takeout place on"—she looked at the map—"Portland Street?"

"Oh, yeah. Way the hell out there?" He shook his head and pulled out.

When Viv said she'd been sexually assaulted, Janice had gasped. She'd wanted to know when and by who, but there were people walking in and out of the washroom. Viv needed to see Janice in person, not just spill her guts in some toilet cubicle.

Benji cranked up the hard-rock station. Viv took out her water bottle. She guzzled back a hit of the booze she'd stolen from her mother's liquor cabinet. It was gross but it helped.

They'd been driving about twenty minutes on a mostly empty road when Benji turned into the parking lot of a shabby strip mall. Bon Pho's was the only business without a CLOSED sign in the window. Viv paid Benji then asked him to say hi to Stu for her. He said, "Yeah," but she knew he wouldn't.

It was a few minutes before Janice pulled up in a dark blue subcompact. Viv climbed in and they drove down an alley at the side of the building, parking at the rear. It was pretty grotty back there—weeds growing through broken asphalt, piles of rotting cardboard boxes—but it was private.

"Honey." Janice took Viv's hands. "Tell me."

"It was Dr. Keppo."

"Ivan Keppo?" Janice lurched back as if they couldn't possibly be talking about the same person. "You're sure?"

Viv was determined not to cry. "He assaulted me."

"When? How? He's so busy! . . . Did you—what?—meet him after hours?"

"Yeah. In his office."

"You . . . you had a relationship with him?"

The question stunned Viv. "What?"

"A romantic relationship?"

"No. He was my . . . my doctor. I was having problems and he took me to his office to talk about them. I mean, that's why I thought he did."

Janice was nodding but frowning too.

"I was drunk." Viv made a sound like a laugh. "Like, passed out cold. You saw me once. A few weeks ago. Remember? You woke me up. That's when it happened. Or maybe another night, but I was definitely out of it, because I don't remember a thing. It can't be consensual then, can it?"

"No. If you're unconscious, it's assault, no question." Janice looked at Viv kindly. "If you don't remember, though, how do you know it happened?"

"I didn't at first but then my boyfriend came home and saw hickeys. On my breasts and butt and, like, crotch. He thought I was cheating on him. That's why I ended up back at Dr. Keppo's."

Viv pictured Dr. Keppo brushing her hair away, studying the hickeys as if he was seeing them for the first time.

"Sweetheart." Janice rubbed Viv's arm. Her hand was cold and bony. Viv was glad when she stopped. "I believe you. I really do. But I've known Dr. Keppo for years, seen all the wonderful things he's done for his patients and students." She put her chin in her hand and looked away for a moment. "I'm sorry, but couldn't it have been someone else?"

"No." Viv said it louder than she meant to. "I have a tattoo. I designed it myself. I just got it recently and it's on my butt so only three people have seen it. My boyfriend, my stepsister and Davida. I found a letter addressed to Dr. Keppo with a drawing of that exact tattoo in the margin. My boyfriend was away, my stepsister is five—and how would my friend get her hands on a letter addressed to Dr. Keppo? He's the one who drew it. I know it."

She rooted through her backpack.

"Here." She unfolded the letter and tapped the doodle of the pizza. "My tattoo. That's it."

Janice turned on the interior light, studied the paper for a few seconds, folded it back up and turned off the light.

She took a big breath and squeezed Viv's hand. "We're going to make this right but I've been to the police with girls in your situation before. If you want to press charges, you'll need to be prepared for some uncomfortable questions."

Viv was trying not to be scared. She nodded.

"For instance—You really think you could have been so drunk you don't remember being sexually assaulted?"

Viv had wondered the same thing. She'd gotten pissed before. Passed out before on benches, in the back of Stu's cab, at home, but she'd always had some memory, hazy maybe, but something that eventually floated back to her.

"You don't look well," Janice said. "Can I get you something? I've got some water here." She leaned into the back seat for her bag.

And then Viv remembered. "Tea."

Janice gave an embarrassed laugh. "Sorry, dear. I don't have tea. All I—"

"No," Viv said. "I mean both times before I passed out, Dr. Keppo gave me tea." The apple-y smell, the liquid so scalding she could barely taste it.

"Oh, Vivienne! He gives everyone tea. I've had it myself."

"But there was something in it. That's why I don't remember. I wasn't just drunk. I was, like, *gone*."

"Something in it? You mean like a sedative?"

"Yes. I'm sure."

"Have you spoken to anyone else about this?"

"A friend."

"Eva?"

"Eva? No. I barely know her. Tim Zanger. I told him I'd been assaulted but I didn't know by who. When I realized it was Dr. Keppo, I tried to reach him, but he was out so I called you."

"Did you leave a message?"

"No." That wasn't the type of thing you'd leave as a message.

"Good. Let's keep this quiet. We don't want to give Ivan a heads-up before the police can arrest him. Now we just need proof."

"The drawing. It's proof!"

"Yes. At least what *we* think of as proof—but from a legal viewpoint? A doodle? A lawyer would say that could be anything, by anyone. What else? The tea? The assault happened weeks ago, so it's long out of your system. We need something hard and fast to make this stick . . . Did you ever see Dr. Keppo do anything suspicious?"

Viv thought for a moment. He'd always been so . . . *perfect* was the only word she could think of. "No."

"Vivienne." Janice shook her head sadly. "Let me be honest. I'm not sure what there is to go on."

"DNA?" Viv said.

"Too late for that, I'm afraid. Rape kits have to be used very soon after the actual act."

"Not DNA from sex," Viv said. "I think I'm pregnant."

Janice put her hand over her mouth.

"Wouldn't they be able to tell from the fetus who the father is?"

"Absolutely." Janice patted her face as if she was checking to make sure it was still there. "Fetal DNA would be incontrovertible proof . . . Ivan won't be able to get out of this one." There was a long pause. "How do you feel, honey?"

"Feel?" Viv sucked in her breath. "Every time I think of what happened or might have happened when I was too whacked to know what was going on, I feel like throwing up. I'm terrified my parents are going to find out. I'm terrified my boyfriend's going to find out. I'm terrified I picked up some disease. I'm just plain terrified."

"Oh, sweetheart. You're shaking like a leaf." Janice held Viv's wrist as if she was taking her pulse. She put her hand on Viv's forehead. "You're having a panic attack. Poor thing. You don't deserve this."

Janice hugged her and kept holding on even though Viv was making her shake too. "It'll be okay. It'll be okay." She said it over and over, almost humming, until Viv could breathe again. Then she said, "I'd like to make a suggestion. It's late. You're fragile. We can go to the police now—but it would be a very long night. Or we can go tomorrow after you've had some sleep. It's up to you but, personally, I'd suggest tomorrow. Nothing's going to change between now and then."

"Yes. Tomorrow. That's better."

"Good. Can I keep the letter until then? I'd like to prepare something for the police. Show them we mean business."

Viv nodded. Janice held her at arm's length and smiled. "In the meantime, I have something that will help with your panic attack. I'm a nurse, as you know, but what you may not know is that I suffer from anxiety myself. This is from my own 'stash.'" She gave a little laugh. "I wouldn't want you to make a habit of this, but one little pill now could do a lot of good. A peaceful night and some sleep and you'll be all ready for tomorrow."

She reached into her purse and pulled out a small blue pill.

"Will it hurt the baby?"

"You're going to keep it?" Janice sounded shocked.

Viv shook her head, shocked at what had just come out of her mouth.

"I don't know why I said that." But, in a flash, Viv did. A baby would love her no matter what she did, no matter who she was. She wasn't sure anyone else would.

Janice had her nurse voice on again. "No. It won't hurt the baby, if that's what you want, but don't take it here. Wait until you get home. You should take it with food, otherwise you'll feel ill."

"There will be food at the party."

"A party?" Janice almost laughed.

Viv did too. "I know it sounds stupid, but I should go." She couldn't bother explaining it any more than that.

"Really?" Janice said.

"I promised I'd go."

"Well, then. Fine, I guess. But, please, don't mention where you got this—and don't give it to anyone else. I could get in a lot of trouble. I obviously should know better than to give prescription drugs away."

"I won't."

"Okay." Janice smiled. "Where to then?"

Viv gave her Ariana Cohen's address. While Janice drove, Viv texted Tim and Davida. She did her best to sound normal.

Good news I got barking robot internship. Bad news jack and I had a fight but so what. On my way to party now!!!!

Janice stopped to let her out a block from the party. "Promise to take the pill?" she asked.

Viv promised.

"Good. Do it right away, before you forget. You'll feel so much better. We both will."

Viv thanked her and walked up to the house. The party was already roaring. Everyone screaming, laughing, drunk out of their faces. She took a deep breath. She was going to need a little help to get through it. She was so glad Janice had given her that pill.

Davida

I wait in the foyer until I hear the van pull away. Then I run up to my room and throw myself on my bed, crying, like I'm five or something.

Everything I thought was wrong.

It's suddenly so obvious and so devastating.

I could tell by the look on Tim's face that he wasn't trying to hurt me. I'm not even sure anymore he was making out with Viv, even though I saw it with my own eyes.

Something happened—between Viv and Tim, between Viv and someone else, between Viv and herself—and she decided to make it go away and took a pill. That's all I know.

I sit up. Wipe the tears off my face with the back of my hand.

I stare at the wall. I'm just trying to make everything go blank but for some reason I focus in on my bulletin board. The ticket to the Knights of the Round Table tacked there. I jump up and tear it off. Stupid oaths. Stupid happiness.

I tear off the program for the taxidermy show too, and a Polaroid Mandy took of my burn, and a napkin from DeJong's Dutch Bakery where Tim's favourite *oliebollen* come from. I tear everything off until all that's left is a photo of my mother holding me when I was a baby,

313

a postcard from Steve and my half-brothers when they went to Iceland, and a doodle of a ruckus.

A ruckus.

That's what started this whole thing.

Dr. Keppo drew it for me after my fainting spell on my first day at the SP program. He'd asked what I thought had brought it on and I said, "the ruckus." Eva Federov had been screaming in the hall. It was a weird word to use but I wasn't feeling very well and that's what popped into my head. When I felt well enough to go, Dr. Keppo gave me a yellow prescription slip with his cellphone number on it in case I needed to talk again. Underneath, he'd drawn this cute little character with its mouth wide open and motion lines all around it. When I'd asked what it was, he said, "A ruckus. See? Not scary at all." That made me laugh.

I almost scrunch up the paper and throw it away too, but I change my mind. I find my phone and call the number. Dr. Keppo picks up immediately.

"David-with-an-A!" he says. "How are you?"

I tell him.

"Ooh," he says. "I know it's late, but why don't you drop by my office for a chat? I'm free now."

Excerpt from police interview with Janice Drysdale, 5 days after the party

Lt. Alan (Pidge) Eisenhauer: Did you know Davida Williamson was coming by that evening?

Janice Drysdale: No. Dr. Keppo and I were both working late. He was upstairs in his office and I was downstairs in mine. He hid it pretty well, but I knew he'd been upset about Vivienne. He had a lot to worry about. Would she come out of the coma, and if so, how much would she remember? The prognosis wasn't good, but miracles do happen. Anyway . . . I'd arranged for him to go away for a few days after the overdose. He'd used the time to meet with some former students and had come back with a large donation for the med school. I thought that had done the trick. He'd seen again that he could be a force for good. The man has his faults, but his capacity to inspire is truly moving. Just last week, we had another baby named after him. Keppo Cruikshank. Cute, isn't it? Anyway, I was hopeful he was back on an even keel, but then I heard voices in the lobby. I saw the security guard talking to Davida.

Davida

4 days after the party
9 p.m.

The security guard lets me in and says Dr. Keppo is waiting for me. "Know the way? Sixth floor. Probably the only office with lights on."

When I get there, Dr. Keppo's sitting at his desk with his laptop open. The sun has gone down, but it's not totally dark yet. The big window behind him is a deep blue.

He stands up. "Davida. Have a seat." He points to the chair in front of his desk. He leans his head to the side. His face is sad. It's almost too much. "Tell me how you're feeling."

"I'm . . . I'm so confused."

My eyes fill with tears. Not for Viv—for me. I want to tell him all the bad things I've been thinking about her, but I don't think I can.

He reaches across and pats my hand. "Hey. Hey, now. How about I get us some tea? Then we can make ourselves comfortable and have a chat, okay?"

I nod. He heads over to the sink on the other side of the room and plugs in the kettle, talking the whole time. About the weather, about the types of tea he has, the types of cookies. I'm barely listening. I realize I've made a mistake. I want to go home. I don't want to talk about this. I just want to forget.

I'm staring out the window, wondering how I'm going to get myself out of here, when I notice something. Notice *two* things.

The first is that all the framed pictures on the window ledge are lying facedown. It's kind of a nothing-thing, so I don't know why it catches my eye. I wonder if someone had been cleaning the window and laid them down so they wouldn't get knocked over.

I look up at the window. For proof? I don't know. It might just have seemed nosy looking anywhere else.

That's when I notice the second thing. The sky has gotten darker and turned the window into a mirror. I can see my reflection. I'm hit by how Dr. Keppo must see me. Small. Timid. My shoulders up around my ears. My fidgety hands.

I can also see what's playing on Dr. Keppo's laptop. The sound is off, but the video is reflected in the mirror clear as can be.

The kettle whistles. "My own special blend of tea all right for you?" he's saying. "It's very good."

"Sure."

It's the hair I notice first. No one can mistake Viv's hair. It's not just blond, it's yellow. It's thick and wavy and almost down to her waist.

In the video, it's the only thing covering her. She's naked and her head is flopping around and there's a man hovering over her. He's wearing the same shirt Dr. Keppo is wearing now.

I sort of know exactly what I'm seeing, but I don't too. It's more an instinct than anything. I grab the laptop and take off. I knock over my chair. Everything is happening very fast and very slow too. I see Dr. Keppo turn with the kettle in his hand, and watch as his smile stretches open into something horrible. A taxidermied wolf about to attack, that's what I think. He lunges for me, stumbles over the chair leg. I hear him shriek but I'm out the door by then and running down the hall to the elevator.

Which won't be there.

I realize that immediately. I'll have to hit the button and wait for it to get to the sixth floor, and by then he'll have gotten up and caught me, and that'll be the end—but I don't know where else to go. I don't know where the stairs are. I just keep running in the direction of the elevator then I turn the corner and there's Janice Drysdale.

She grabs me. "Give me that." She snatches the laptop.

It's like she was waiting for me.

Excerpt from police interview with Janice Drysdale, 5 days after the party

Lt. Alan (Pidge) Eisenhauer: You hear Davida and the security guard talking so you follow her?

Janice Drysdale: No. Not follow. It took me a few minutes to decide what to do then I took the stairs.

Eisenhauer: Why?

Drysdale: I didn't want him to hear the elevator? Not sure. I was anxious. I wasn't thinking clearly.

Eisenhauer: Then what happened?

Drysdale: I heard a commotion, someone running, and Davida came around the corner. She was so relieved to see me, poor thing, I almost felt sorry for her. She handed me the laptop without a struggle. She was talking a mile a minute. "It's Dr. Keppo!" "He raped Viv." "He videotaped it." That sort of thing.

Eisenhauer: What did you say?

Drysdale: I don't recall. We could hear him at the other end of the hall. I found out later he'd stumbled and spilled boiling water over his crotch. That must have slowed him down. He didn't seem to know which direction she'd gone. We were hidden around the corner from the elevator. We could hear him swearing and cursing as he ran our way. Davida was holding my arm, shaking like a leaf. She obviously didn't realize which side I was on. But then again, neither did I.

Davida

4 days after the party
9:10 p.m.

Dr. Keppo's screaming at me. I can hear him coming. I tell Janice he assaulted Viv. She's naked. He's on top of her. It's on the laptop.

I'm worried that she won't understand, that she won't believe me—but she doesn't even blink.

She's not surprised.

She knows.

I understand that immediately. She knows what he did.

And now she's got the laptop.

I grab it from her but she's holding it so tight her fingers have gone white. We're tugging back and forth. She's staring me right in the eyes and she looks so mean, so *cold*, and I really, honestly think it's over and it's useless and now he's going to get me too—but then this thing pops into my head. Something Tim said to me. Something we'd both promised.

"To defend the defenseless."

Viv, that's who I'm thinking of. Not me.

I'm not defenseless.

Excerpt from police interview with Janice Drysdale, 5 days after the party

Lt. Alan (Pidge) Eisenhauer: Dr. Keppo came around the corner and then what?

Janice Drysdale: I'm not sure. Perhaps I loosened my grip, but maybe not. In any event, that little Davida was surprisingly strong. She got the laptop from me and—just like that—smashed him in the face. The sound! You should have heard it. I didn't have to look to know his nose was broken. Ironic, isn't it? All the years of me thinking those videos would do him in—and, in the end, they kind of did! I saw him on the floor and you know what I thought?

Eisenhauer: What?

Drysdale: "Now who's out cold?" It made me laugh.

Eisenhauer: How long had you known about him?

Drysdale: Depends what you mean by "known." Had I seen videos? Yes. I stumbled across the first one, oh, probably fifteen, twenty years ago. I was doing administrative work for him and accidentally opened the wrong file.

Eisenhauer: What did you do?

Drysdale: Confronted him. He said, "Jan . . . ," in that way of his, smiling, shaking his head, like it was all some silly misunderstanding. They were for research purposes. Medical research. That's what he said.

Eisenhauer: And you believed him?

Drysdale: I'm a nurse, not a fool. I'd seen plenty of medical research. I knew what they were. But . . .

Eisenhauer: What?

Drysdale: I'm going to sound incredibly naive but here's the thing: at that point, the videos were just of naked bodies. The subjects were asleep or, perhaps, unconscious. It's not like Ivan was *doing* anything to them. He wasn't *sharing* the videos. No one would have recognized anybody even if he had! He didn't show the faces. So I thought, what's the harm? Or, more importantly, what harm would come if I exposed Ivan? Compare these relatively innocent videos to all the good he was doing. The med school? The SP program? His work in the community? It was no contest. *That*, I truly believed. I did my best to keep Ivan out of temptation's way and then just . . . turned a blind eye to what I couldn't prevent.

Eisenhauer: You really think these videos are harmless?

Drysdale: Not *these* videos. *Those* videos. The old ones. He wasn't touching anyone. He was just looking! Just looking at young adults. Sexually active young adults who'd wake up from a nice long nap none the wiser. You know what they say: what you don't know can't hurt you.

Eisenhauer: You're joking.

Drysdale: Not really. Many successful former members of Dr. Keppo's youth initiatives have suffered absolutely no ill effects from his little hobby. Take George Pineo. I've mentioned him before. He drank his share of "tea" as a teenager. Would he be better off to live out his life in public housing— or to have unwittingly been the subject of a few private videos and then gone on to med school? You tell me.

Eisenhauer: I'm going to let that go. Keppo's activities recently became less "innocent," didn't they? What changed?

Drysdale: Eva Federov. She found out what he was doing with her. I don't know how. She came to earlier than expected or stumbled across the videos somehow, but she figured it out. Before I had a chance to intervene, Ivan had come up with a story. He convinced her that this wasn't what it looked like. This was *love*. I don't need to tell you how dangerous a strategy that is with an emotionally unstable eighteen-year-old girl. What a mess. Especially once Ivan tired of her. She went into a tailspin. Started harassing him. Suddenly, everything was at stake—his marriage, his reputation, the school. The only saving grace—if I can call it that—was that Eva had a history of instability and no family support. It wasn't easy convincing people her ravings were the result of mental illness, but it was doable. I'd just got that somewhat under control then Viv came along. I'd had the security guards on high alert to make sure Eva didn't get in after hours, but she's a clever girl. She found a way in through a basement window in the Bunker. She crawled in one night and caught Vivienne and Dr. Keppo at it.

Eisenhauer: Sorry. Vivienne was not "at" anything.

Drysdale: Fine . . . In any event, things suddenly got more complicated. I was so angry at Ivan for getting involved with someone like Vivienne, of all people. She wasn't his type at all.

Eisenhauer: What do you mean?

Drysdale: Smart. Credible. Loved and supported by her family and friends. If she talked, people would believe her. Ivan risked everything he'd built—everything *we'd* built—over the past twenty years for what? Sick sexual gratification. It was enough to make me ill.

Eisenhauer: So you decided to kill her.

Drysdale: No. I did not decide any such thing. I agreed to meet her. Ivan, in his bare-bones way, had alerted me to the possibility of a problem. I gleaned that he'd been more active with her than others but that it had happened several weeks ago and, given her issues with alcohol, could be readily explained away. I thought I'd talk her out of it—I thought I *had*; I even managed to convince her to give me the drawing—but then she asked about identification through fetal DNA. I knew it was over. Ivan couldn't wiggle out of that. It would be the end, not just for him but for the school. For me. For everything I'd worked for. In one second, I saw my whole life disappear before my eyes.

Eisenhauer: Luckily you just happened to have oxy with you.

Drysdale: I don't know about "luckily." You can return unused prescriptions to pharmacies, did you know that? I'd brought Mother's leftover pills to the office to return several weeks ago. I got busy, though, and didn't get around to it, so I put the bottle on my desk as a reminder. Eva just happened to come into my office one day after that—raving, of course—and I noticed her noticing them. On a hunch, I made an excuse to leave her alone for a few moments. I checked after she'd left and five pills were gone. I figured if she didn't solve the problem for us herself, we'd at least be able to establish drug use as a contributing factor.

Eisenhauer: But she did you a favor. Being told you're crazy over and over again can take its toll, I guess.

Drysdale: I just heard. Where did they find the body?

Eisenhauer: That's none of your concern . . . So with Vivienne, in other words, you came prepared.

Drysdale: Not intentionally. Ironically, I actually had the pills in my purse in order to finally take them back. I had no intention of giving one to her, until she mentioned the pregnancy. She had incontrovertible proof of Ivan's involvement. I had to do something immediately. I smelled alcohol on her breath and reasoned a slender, opioid-innocent teen who'd already consumed a depressant—that was probably enough to do the trick.

Eisenhauer: You're shaking your head.

Drysdale: It's sad. Such a waste! I understand now that her period was just late. She wasn't even pregnant! It breaks my heart. Why would she say such a thing if she didn't know for sure? All this could have been avoided.

Eisenhauer: Yes, it could have.

DEAN OF MED SCHOOL CHARGED

Dr. Ivan Keppo, dean of education at the MacKinnon School of Medicine, has been arrested on multiple charges of sexual assault, administration of a noxious substance, attempted murder and possession of child pornography. Police have confiscated computers from his home and office. More charges relating to crimes dating back several decades are expected to be laid. Dr. Keppo is recovering in hospital from undisclosed injuries.

Janice Drysdale, coordinator of the school's Simulated Patient Program, has also been charged on numerous counts. Sources say charges may also be forthcoming regarding the overdose death of Eva Federov.

The MacKinnon School of Medicine declined to comment.

Davida

7 days after the party
Visiting hours

They're only letting in one person at a time because Viv's still pretty fragile. Dad didn't want me to go to the hospital. Even Steve thought I should wait. They say I'm pretty fragile too.

I *am*, but not in the way they think. Everything's been so crazy the last couple of days. My picture everywhere. Journalists from Japan and Finland asking for interviews. People calling me a hero. It's stupid.

I'm not a hero—and I'm not just being modest either. I only went to Dr. Keppo's because I needed help. I wasn't doing it for anyone else. I only grabbed the laptop because I wasn't thinking. If I'd been thinking, I would have run for my life.

Everyone's worried about the violence—the so-called trauma of me actually having to take a guy down—but that's not what bothers me.

It's picturing Janice. She fought me like a crazy person, but then she laughed when I hit him. She sobbed when they arrested him, but then she called him a prick and a pervert. It was like seeing someone split in two. Love is horrible. That's what scares me. I mean, if that's what love is. (Tim says it isn't, but he doesn't know any better than I do.)

The door opens and Tim comes out of Viv's room. "Your turn," he says.

I smile but I'm terrified. I keep reminding myself that Viv never knew any of the terrible things I thought about her. She never knew we'd stopped being friends. She never knew I hated her.

He puts his arms around me. "Go on. It'll be fine," he says. "She's still Viv. Trust me."

I do. I should have trusted him all along.

When I don't move, he gives me a kiss and a nudge and says, "Just pretend it's moulage. Works like a charm."

I push the door open a crack. Viv's lying in bed, her arms flat at her side, her head propped up on her pillow. I can't tell if her eyes are open.

"Viv?"

She turns her head. She looks like death. I'd heard the expression before but now I know what it means. She's so thin and pale, like *vampire* pale, that I have to suck in my breath to keep from crying.

"Davida." Her voice is raspy. "You're here."

She smiles and struggles to sit up. I rush over and take her elbow, but she gives me a little push. Her hand is purple from the IV and I can see where the tape was.

"Hey. I'm not *that* feeble." She laughs and falls back on her pillow. "Or maybe I am."

"Can I help?" I feel useless.

"Yes." Her eyes are closed, maybe from the effort, but she's smiling. "Absolutely."

"How?"

She turns and looks right at me. "By telling me what the hell happened."

I pull up the chair. I don't know where to start.

6/22 - 0